EVERYWHERE BUT HERE

EVERYWHERE BUT HERE

Jacqueline Silvester

SIMON & SCHUSTER

London New York Amsterdam/Antwerp Sydney/Melbourne Toronto New Delhi

First published in Great Britain in 2026 by Simon & Schuster UK Ltd

1 3 5 7 9 10 8 6 4 2

Simon & Schuster UK Ltd, 7th Floor,
199 Bishopsgate, London EC2M 3TY

www.simonandschuster.co.uk
www.simonandschuster.com.au
www.simonandschuster.co.in

The authorised representative in the EEA is Simon & Schuster Netherlands BV, Herculesplein 96, 3584 AA Utrecht, Netherlands. info@simonandschuster.nl

Simon & Schuster Australia, Sydney
Simon & Schuster India, New Delhi

A CIP catalogue record for this book is available from the British Library.

PB ISBN 9781398536395
eBook ISBN 9781398536388
eAudio ISBN 9781398536401

Printed and Bound in the UK using 100% Renewable Electricity at CPI Group (UK) Ltd

FSC www.fsc.org
MIX
Paper | Supporting responsible forestry
FSC® C013604

To my love David,
For all the many miles.

'People don't take trips,
Trips take people.'

John Steinbeck

From: Lucille@CreatorLabs.FR

We have an update on the last email!

This spring the iconic international hotel chain Maison Partout will be hosting an influencer competition as a part of their '*the Home Is Where Your Heart Beats'* campaign, designed to promote their recent absorption of various boutique and luxury hotels around the world and to 'cement them as a romantic luxury destination where everyone can feel at home'. (pulled from their brief)

Influencers with over one million followers and a travel, romance or lifestyle niche are invited to enter the competition. Maison Partout will narrow down the list and selected influencers will be flown out to Bali for the competition (we don't have exact details on what the competition entails yet – sorry!). Once in Bali, two winners will be chosen and sent on a brand deal trip across the world. Exact locations are being kept under wraps – presumably to drive hype.

Travel and board are covered for the trip, with a daily spend of 250USD per participant, a merch package, fifty per cent off bookings for five years and potential for future collaboration for those who don't win.

Either way, the exposure on this project seems amazing. ☺

If you would like to be put forward for this campaign, please let Sophie know ASAP.

Thank you,

Lucille, Head of Bookings
Creator Labs, Agence de Talent, Boulevard Voltaire, Paris 11ème
CreatorLabs.FR

UBUD, BALI

CHAPTER 1

MARGOT

I scroll past the crying girl.

My thumb flicks upwards almost automatically. I've learned the hard way that once you linger on the sad stuff the algorithm learns to serve it to you often and plenty, like hot, little, personalized trauma cakes. Social media can be like a car accident – you tell yourself to keep driving past the smoke and sirens but a minute later you're slowing down, glued to your window, unable to look away from someone else's trauma. Oddly relieved that trauma isn't yours.

It's easier to just keep scrolling.

I click the heart icon on the next video of a tutorial for cakes shaped like sausage dogs. I'd rather the algorithm believes I like baking than tears.

'You are not meant to be scrolling, you are meant to be the stuff people scroll,' Dimitra says in her Greek accent as she walks in and stretches dramatically, exposing her toned midriff. My temporary roommate smiles at me across the spacious living room of our Balinese villa and tousles her curly brown hair into place. She's wearing the same Balinese trousers as me – they were in our hotel welcome baskets, the *Maison Partout* hotel chain namesake stitched in gold across the emerald-green front with its hot-air-balloon logo.

'You know, with our type of hair we should be sponsored by Detangler,' I say, automatically opening my Instagram and scrolling through the haircare brand's business account. My hair is bright red and as thick and wavy as hers. Both of our manes take ages to detangle. I tap the contact button.

'Do you ever stop talking about work?' She gestures playfully to the cobbled veranda outside, rounded out by a small freshwater pool that's framed by the lush jungle beyond.

'Sometimes.'

'We have arrived in paradise,' she says, and then yawns because even heaven doesn't stop jet lag. 'You can take a break. Hey, remember the time we were getting drunk in Warsaw and you stopped to ask the bar if they were looking for content creators?' She laughs.

I grin. 'I remember. I'm just seeking inspiration.' I keep scrolling. It only took twenty minutes after checking in to the beautiful Royal Rita Hotel in Ubud before anxiety started bubbling up inside of me, chalky and thick, like the sticky residue of a soup forgotten on the hob. I don't even know *what* the competition is yet but I'm already scrolling for ideas on winning content. I could stop and play, but a part of me feels like I can't afford to stop. I'm not about to tell Dimitra that. Who wants to admit they get anxious even in paradise?

'Can you help me film this trend?' I ask, pointing my screen at her to show two friends slapping each other's hands. At each slap the scene changes, as if they're teleporting from location to location. 'We can do one in the room, then main poolside, restaurant, then somewhere else . . .' Dimitra yawns again.

'That's a little outdated, no? I'm tired. Let's get breakfast first.'

We rushed a little through check-in because I was eager to change out of my clothes, damp from plane sweat and soaked with the smell of those little tin-tray meals. If I'm to meet anyone from the Maison Partout team, I want to smell like the sample of Mademoiselle Chanel I got from Duty Free and not like chicken parm.

'Five more minutes? I need inspiration!' I plead, picking my phone back up.

A post comes up from a friend: she's at a protest in our home town. A sort of light, frothy guilt sloshes in my stomach like latte foam. *I'm not there.* I've helped make cardboard signs for my friends and signed petitions to protest the water company that ruined our town, but I haven't attended many of the actual protests. I should post something in solidarity with the protesters or I should share her post. But every time I post something off-brand – something that isn't slow living or flowers or countryside – I lose followers. I quickly swipe up and save two viral sounds instead. Then I open my mail app and email Lucille, my contact at the Parisian agency that got me here, letting her know I've arrived safely. Almost instantly, I get a reply from Sophie, the intern I've only seen on Google Meets, wishing me good luck. If I do win the $100,000, they get a sixteen per cent cut – but without them I wouldn't have even known about the competition.

'I have to get as much content as I can before I leave,' I tell Dimitra. 'Keep my socials sunny when I'm running low,' I add. Obviously, I'm hoping to win and so is she; there's even a chance we're both chosen to represent Maison Partout, which would be a dream, but what are the odds of that?

'Or till winter when everyone and their mother is posting St

Moritz slopes and moon boots, and your Balinese breakfast is old news.' Dimitra winks at me.

'People back home like to daydream about the heat and plan destination trips, even in winter.'

'Oh yeah? People in *Puyfleur* plan a lot of trips to Bali?'

I squint up at her, impressed at her pronunciation of my French town, annoyed at the rest. I know that Dimitra's question is innocent. I could ask her the same thing. We both come from small rural towns, the type where people never leave.

'That's why I said daydream.' I nudge her in the side so that she lets me get to the full-length mirror. People love escapism in the form of a tiny screen.

Especially now that unrest in my town is brewing.

'Also sixty per cent of my audience is abroad.' I pout at Dimitra in the mirror as she takes a photo of us. 'Look, I want to do this trend. Please, please, please, please?' I hover over her shoulder, flicking through the trending sound at an angle where she is forced to look at my phone. 'Don't make me beg.'

'You are already begging. Fine! I'll do it, but you have to go to the hotel's complimentary Pilates class with me.' She winks at me in a mischievous way that I have learned to fear over the course of our five-year friendship. We met at a young influencer meet-up online when I was twelve and she was fourteen. We've since encountered each other IRL on brand deals in Barcelona and Warsaw. This is only my third brand trip so far.

I hate these infernal reformer Pilates straps and being told to tighten my core by a faceless voice somewhere out of my line of sight. But fine, it's worth it for a collaboration video. At two million, Dimitra has nearly double my following and I really want my numbers up if the Maison Partout team decides to browse my latest before making their decision.

'That's the last of my scrolling for the day,' I declare, putting my phone away and following her to the door.

CHAPTER 2

THEO

All I want is normal eggs. Not eggs that come suspended in a tiny net, or adorned with purple purée, or in the shape of a cute animal. Normal, serious eggs, meant for a grown man. Or a grown nineteen-year-old at the very least.

'Just eat the eggs.' Jodi glares at me. 'They tried.'

'They absolutely did not try – I said plain omelette with ham and cheese. What is this?' I hold up a large flower.

'Edible flowers.' Jodi takes a bite of a huge dandelion. 'When I came to visit you in Courchevel you made me eat a gallon of cheese. It was served in cute tiny dishes. I vomited for hours. You are in no position to make critiques.'

'Raclette,' I confirm. It's true, when Jodi visited me at my ski chalet, he was adventurous – he tried everything, and did it with a smile. I guess that's why people love following him – that and the fact he takes every chance to show off his six-pack. I thought the depths of winter would render this impossible but when I gave him a tour of our saunas, he snuck a selfie in.

Jodi pushes another dandelion into the place of the former and takes a photo. Then he pulls his phone over his plate to get an aerial shot of his pancakes. 'If you weren't so grumpy, you'd notice that the food is good, the view –' he gestures out to the rice paddies beyond our Balinese terrace – 'is novel worthy. And the girls . . .' His eyes wander to two long-legged German TikTokers relentlessly trying to nail a shot on the café's rice-paddy swing. 'Chef's kiss,' he concludes, kissing his fingers like an Italian chef. 'Just try to enjoy living while you are actually alive.'

'Deep.' I use my fork to push the flora and fauna off my eggs.

'Also, my friend just opened this brunch spot so a little story or two is much appreciated.' Jodi winks at me. The nerve.

'So that's what this is. You know I'm not much of a post-my-breakfast-to-my-stories kind of guy.'

'Force yourself,' he says with a smile, and it's hard to not be charmed by someone like him. 'A part of the proceeds goes to the local animal shelter.' Jodi picks a postcard up off a nearby table and slides it over to me. It's a picture of a little silver-grey stray pup, giving the same puppy eyes Jodi is giving me now.

'Do it for the pups, Theo,' he coos. 'And, more importantly, do it for my friend's hot sister who is more likely to date me if I help hype up her brother's restaurant and their family charity.'

'Okay, okay,' I laugh. 'I'll post a story about the dog thing, not the eggs, that's where I draw the line.'

'See, that's the spirit.'

I'm projecting; I don't care that much about the flower on my eggs. Something in the air has me nervous ever since I arrived. Even though the Air France new business beds were comfortable, there's a kink in my neck I can't shake and a headache kneading my forehead. My phone beeps and I check the notifications. The likes keep climbing on my last YouTube video. A challenge where I rode every means of transport in Portugal and rated it. My thumb scrolls seamlessly through the comments before I tell it to stop. I check the shorter version of the post on TikTok and, before I know it, I'm phantom scrolling, my thumb jerking upwards without my permission.

The pit in my stomach tightens as clips surface from home – protests, vandalism, smoke. I blink groggily and try to settle my nerves. Maybe it's the jet lag. I've just arrived, and though it was kind of Jodi to pick me up from the airport and take me straight to brunch, I'm not even sure my stomach can handle it. I watch a video of an angry farmer covering the Puyfleur city hall in manure. It triggers a row of memories, calcified somewhere in my brain, as if I'm sifting them out from muddied water.

'For Christ's sake,' I mumble, setting the phone down.

'The news? Or your dad?' Jodi watches me.

'My dad *is* the news.'

I stretch and my back answers painfully; maybe I should be doing yoga like the rest of the island.

'It will quieten down,' I say, more to myself than Jodi. 'People always move on to the next thing in the news cycle.' But I'm not sure who I'm trying to convince today; I know that my father's impending trial is bigger than whatever else has landed him in the news before. People are unlikely to move on from this anytime soon.

'Don't worry, bro. Hey, do you want to film a few videos before we head over to the Royal Rita?'

Jodi and I met a year ago on an influencer trip to Bavaria with a luxury car company. Now I've come to Bali to partake in a big influencer competition, and he just happened to be back home to visit his parents and will take part in the competition too. I don't know if he got in fair and square or if his deep-rooted connections in Bali got him here, and I didn't ask. Jodi's dad is a big-deal politician in this country. He understands at least part of what I'm going through.

My phone buzzes again. It's my mum. My heart sinks even more.

I don't think I can go, her text says, referring to the expensive doctor's appointment I've already booked and paid for her a few towns over, under a fake name so as not to alert my father.

Maman, this appointment wasn't easy to get . . .

My father could pay for any specialist in the country, but he won't. For a myriad of reasons, least of all the fact that he just doesn't feel like helping his ex-wife.

This specialist cost me a lot. I try the guilt route. Watching the '. . .' hover on the screen as she types and deletes her reply multiple times over.

Don't drink the water over there by the way. I saw a video.

I grimace. Of all the things in the world, she mentions water.

Can't be as bad as it is back home, I write.

Delete your message! she writes back, and I oblige. I don't need to give her any more reasons to be paranoid.

I sigh. Check my bank and crypto accounts on my phone, and sigh again. Getting her a comfortable apartment outside of my father's clutches, and getting her treatment all without my father's help, is going to cost a lot more than I've been able to squirrel away with brand deals. I *need* this prize money yesterday. I open my emails and scan for sponsorship offers I might be able to knock off quickly while in Bali. Before I left, I sent out a bunch of enquiries. There's nothing but AI-penned offers and a brand deal for dandruff shampoo back home.

'I need to win this competition,' I say, leafing through a Bali tourist magazine on the coffee table in front of me for inspiration. My drone is charged and ready to go. 'What kind of content do you think they want? Probably something pathetic like those flower-filled bathtubs.' The brief mention of luxury and romance, and a half-meandering slogan – *Home Is Where Your Heart Beats.* But that can be interpreted in a myriad of ways.

'You know you're a real downer today,' says Jodi. 'Maybe if your pancakes came shaped like teddy bears you wouldn't be so grim. Look at this magazine.' He pokes it with his index finger. 'How often in life do you look at a travel magazine and know you're currently where the cover was shot?' He points at the paddy field. The same one on the cover.

'It *would* make a great drone shot.' I cock my head.

'Exactly.'

'I don't know, maybe I'm being paranoid. I just have this bad feeling lately.'

My phones buzzes again. Notifications. Protests near my dad's main water plant have doubled in both size and coverage overnight. The more coverage something gets, the more it grows, and the bigger it grows, the more the papers scramble to cover it. It's a toxic cycle. I close my eyes against the memory that sweeps in. A quiet night, a thundering noise. My mum's body pressed against mine in a panic room. Another headline the next day. *Vandalism and break-in at billionaire's home.* I blink it away, finger hovering over my dad's avatar in the text app. But his name doesn't anchor me; instead it feels like being out at sea, watching someone blur on the shoreline, knowing they can't save you from drowning.

The knot in me tightens.

I put the phone away. I don't want to be like my mother, living through pixelated fear. Everything will be fine. I manage a smile in Jodi's direction.

'Let's go get some footage,' I say.

'And a couple of phone numbers,' he replies.

CHAPTER 3

MARGOT

All problems in life can be solved by the sun. Renewable energy. Check. Growing the perfect fruit. Check. And restoring my mood. Check.

'Engage your powerhouse,' says the beautiful Balinese woman teaching our morning class. I oblige but still angle my face to the sun, soaking it in like some contortionist desert bird.

'That's right,' the teacher says, her voice schooled into a relaxing melody even though I feel anything but relaxed. 'Collarbones wide. Focus on your core. Let your mind focus on your alignment. There are no worries here. No phone calls. No phones. Nothing but the present moment and the deep, deep stretch.'

Her mention of phones reminds me of mine. Tucked secretly beneath a towel, under my hellish Reformer machine. Everyone's eyes are trained on the ceiling and the trainer is busy helping someone – this is my chance. I release my ropes and quickly snatch the phone. Then I angle it for a story. As I film in line to try and get the whole class in, and the glorious jungle beyond the rows of raised legs, my camera lands on the teacher. Her eyes are not on her student, and she does not look pleased. She smiles but it's forced; she probably has to be extra nice to us content creators. I flash her an apologetic smile and shrug, then tuck the phone away again.

The moment the class ends I duck behind a palm tree and post my video. Then I film a few shots of myself which I will use for the 'come and try Pilates in Bali with me!' TikTok. Notifications flood in over my views and comments. I do the usual quick-fingered heart emojis and *thank you*s on my last TikTok, where I was swaying on some beautiful Bali swings that we had passed on our way to the class with a caption that read 'don't spend today thinking about tomorrow', paired with the latest viral K-pop song.

'Did you see the guy to the left, front row? Looks like he was built in a lab?' says Dimitra.

I roll my eyes. 'Even during Pilates, you manage to thirst on people.'

'And even during Pilates you manage to post.'

Dimitra might be a content creator like me but she's taken a more cultural route. She does exposés on galleries and visits every biennale art show around the world. Titling her videos cleverly like *I spent three days staring at one famous painting – here's what happened.* Aside from that she does amazing wellness content, like spas in Budapest and eighteen-step K-Beauty regimens. I, on the other hand, do salt-of-the-earth-type stuff, like pouring myself coffee on a misty morning, or boiling vegetables on a hearth. I like to think of myself as Frodo Baggins with an iPhone. I look at the little hearts flooding my phone from our shared selfie earlier in our matching green trousers. Three million people around the world could potentially see our shared story – not too shabby for a pair of farm girls.

'Solo jungle background shot?' I ask Dimitra, but she's already reaching her hand out to me. She read my mind.

We go into the beautiful studio, lined with caramel bamboo, and encased in glass walls that reveal a backdrop of luscious jungle canopy. I give Dimitra a few of my signature poses. I make a mental note to change into my trusty cottage core white dress at some point, the one that carried me from the low thousands to a million followers, but this is a Maison Partout brand trip so the embroidered trousers will do.

'Turn more to the light, three quarters, yeah, just like that,' she says.

I try and extend my neck like I'm a swan trying to drink up the rays of light.

'My right side is my good side.'

She rolls her eyes. 'You don't have a bad side, Margot. Just good and better. Extend your left leg though, it's doing something weird.'

I oblige. After a few more minutes of this she turns the phone around and shows me the results. I scroll through the camera reel, looking at nearly twenty identical shots of me posing in the studio.

'Perfect.' I beam at her.

'We have to go,' she says, glancing at her watch. 'They will be rounding up the creators soon for a meet and greet.'

'You're just hoping the *built-in-a-lab guy* is a participant and not a hotel guest.'

She laughs, her olive-skinned face beautiful in the sun.

'No, I'm actually trying to be organized. I want to win too, you know. I'm saving for a deposit for a new flat in Athens.'

'Ooh la la.' I wriggle my brows at her. 'Can I visit?'

'Anytime,' she says over her shoulder as she heads for the door.

Dimitra is already able to support herself with her influencing alone, which means relocating from her small town to the capital, and thus a major airport, was the next logical step. As much as I would love to move to Paris and pursue opportunities there, I'm still quite a few brand deals away from being able to stroll through the Jardin des Tuileries on a whim. Dimitra, already halfway out of the building, brings me out of a stupor by calling my name.

Before I head after her, I quickly flick through the breaking news notifications on my phone, but there's no update yet on the biggest news story concerning me and my town. Then I follow.

CHAPTER 4

THEO

I watch the canopy of jungle swallow our SUV and spit us back out into a sunny patch of thin rice-paddy-lined road. I would have loved to show this to my mother. And inevitably that thought leads me to how that will never happen. Not because my mother is sick, but because she lives in fear. Fear of being photographed, of her plants dying, of aeroplanes, of strangers. At some point after her very public divorce, fear took hold of her, and its grip is ironclad, a boa constrictor compressing around her neck – sluggish but deadly.

It's not for me, Theo, she would say, with resigned exasperation. *All these things you do, it's not for me.* As if I were a jewellery thief instead of a content creator. *It's just not for me.* I picture her, sitting in one of her well-maintained Loro Piana cashmere sweaters, either glued to her tablet – sucking up rows of YouTube news clips – or fastened to her solitaire app in my father's city apartment. In an alternative universe, she could brave the flight and be here with me. But alternative universes are built for fools.

Though I did get her out to Türkiye once, to an all-inclusive resort, early on in the divorce proceedings. She enjoyed it, but when tabloids posted bikini photos of her side by side with my father's new wife she said she wouldn't go travelling again. That was the beginning of the end.

'I feel good at home,' she told me. 'Safe.' Encumbered with her shows. Surrounded by trinkets from a former life with my father, before the renowned water and gas tycoon who privatized a third of the Swiss French border became as much of a villain off paper than he already was on paper.

He went on to live a life of even greater excess with his new wife, a twenty-five-year-old rising actress, and my mum went on to live her life in fear, cocooned in the soft cotton of memories like a nesting chick too afraid to fly.

I watch a row of black-and-white birds perching on a telephone wire, causing it to sag. I sigh and try to steady my breathing, then I film a small segment of passing trees. The hypocrisy of an influencer judging people for living their lives on their screens isn't lost on me. I just want better for her. I want the woman who gave me life to have a life worth living.

Agoraphobia, the internet said when I looked it up. But now I need specialist help, not just online diagnosis and tailored doomscrolling that makes me believe she will never get better.

The internet can't give you the antidote, it can only give the poison a place to go.

Twenty minutes later the car is cast into the shadows of the jungle canopy, and I'm still lost in thought. Caught somewhere between hating home and missing it.

'Your head looks like an awful place to be,' says Jodi from my right. I nod, because he's right.

'It can be an awful place, or an entertaining one. Depends on the day.'

'Well, today is a great one, brother,' he says, pointing out the window.

We veer down a serpentine driveway, hugged by frangipani flowers on all sides, until our hotel, the famed Royal Rita, materializes in the jungle like a haze-cloaked mirage.

Jodi lets out a low whistle. 'Damn. You know a local prince used to own this? Before they sold it to the Maison Partout chain. It's stunning.'

I press closer to the window. It's true – it's magnificent. It looks like a Balinese fortress. The reflection of its red stone façade is sliced in the middle by a floating walkway, lined with ponds of giant lily pads and protruding short stone statues speckled with moss. Luxury cars crowd the circular drive, looking at odds with the ethereal building.

'Freshly renovated, dates back two centuries, five stars, rooms starting at eight hundred a night,' I recite from my info packet. I came prepared and did all my homework on the flight. Jodi rolls his eyes at me.

I thank and tip the driver and unload my gear. Cameras, drones, tripods. Jodi unloads the suitcases.

'You didn't need to bring all of that,' he says.

'We still don't know what the challenge entails – I wanted to be prepared for anything they throw at us.'

'*Nerd*,' he mouths.

The air is thick with the scent of blooms, despite it being early March. A young lady and man in traditional Balinese dress welcome us and hand us cups of iced tea. Our luggage has already disappeared, with the efficiency you expect from a five-star resort, as we are guided into the sprawling open-air lobby which glows with endless white marble.

My sandals smack the pearly speckled marble that stretches onto the terrace. We are guided there for our welcome drink and that's when I see that we are not the first to arrive. I recognize a few faces from the influencer world. A Japanese guy. A German couple.

'Hello, my name is Sarah. May I give you a short tour while you enjoy your welcome drink?' asks a Balinese woman in a beige kameez.

Jodi and I nod, thanking her, and begin following her around like baby ducklings as she explains the history of the intricate wooden carvings and trickling fountains, then deposits us on the enormous terrace. I glance over the balconied edge, onto a sprawling jungle, dotted with thatched-roof villas and three cascading infinity pools that seem to float in mid-air like something from *Avatar*. At the bottom of the hill, more villas lie clustered around a narrow river, flowing and ebbing and foaming wildly. I watch as two red rafts come barrelling down, passengers screaming with glee.

'A complimentary river-rafting session will be included in your package,' says another woman, one with a nametag that has flags for all the languages she speaks.

'*Matur Suksma.*' I thank her in Balinese, feeling slightly uncomfortable as she and Sarah deposit welcome packets in front of us and bow, before retreating. Jodi says a few more phrases in Indonesian; my knowledge has tapped out at *thank you*.

'Perfect service,' says Jodi, almost as if he is making a mental note for his vlog. He already has his phone out and is filming the terrace. I wave him away as he gets me in the shot.

I'm uncomfortable with bowing. When I visit my father in his sprawling château – my childhood home outside of Puyfleur – his life is like this too. People bowing and depositing things by your side before you have a chance to ask for anything. It's not like that at my mother's apartment where I choose to live. A modest two-bedroom on the north side of the city, one of my father's many assets and the one she was forcibly relegated to after the divorce.

'Almost as good as the service in the château,' says Jodi. He visited me there after our trip to the chalet. Visitors my age weren't that common in my childhood, and I was excited when Jodi wanted to come by. With that in mind, I wanted to be the best possible host so I involved my dad and his staff. It meant I could give Jodi the absolute five-star experience, something I felt he was used to, but there was hell to pay when one of Jodi's videos accidentally showed a pile of trash outside my dad's factory. My father forced me to mount a performative clean-up campaign on my socials. It was one of the last times I ever asked him for favours.

'Yes, I guess,' I agree. 'But I don't enjoy it that much.' I scratch the back of my head. I haven't told Jodi everything that's been happening back home: how much my mother has changed this past year from the woman who commanded secretaries around and planned elaborate dinner parties, to a woman who now spends more time in her pyjamas watching natural disaster videos.

'This welcome bag is amazing,' says Jodi, picking through the bamboo bag embroidered with the *Maison Partout* logo. I peek into my own, momentarily distracted by the soaps, coconut scrubs and hemp body milks. Though I probably won't use them, I've always found reading the back of those things relaxing. It's hard to feel stressed when you smell eucalyptus and read phrases like '*a magical forest of invigorating mint*'.

'Not sure why you're looking at that shampoo bottle with more adoration then you did at Helga this morning.' Jodi elbows me in the side, reminding me of the German influencer from brunch.

'I could never date an influencer,' I say grumpily. 'Can you imagine it?'

I think for a second and then point at him. 'Well, it would be like dating *you* . . . Photographs at every meal, those awkwardly posed reels where you make hearts with your hands,' I scoff.

'May I remind you that you too are an influencer.'

'Content creator,' I correct.

'What's the difference?'

'I don't do any of *that*,' I say, waving grumpily at a group that are trying to film themselves jumping in the air in front of the Maison Partout wall installation. 'The eventual goal is to be a videographer. The influencing funds my expensive travel habit.'

It's an easier lie than telling him the truth, that influencing is my exit strategy. While I'm not one hundred per cent sure who I want to be yet, despite my love of filming, I *am* certain that I need a way out – out of my father's spare flat where he used to harbour his mistress and has now relegated his former wife. A way out of his toxic financial influence. Right now, I can only get paid for ads but eventually I'll be able to pay for my own education and become a director of photography, a *DOP*. When that day comes, I'll never use another hashtag ever again.

'Your father has a jet,' Jodi reminds me. I flinch. Sometimes it's difficult to be transparent in front of someone. To have someone know so much of you – from newspapers, Wikipedia, gossip sites – it's as though your skin has been left out to dry on a rack in the sun like cod. And yet Jodi doesn't know the fine print. I shrug. 'I . . . I don't want to use his jet.'

'If I had a jet I would use it,' says Jodi, examining a set of loofahs from his gift bag and staging a perfect shot of his gifts on the coffee table, paired with his iced tea.

'Everything with my father has strings.' If I ask my father for the money I need, he'll want me to work in the company. One of his long-term ambitions. And I would rather eat one of these loofahs than work at Eau Jeune and be trapped under my father's thumb for the rest of my life.

'Besides,' I add, 'I'm not interested in maximizing my carbon footprint.'

'Right. Lots of strings. Though call me Pinocchio because I just do whatever the big man says. I don't mind the strings.' Jodi is referring to his father, who I've never met but from his stories sounds a lot nicer than mine. 'Sometimes,' he continues, 'the strings are worth it.'

I let his words go. Let him believe it. No one knows until they are in your specific gilded, tightly laced shoes. The gift horse looks pretty till it bites you.

There's more Jodi doesn't know. Which is that each thing my father bestows, he takes a little bit away in return. Sometimes a lot. He bought me my first set of camera equipment and in exchange I had to go to a gala fundraiser where I was dressed and coached on what to say and when. My knowledge of foreign languages was used to impress business partners. One time, I begged him to take my mother and me to the Maldives, and afterwards he told me I had to go on a date with a head of state's daughter who was in town.

My travel content was just a hobby at first. It blew up because people were already following me due to the Delacour family name, but it wasn't until I was offered my first brand deal in exchange for cash that I realized this could be my ticket to independence. That's when I started vlogging for real.

I can't stand to be a part of his machine. Not after what he did to my mother.

Jodi suddenly sits up. 'The real competition is here.'

We've been ignoring the other vloggers around us in benefit of our tête-à-tête. I move to remind him there were German vloggers here when we arrived, but then I see what he means. Vincent Coles, a famous English vlogger, enters the lobby, visible from our viewing spot on the terrace, his driver dragging his Rimowa luggage set dutifully behind him. Vincent is the obnoxious type, a man who wears aviator sunglasses, swoops his hair perfectly and prefers to focus his content on things like ski resorts in Gstaad and weekend escapes to Biarritz. But the vain luxury content has brought him four million followers, and when it comes to brand deals like the Maison Partout chain, he is real competition.

'What a pompous prick,' I say.

Jodi nods his head but seems less repulsed by Vincent Coles than I am and more admiring. 'He did this video where he just rented a spa all for himself,' he says.

'How novel!' I say grumpily. He stands for everything I don't like – vapid, lavish success and shiny things. Like all the people my dad always wanted me to be friends with when I went to boarding school. I scowl and focus on my magazine as Jodi launches into a near high-school level of who's who as the newcomers continue to arrive and mercilessly pelt us with the competition.

'That Portuguese vlogger there only does content with his girlfriend, see? She's right behind him. So, if they win it,' he explains, 'it will be for something romantic and they will win as a pair. That American with the moustache does a lot of viral TikTok stuff. Started with pranks and grew into a sort of food vlogger. The Japanese girl has a huge following back home but not much in the Western market.'

My eyes scan over the people, recognizing a few of them from my own feed. The TikTok star from Brazil who makes videos about local crafts then makes stuff which she sells online. The Japanese ex-Olympian who now makes fitness videos in exotic locations.

The palm trees sway overhead and I watch a monarch butterfly land on a nearby satin cushion. Opening and closing its wings a few times, as if stretching.

'I have to admit, it's pretty brilliant all of this, genius actually.'

Jodi looks at me. 'Which part?'

'Well, with such a large competing base they are really hitting a lot of categories and markets just with the competition alone,' I volunteer, turning my strategist hat on. I look over to a woman in a linen suit, who seems to be the Maison Partout representative, busy greeting guests in a flighty PR manner. 'Maison Partout will get so much content generated just from the people here this weekend. Sure, they had to spring for airfare and stipends, but from this single competition they will hit all markets – Asia and the West, central Europe, everything. The exposure is pure gold.

'But by the time the competition is concluded, the whole follower base for the other vloggers will be invested in the story. You get all those eyes, and the followers of every participant, following you for the price of one. Anyway, when the two of us win . . .' I shoot for optimism. 'We will also get everyone else's followers as a bonus.'

'Something tells me they will want both female and male

demographic,' he says. I nod my head. I knew that, but it's fun to imagine.

'Besides,' he adds playfully, 'I don't know how to handle a huge brand deal trip with your grumpy ass. I think I would rather win with her.' Jodi points at a pretty vlogger with braids.

'I doubt they make you share a bed . . .' I say.

'I've changed my mind,' says Jodi. 'I'd rather win with *her*.'

He fans himself comically, as if from the heat, but I've turned my head and I can't respond to him. I take in her large mane of red hair, the signature freckles and cold green eyes. I'm speechless. Because the last person I ever wanted to see has just walked in.

CHAPTER 5

MARGOT

Back in the lobby, I'm greeted by the thick smell of hibiscus and the sound of a waterfall I hadn't noticed at check-in. But on closer inspection, I can see that it's a bustling river beyond the furthest veranda, slicing its way through the thick gorgeous jungle that borders our villa like a rust-coloured snake. I angle my head over the balcony and take in the floating pools.

I take a few quick photos and send them to my mum, then my cousin.

A woman in a suit introduces herself as Georgina.

'I'm the head of marketing for Maison Partout,' she says with a too-white smile and an English accent, as she gestures to a few women who give us welcome bags. I'm schooling my face into neutral. Pretending I've been to places like this. That I'm used to the luxury. That this isn't my first major brand trip. I will nonchalance to ooze from my pores.

'It's so nice to meet you. This is a stunning location,' I volunteer, as Dimitra gestures secretly that I'm smiling a little too wide and I school my features back to normal. I hate that feeling when you meet important people and suddenly your body forgets how to human.

Georgina gestures for us to take a seat on a luscious green couch and hands us two information packs that read *Maison Partout – Home Is Where Your Heart Beats*.

'We are excited to have you, Margot. Your content is so feminine and inspiring – we are delighted you are here. And you Dimitra – we at Maison Partout love your wellness content. We are offering free spa services during this weekend. Just book in.' She taps the info packet with a perfect nail.

Like any marketing person, she puts a lot of emphasis on words like *delighted* and *excited* and *love*. There's a cool mist in the air and the smell of rich soil; an earthiness hangs heavy. Georgina tells us about the welcome dinner where we will learn about the challenge at hand, encourages us to document our day in the villa, and says her swift goodbyes as she hurries over to another group of arriving content creators.

'Stiff competition,' I say, eyeing up the new arrivals, one of whom I recognize from the TikTok Awards. A beautiful American girl with a knack for transitions. Imposter syndrome tightens its knotted grip around my throat. I don't belong here. I've barely travelled and most of my following comes from the fact I like to get very messy and creative.

'You're better than all of these guys,' says Dimitra, taking in my expression.

'Either way.' I wave my hand in the air, feigning disinterest. 'Whether we win or not, we still get three whole days in paradise. All paid for. We've already won. Let's hit the spa.'

'You're full of crap,' she says, smiling, and it makes me giggle.

'I was going for nonchalant.'

'This lobby literally feels like a spa – imagine the actual spa,' says Dimitra, beaming as she leafs through the services in her pamphlet.

'True.' I nod vigorously. *Lots to be grateful for here.*

'Full-body lychee scrub and a four-hand massage for each of us,' she declares, hurrying off to the check-in desk to book the services.

I scan the lobby, half smiling, until my gaze locks on a pair of cold blue eyes, a buzzcut and an oversized hoodie. It takes me a beat to move on from his face and pretend I didn't recognize him. Of course, I recognize him. Everyone in my country would recognize him. Son of one of our most powerful businessmen. Son of a monster in a cog of monsters.

Hate boils up in me, evaporating the gratitude like hot steam. I can't stand him and everything he stands for. From the corner of my eye, I can tell he's still staring at me but I don't look back. Won't give him the satisfaction. And I'm more determined now to win the challenge. More than ever. Ignoring him, I saunter off to join Dimitra.

He might matter back home but here I'll make him insignificant.

CHAPTER 6

THEO

I unpack my gear in the palatial open-air villa that was assigned to me, making sure to organize my camera equipment and charge everything in the wake of tonight's welcome dinner where they will finally explain how the winner will be selected. Jodi is outside my villa, already in the stone pool. I try not to think about the way that Margot girl looked at me, but that kind of piercing hate is hard to shrug off. It clings to my skin. I'm glad to be away while the protests are unfolding back home as the trial against my father begins. They say news cycles die but they don't, they go dormant, to be woken again by any development.

The news cycle resurrects itself.

'Time for a swim,' Jodi calls. 'Enough polishing your lenses.' I flinch as my FYP shows me an interview with a young mother who got sick because of my father's business. I exit all news; *it's just the internet* is what I've told myself since I was old enough to hold a phone, every time I stumbled across a nasty article about our family. Or articles confirming that the people my father did business with were not good people.

It's just the internet, I repeat. And then I jump into the warm water of the pool.

*

The rain pelts us as we hike up the ancient-looking stone stairs that lead to the grand terrace where dinner is being served. I feel something glide along my feet, then I hear a *plop*, *plop, plop.* I trip as something slippery slides against my sandals, then I aim my phone torch at the ground. Jodi shrieks by my side as we see a dozen or so frogs making their way down the steps in cascading formation.

'Vile,' he says.

I aim the light at my face and grin.

'Ribbit.'

Jodi doesn't share my enthusiasm and curses as more frogs dart between us, then he races up ahead and I follow.

We are both soaked by the time we arrive in the grand dining hall. Georgina rushes to meet us.

'Oh no. You're drenched. There's an elevator,' she says. 'At the ground pool. I'll have someone from the staff show you later. Come, your table is right this way.'

Water drips off my shorts and I run my hand across my buzzcut, sending dribbles of water ricocheting to the marble floor. Camera flashes go off around the room and slowly I become aware that half the influencers in the room are dressed like they are going to a wedding. I catch sight of myself in a passing mirror. Linen combo and sandals. *Never taking anything seriously*, my father would say. I already feel a heat creeping up in my cheeks when Georgina stops and gestures to our large table, pointing to an empty seat next to Vincent Coles, diagonally opposite the vlogger from home.

CHAPTER 7

MARGOT

I stare at him. Unable to help myself at this point. It's akin to seeing a celebrity in the wild. One you don't particularly want to see, and yet . . . You know so much about them, it's an odd creeping sense of unwelcome familiarity. Like seeing a childhood friend at a grocery store all grown up and feeling overcome with the desire to duck into an aisle. I know that he has a private jet and doesn't care about the environment, I know that his pompous sixteenth-birthday party was hosted by a glossy magazine, and I know that he has corgis named after French royalty. I know everything I need to know, and more than I'd like. And I can't stand him.

I don't understand why he is so dishevelled, and wet. His head freshly shaved when usually photos of him have his hair neatly arranged to one side. Knowing so much is uncomfortable, and I fidget under his gaze. The public nature of his parents' divorce, staged photos of his childhood self next to an imported Shetland pony. I'm caught in thought when suddenly I'm being introduced to him.

He nods in my direction but I don't really reciprocate and soon the greetings have moved on to Dimitra on one side, the pretty blonde on my other, a man who just sat down who is introduced as Vincent, a Portuguese couple, and finally a Balinese vlogger named Jodi who seems to be Theo's friend. I've never seen his content and vow to check it as soon as I get the chance. The two late arrivals sit down.

'Theo is from France, like you,' Georgina says helpfully, beaming down at me.

'I know who he is.' It comes out meaner than I intended. 'I mean, everyone knows who he is.' I shrug my shoulders and Dimitra gives me a weird look.

Theo shuffles awkwardly, which, again, I didn't expect. I thought a boy like him would be comfortable with the attention. He's clearly aware he's attractive, and very rich, and hugely entitled. I'm sure the uncomfortable stare is a disarming technique he uses to pretend he's shy.

'Anyway, welcome, everyone,' Georgina segues quickly. 'The presentation will begin shortly.'

The bread course comes swiftly, almost as if Georgina summoned it to melt the unease. Soon there's chit-chat, accompanied by the clank of knives against the china.

'So, we don't like him?' whispers Dimitra.

'You remember the whole thing with the poisoned water in my town? Where loads of people got sick and died?' I whisper back, and she nods; it dominated our national news but was not that interesting to the international circuit until the trial. Nothing gets national attention like a billionaire scandal – not least because his new wife has been deemed to be the next up-and-coming Hollywood actress since her appearance in *Emily in Paris*. Nonetheless, I had sent Dimitra a few screenshots of what was going on.

'He's the son of the guy that privatized our water plants – the man's a monster. And he's the little nepo baby that got everything handed to him, including his following.'

'Jeez, how do you really feel?' says Dimitra into her juice. But I know she's here for the gossip and loves it.

'He's kind of hot,' she adds. 'You know, in an evil way.'

'I guess.' I can't deny he's conventionally good-looking, but I've never thought about whether Theo Delacour is hot; I've just hated him ever since he popped up on my FYP, outraged that the son of such an awful man was landing brand deals with Mercedes. As if he even needs it.

'The whole water scandal …' Dimitra ventures. 'It affected tourism in your area, right? Causing a drop in occupancy at your family's inn? I have the memory span of a goldfish.'

'Something like that.' I shrug my shoulders. I'm not prepared to delve into the details when I'm at a fancy dinner wearing satin, but the Eau Jeune water scandal took more from me than I care to admit publicly or to my long-distance friend.

It took everything. And this boy's father was responsible.

I shake my head and chomp down aggressively on my buttered bread. I can't spend my time thinking about Theo Delacour or his father right now. I need my game face on.

I take stock of the room – a few tables away there is a Chinese vlogger who does a lot of challenges and a lot of hype content, like diving into the deepest swimming pool in the world in Dubai or skydiving in odd places. In the corner of the room, I recognize a Korean guy who used to be in the military and does a lot of nature content. Pretty good stuff – mostly camping and hiking. I assess each person and weigh up my chances. My eyes catch Theo watching me. Is he assessing me too? I wonder what he thinks of my content. Has he seen any of it?

The brief for the rebrand was short. No matter how I spin their emails in my head I can't get that much out of *Home Is Where Your Heart Beats*. If they want high-end glamour, I'm screwed. It also depends on what platform they prefer. I'm not strong on YouTube – people like Theo are the ones who have cultivated a long-term YouTube channel. I'm not huge on spilling my heart to the camera. But then neither is Theo Delacour; I don't think he's ever revealed anything about his private life. It's all tabloid speculation of how he will inherit his father's blood empire and which Paris Fashion Week model he's dating now.

'It just dawned on me,' Vincent announces across the table. 'You're Delacour's son. Like *the* Delacour. The French billionaire that's always in the news.'

CHAPTER 8

THEO

I wish I could bury Vincent on the spot. I didn't need the introduction. And I can see that Margot's green eyes are trained on me like a cheetah's, digging its claws into the soft ground, ready to pounce. *The French billionaire that's always in the news . . .*

'I've been to your part of France,' Vincent volunteers, even though no one freaking asked and he could take the awkward silence for a damn hint.

'That's nice.' Margot nods her head. 'Where did you go?'

'St Jacques Castle near Puyfleur. I was invited to a diamond conference,' says Vincent, chest puffed out. *A diamond conference.* I push my lobster starter around on my plate. I grew up around boarding-school boys like him – pompous and proud. Standing tall on towers built for them by someone else.

'Puyfleur.' The German girl introduced to us as Emma furrows her laminated brows. 'I've heard about that place. With the water scandal.'

'Yup, that's the place.' Margot's eyes are burning. I avoid her gaze.

'I've been there too, as Theo's guest. Absolutely amazing,' says Jodi, doing his best to break the icy edges of the conversation. 'We also spent a night at St Jacques Castle, where they do the wine tours. I really recommend it.'

'As long as you don't drink the tap water, isn't that right, Theo?' says Margot. My eyes flick to hers. She's smiling, but the way her lip has curved makes my skin crawl, like I'm some vulture or something. I've tried to reason with my father many times, most of all over my mother, sometimes over how he's handled the scandal, but it's all led nowhere. Where does she get off trying to humiliate me like this? She doesn't know the first thing about my relationship with my father *or* his businesses.

'Margot lives on the western outskirts of our city. It's nice there, too – so rural,' I say in Vincent's direction. 'Cows, sheep, very disconnected from the realities of the world.'

Vincent's eyes settle on Margot, waiting for a reaction, but she doesn't give one. The second course arrives and she photographs her meticulous plate, frowns at the photograph, picks a flower from the centrepiece and arranges it in her soup. Why? TikTok girls are the weirdest breed of people.

'I haven't been to Puyfleur,' says the Portuguese man, unable to pick up on the social cues and the awkwardness. 'But I would love to go.'

'Probably not a good time right now.' Margot's emerald eyes flash to me again. There are nods around the table. By now, everyone has loosely heard of the mounting protests, the yellow-vested farmers and residents from Margot's town, chaining themselves to government buildings and stopping traffic to protest the polluted local waters. Waters that have been making people sick for ten years.

Pollution that my father is, in their opinion, partially responsible for. Something he denies. But hey, I might as well be guilty just by association. Accusations stick to the skin like honey. And I can tell Margot isn't interested in getting to know me; she's already made up her mind.

The conversation tapers off. My hands itch to check my phone, check the situation. This week the protests are larger than ever before. But equally, I don't want to be the guy reading the news at the table.

'Is it everyone's first time in Bali?' Jodi asks, desperate to break the silence that has erupted from my and Margot's very clear hatred of each other.

People launch into their experiences of Bali as a procession of courses begin to arrive. Half an hour and an ocean of influencer small talk later, dessert – mini chocolate cakes shaped like hot-air balloons – is deposited in front of us. On my third mouthful my eyes land on Margot's and we both hastily look away. Both Vincent and Jodi notice.

As if she has a sixth sense for difficult situations, Georgina saunters over. 'How is everyone doing over here? Have you two met, by the way?' She points her perfect fingers at me and Margot and silence descends.

All the faces previously consumed with awkwardness and boredom suddenly light up at her appearance. Georgina is the person to impress around here, to suck up to. She is one of the judges, after all, and the only one we will be meeting. Neither of us answers her.

'I was just telling Margot and Theo of the time I was invited by the French Minister of Tourism to a diamond conference in their region,' says Vincent.

The urge to say *no one asked you, Vincent* is overwhelming.

Georgina fake smiles at him but her eyes narrow on us, noticing that she has been ignored. 'Right . . . but have you *two* –' she points her finger at me and Margot – 'been properly introduced? You are both from the same region of France!'

'That's the only thing we have in common,' Margot says with an icy giggle.

Maybe she meant it to sound cute but it doesn't. It sounds defensive. Georgina flinches, and I'm surprised Margot has the guts to give attitude to one of the people who decide who wins the competition.

'Oooops, I completely forgot to speak to the kitchen about the champagne toast,' Georgina says before sauntering off, doling out compliments to influencers left and right as she goes, like a publicity butterfly.

'She's hot,' says Jodi under his breath, looking at Margot, who has moved on to talking to the German vlogger next to her. 'But she really *really* hates you, dude.'

'Thank you for stating the obvious,' I mumble into my dessert. 'Of her hating me, not of her being hot,' I correct. The latter is objectively true as well, what with the red hair and bright green eyes, but her negative vibes are putting me off my food.

'You know,' says Jodi, eyes twinkling, 'Shakespeare said the lines between love and hate are thin, or something like that.'

'Shakespeare didn't have algorithm bias.'

In this girl's world I'm the villain, plain and simple. There are no thin lines.

Jodi nods, catching my drift. 'So, you think she's been affected by the whole water thing?' he says, voice low.

'Maybe, or she just hates us because she's been told to. We are all one TikTok away from hating someone we've never met.'

As if she can feel that we are talking about her, Margot's eyes snap to mine. Through habit, I offer her a hesitant nod – it is not returned. I glance at Jodi's fancy watch he got in a brand deal, as waiters deposit flutes of champagne at every table and Georgina takes her place at the podium.

She taps the microphone. 'Welcome, everybody, to our first Maison Partout Content Creation weekend. We at Maison Partout are happy to welcome so many amazing vloggers from around the world. Your content inspires myself, the rest of the marketing team, and the board, and I thank you for making the long trek out here.' She pauses, her eyes twinkling in the spotlight as she scans the crowd before continuing.

'The Maison Partout chain was founded in 1951 and has, for a long time now, focused on opening large family-friendly hotels around Europe. In recent years, the Partout company has been acquiring various new properties around the world, from small boutique hotels to large business hotels, and we are working on placing that under the umbrella of Maison Partout – and that's where you come in.'

Another dramatic pause, meant to drum up excitement. I take a swig of my champagne in the lull.

'Our goal for this weekend is to invite you all here to discover our latest acquisition, the Royal Rita Hotel. We hope you will enjoy your three days here and share this beautiful hotel with your following. Please use our hashtag.' She winks as if she has made some inside joke. 'But more so, this weekend is a chance for us to select two wonderful vloggers who will travel to the other hotels we have acquired around the world and introduce them to the world as our new additions to the Partout brand. Though these hotels are all vastly different, we believe they can be unified under the idea that a Maison Partout hotel is a home away from home, and that – *Home Is Where Your Heart Beats.* You will receive an envelope over breakfast tomorrow that explains the details of the challenge and the rules. Until then, please enjoy your welcome dinner and have an amazing time.'

The Portuguese couple shoot one another a meaningful nod. I suddenly feel like I'm in the influencer Hunger Games.

'To Maison Partout hotels!' Georgina raises her glass. I raise mine again and drain it.

I watch Margot as she throws a look of complete disdain my way, wondering what she's planning. Then she and her friend get wrapped up in conversation.

'I know what it's like, you know,' a voice next to me says. I fight the urge to roll my eyes.

'What *what* is like?' I say, disinterested.

'People not understanding your family business, the sacrifices it takes,' says Vincent in his incredibly annoying way. 'I dated a vegan once.'

I gawk at him. 'What does that have to do with anything?'

'Coles,' he says, as if I'm the dumbest person in the world. 'Like *Coles Meats*? The biggest producers of meat in the UK.'

Though I want to say *why would I know that?* I must admit the name does ring a bell or two.

'I meant,' says Vincent, taking a swig of champagne, 'being hated unfairly is not new to people like us.'

I nod, but instantly hate myself for it.

One billionaire's son telling another that they are hated for no reason over a glass of champagne suddenly makes me feel like an absolute cliché.

CHAPTER 9

MARGOT

It's a strange thing waking up in heaven without needing to die first. There's a large mosquito net ballooning over me, creating an ethereal feeling as the room bathes me in white. I nestle a little deeper into my fluffy duvet, shimmying into the creamy feel of the luxury sheets. When I've had enough, I rub my eyes and wander into the large en suite and switch the water on in the heart-shaped bathtub. I look up at the highest point of the domed thatched roof.

The dollops of bougainvillea sway a little outside my window in the jungle breeze. By the time I make it out into our open-air living room in my bathrobe, Dimitra is already there, filming herself doing yoga. I don't interrupt her; instead I tiptoe around her tripod and onto the veranda. Our pool is gorgeous – made of stone and filtering in water from the rushing river right outside the boundaries of our villa. I film the outside and wonder briefly what my followers will make of all my Bali content.

I started with cottage core videos. Me in flowing dresses dancing around fields of poppies and rapeseed. Me and my friends in the sunflower fields. Baskets of baguettes and jams in the summer, soups simmering in cast-iron pots in winter. People loved a glimpse into our lives in the French countryside.

I go back inside and leaf through the few dresses I brought. I own two main dresses that I film in, both of which I had to save up for and neither of which is truly forgiving in the heat. What am I going to wear? I think of the Portuguese couple and how they were dressed like they were going to Milan Fashion Week. What if I get judged for having the same dress on in the videos? What if that couple has, like, ten outfit changes in a reel? Will it matter to the board and Georgina?

You belong here, you're not an imposter, you made it here fair and square, I remind myself.

I worked blood, sweat and tears to get where I am. Unlike that vile Theo who had it handed to him. My blood boils when I think of him and his entitlement. Too good to even wear a shirt to our welcome dinner, even though he probably owns a walk-in closet full of luxury clothes that would make a better impression. Bet he thinks he has this in the bag based on who his dad is. I can't wait to prove him wrong.

'I ordered breakfast to the pool,' Dimitra says, popping her head into my room with a grin.

Well, that puts a pause on the outfit dilemma for now. I quickly change into my bikini and go out to the pool.

I watch as a gleeful group speed by on their wild river-rafting tour, squealing with excitement around the bends. I snap a few photos of the scenery and post them with the hotel's hashtag. Sparrows drinking from our pool. Bees feeding off white orchids.

There's a knock on the door and the hotel's famous floating breakfast arrives, carried by two men. Circular floating trays loaded with croissants, silky fold-over omelettes, tiny yoghurt bowls, fruit cut into shapes and purple smoothies. The men greet us and set off both breakfasts floating into the pool like mating swans.

Dimitra gets in first.

'*Ooh la la*,' she sing-songs, holding a golden envelope in the air.

I pick up my matching glittering envelope and take a photo of it, with its hot-air balloon wax seal, against the backdrop of the pool. Then Dimitra does the same before finally tearing it open and clearing her throat. Nervous, I bend over the lip of the pool and reach for a tangerine from one of the trays, peeling it as Dimitra takes her sweet time reading.

Excitement twists inside me, right next to the little clock that's been counting down the hours till submission. 'What does it say?'

'Dear tastemakers . . . *huh.*' She pauses. 'I like that. Tastemakers. Way better than Instagram sluts.'

I throw a tangerine slice at her tray. 'Read on!'

'Dear tastemakers, it is our honour to welcome you at the Royal Rita, the new crown jewel in the Maison Partout global hotel rebrand *blah blah blah.* Ah, here it is . . . The rules of the challenge are as follows . . .' I open my own letter and catch up till I'm following along.

You have to film a piece of content featuring footage of the hotel (shorter than three minutes).

You have till midday on Sunday to submit that piece of content to us and post it on your socials.

You may not partner with another participant for the submitted content unless you were invited as part of a duo. You can, however, feature in each other's videos but they will be separate submissions.

Feel free to film any part of the hotel – get as creative as you can!

The Royal Rita Hotel is *where nature meets luxury* and remember, the theme for Maison Partout is *Home Is Where Your Heart Beats.*

Good luck! Team Partout

'That's not much to go on,' I say.

Dimitra folds her letter back into the envelope. 'Nope.'

I look down at my beautiful floating breakfast. 'I guess we should start by filming this. Definitely qualifies as nature meeting luxury.'

'Then we pick outfits,' says Dimitra. 'But we will have to diverge; we can't have all the same content.'

I nod in agreement. Business is business, and as much as I love Dimitra, I have my eye on that prize money. 'But I'll help you if there's a challenging angle.'

She smiles at me. 'Same. What are you going to wear?'

'I'm going for casual,' I say, panicking on the inside.

She laughs. 'Okay, Instagram slut.'

'I think you mean tastemaker?'

Dimitra grabs her camera equipment. 'Let's get a good shot of these breakfasts while the eggs still have steam. Looks good on camera, though I could add it in post.'

'For once I wish I could have my breakfast hot,' I moan, heading for my tripod.

'You know what they say,' Dimitra calls from the other pool. 'An influencer's dish is best served cold.'

CHAPTER 10

THEO

I wander past intricate carvings in the lobby and past the ornate moss-stained sculptures of Balinese gods that line the outside. I stare out at the jungle, almost like I'm trying to crack its secret. *Where nature meets luxury.* I think about what the note delivered to my villa said and gaze out at the jungle again, catching a quick glance of a monkey's tail in my peripheral vision. The lobby is so opulent on its own, maybe that's a good shot. Watching a monkey as I swig my morning filter is enough to entice me, but I have to think of the audience. What would they want to see?

I walk back under the soaring wooden ceiling, past sparkling chandeliers and long velvet couches. Staff dressed in traditional Balinese attire greet me in a serene synchrony on my way to breakfast, and by the time I reach Jodi my head is tired of bowing.

I forewent the floating breakfast and convinced Jodi to do the same. I'm more interested in their kitchen settings, the behind-the-scenes and the average Royal Rita morning than I am in the Instagrammable novelty of a breakfast that floats. Everyone in Southeast Asia has that. I think Georgina and the judges will be looking for something more, something special.

Jodi meets me by the central restaurant where we had dinner last night and we are seated at a beautiful table by the veranda. I set up my tripod pointing at the table and check the view. In a perfect world I would like a casual shot of my breakfast with a monkey scurrying up a tree in the background. A sudden sound of girls giggling sets me on edge.

'TikTok girls,' I say under my breath. 'Such a waste of space. Diluting all things into snippets of these artificial lives.' I wave my hand in the air. 'Taking all the authenticity out of it with their clean girlification of life.'

'*Hnmmm,* sure.' Jodi nods, but is busy staring at them. 'They look real good wasting space though.' He wiggles his brows and I laugh despite myself. 'Theo, I love you, bro, but you're starting to give distinct *get off my lawn!* vibes, only it's about fifty years too early. And saying *TikTok girls* is sexist. It's *TikTok people*. Look at that guy.'

I peek over the edge of the veranda to see who he's referring to. Next to the first of the floating pools, I spot Vincent filming himself with a tripod as he dives into the infinity pool with the precision of an Olympian. A very arrogant and annoying Olympian.

'He's even more annoying than the girls,' I say, just as I spot the girl, Margot, from last night and my stomach gives an unpleasant lurch. Every time I see her, I feel like I've been caught doing something wrong. I watch her approach Vincent and talk to him about something. Is she looking for tips? Trying to sus out the competition? Or is she just hitting on the guy whose six-pack is visible from two balconies away? Either way, I don't have time for this. I roll my eyes when she puts a hand on his arm and turn back to my camera equipment.

*

Back in my room, everything has been cleaned and dusted and in the middle of my bed are two swans made out of towels.

'Very romantic,' says Jodi.

I go and look in the bathroom, just to have my fears confirmed.

'They've filled the whole damn bathtub with rose petals,' I say, picking up some sticky pink mush and flicking it aside.

'Oh, the horror,' Jodi mocks me. 'The monsters! First the floating breakfast and now this.'

'It's not that,' I say, flicking some more. 'But it's wasteful. It's not like I'm here with a partner to enjoy the romance.'

'Speaking of romance. Did you see the legs on that Norwegian girl?'

'Are you ever not thinking about girls?' I say.

'Only when thinking about food.'

I think for a second and sigh. I look at my phone. We've got the rest of the day and tomorrow morning till submission. That includes editing.

'That Margot girl, do you think you could be my wingman, even though she hates you? It might work in my favour. Like, she might hate you so much she ends up attracted to me.'

'Great strategy. *Hi, you seem to hate my guts and everything about me. Would you like to sleep with my friend? He's nice.*'

'No one said anything about sleeping with her.' Jodi flexes his pecs in his mirror and adjusts his linen shirt he chose to wear open. He's lying.

I chuck wet flower mass at him. 'Get your mind out of the gutter, we both need to win. Then we get the prize and travel together for three months.'

'Flower stains don't wash out of linen,' he complains, ignoring me.

‘That sounds like a distinctly Balinese problem,’ I say, clearing the bathtub. I don’t know why the flower mush bothers me this much. Perhaps because it’s wasteful. It’s indulgent. It’s silly. You don’t even get clean bathing in a bunch of flowers. Did they do this because it’s what they want me to film?

‘Like I said, they will probably pick a guy and girl, let’s be real – how the heart beats and all of that,’ says Jodi. ‘Alas, no chance of that romantic bromance trip around the world.’

I’m inclined to agree, which means I have to beat Jodi too. However, we are not in direct competition because our styles are so different: either they want a stylish bachelor who enjoys clothes and the finer things in life, like cigars, or they want a guy with a tripod and aerial shots. One simply cannot be both.

‘Chill,’ Jodi says, rinsing the stain from his shirt. ‘You make the best videos I have ever seen.’

I open my phone and scroll through some of the competition, ignoring messages from my father. Then I look at the bath full of mush. Surely that’s not the most appetizing water. There are so many more intriguing things I could film.

My ears tune in to the water rushing outside, a happy scream. An idea rips through me the way they often do, grabbing hold of my throat, sudden and obsessive.

‘I need to go film the water.’ I grab my camera and go without waiting for Jodi’s reply.

When I was little, my life was full of tutors and extracurriculars. Every weekday signalled a different tutor. I found most topics boring, unable to zero in on information and focus. Until my biology teacher decided to talk to me about fauna and flora and

I found my interest in the outside world unshakeable. I never got bored walking outside, collecting specimens, learning which country housed which plants. That same teacher died from cancer when I was fourteen. My father didn't let me attend his funeral, said it wasn't good for our public image. Or didn't want to approve the additional security detail. I didn't realize at the time my father could somehow be responsible for the death of my tutor. That the water had killed him.

Either way, I think of him now as I walk through cascades of blooms that explode around the property like fireworks. I'm able to name some of them – frangipani, with its pale white and yellow petals. Hibiscus, with its vibrant red, pink and orange blooms. Bougainvillea, with its bulbous bright pink, purple and red flowers that cascade down walls and fences of the stone villas. Lotus – a ritual pool overgrown with its elegant pink and white petals. Finally, orchids, with their intricate and delicate blooms. I film as I go. Scoring high-definition shots of everything. Hours go by like that.

My knees are planted steadily in water, soaking the trousers I was going to wear for dinner. I sink even deeper and set the camera just right, splashing myself in the face. I'm close to being swept away – I feel the pressure of the current against my legs.

A boat rounds the bend and comes barrelling towards me, weighty with shrieking tourists in bright-red life-vests. The instructor screams at me to get out of the way, but I'm close to getting the perfect shot. A giant bearded lizard jets out of the river, tail whipping behind him like an alligator. He felt the vibrations of the oncoming boat. The instructor yells at me one more time to move, and I do, just in time, but not before getting completely splashed. My knee is bleeding as I hurry up to the lawn and rewatch what's on my DSLR. I got the perfect shot. Water rushing at the camera, lizard, everything. Worth the pain.

As night falls, I only have one shot left to get.

CHAPTER 11

MARGOT

I'm taking a much-needed break from shooting, scrolling my phone. I flinch as videos involving water cannons spring up on my FYP. I take a moment to repost a few of them, for awareness. The farmers who have suffered in my area, just like my family, are fighting back against the pollution in the water and the corporation responsible, and it's both painful and beautiful to see. I tap out of a video when I see a man arrested and dragged away, bleeding from his head.

But I can't lose focus. So far all I have is some pretty predictable cottage core content where I walk around the beautiful scenery, running my fingers through flowers.

'How are you feeling?' Dimitra asks, looking out of the window, as if the fading light of the jungle might hold answers.

My fingers ache from browsing everyone's profiles so hard. Scoping out the competition, last-minute Pinterest ideas, but I don't feel that I've cracked it.

All the vloggers have also been engaging with the hotel hashtags and posting about the competition. Someone in the comments said it's like watching a vloggers Eurovision. I have supporters and followers that have created a #teamMargot hashtag. Someone else with no photo in their avatar said I'm too dumb to win. Another account called me a whore. Predictable internet behaviour.

I've learned that on the internet I am a mere pixel – if I flicker out, the greater picture remains whole. That is to say, people don't care when they knock me down. I'm not real to them, just something that contributes to the pretty picture. One they can claw at if they want. Like cats shredding furniture.

The girl from Estonia creates beautiful underwater shots: she has multiple diving licences. She looks like a damned mermaid – she will probably make beautiful videos of the pool. The English guy, Vincent, is heavily into transitions and editing. His videos have an enviable cinematic look to them. I wonder if he has a team back in the UK to edit? Is that technically cheating? No, probably not. I tried to pick his brain earlier today, but it may have come off as flirting. Theo's content has always looked like a feature film, but I haven't bothered revisiting his profile – don't want to give him any extra engagement.

I give everyone's hashtagged content a like and a comment except his. Even if I don't win, I'm planning on building valuable connections here. Then I toss my phone aside.

'Do you think everyone is going to focus on one aspect of the hotel? Or do like an overview of all the amenities?' I ask Dimitra. We separated for a while during the day and she headed to the spa, which I knew she would. Her following is majorly health orientated – not just matcha and slicked-back buns, she's even travelled to Istanbul to look and compare popular one-stop-shop medical centres that do those viral full-body check-ups, and she launched a brand of natural Greek olive oil creams. She's been committed to the point where she has elevated her parents' farm to a boutique wellness Airbnb with scrubs and a hot tub.

Morning green shots and American tourists took some getting used to from her Greek dad who used to walk around in underwear with a cigarette in his mouth.

I admire her hustle, and I wish I could restore my own family's inn to its former glory. Maybe with the prize money I can.

'What do you think the Partout team had in mind for their perfect video? And how are they going to judge it? I mean, sometimes I feel like if you've seen one travel reel, you've seen them all.'

'I think they want creative,' she says, 'unusual and like something no one on the line-up has done. It's all about the shares at the end of the day. Unusual does better now. There's a guy in Korea who just eats noodles in a Spider-Man costume and talks in a funny voice, and his account is blowing up.'

'Where do I get a Spider-Man costume this late in the game?'

She laughs. 'Just eye-catching is what I mean – hook them in the first three seconds.'

With a small degree of insecurity that I haven't seen from her yet, Dimitra glances at the clock near my bedside table.

'There's nothing eye-catching at night.'

I glance out at the canopy. I guess I'll just take a bath and hope for the best. Maybe film myself meditating in the bath for a touch of luxury. I look at the flowers in my now-cold bath. Can I reheat it somehow? Shame to lose the blooms. I think about how my dad dragged an old bathtub outside our farm for me. How we washed it out and filled it with water and yellow flowers. How popular the video of me bathing in it, in a white dress, in the mist is. Basically, today I've recreated a lot of my home content just in a different location. *Very original, Margot.* Might as well redo my bathtub video.

I sit up suddenly, startling Dimitra. 'I've got an idea!'

CHAPTER 12

THEO

I submitted my video yesterday by the skin of my and then spent the day exploring the nearby monkey forest. The insecurity still gnaws at me as I order my brunch at the restaurant. Jodi joins me, looking as unbothered as ever. And, inexplicably, Vincent stops at our table to chat.

'I'm feeling confident,' he says, and I wish it was socially acceptable to just turn away and look at the view instead of engaging with someone who is directly talking to you.

'Oh yeah?' I volunteer half-heartedly. I dig into the most delicious bowl of oatmeal I've ever had, topped with dragon fruit, nuts and maple syrup.

'What do you two have lined up after this?' says Vincent, doing a lean on the wall I thought people only did in movies. 'I mean, I know I might win but I still booked some gigs. I'm not going to risk an empty schedule just for Maison Partout. My agency can cancel it all if I win.'

This man is like a real-life chatterbox and I wish I could find his off-switch.

Jodi answers first. 'I have a brand deal in Malaysia and I'll be in Vegas in a couple of months.'

'I'm not sure,' I say, moving my fruit around my oatmeal. I don't have any specific brand deals lined up. I could go home and do something for the forestry or tourism department like I normally do. I've had a passion for nature-themed content for years and the tourism board is always up for sponsored content. They don't pay the big bucks like car companies but anything is better than nothing. However, the quiet buzzing of news in my pocket makes me not want to go home. The protests are literally happening in my backyard.

'After this, I'm going cliff-diving,' Vincent announces proudly. Jodi mock imitates him behind his back and swigs his matcha when Vincent turns around. 'If either of you want to come?'

'Hmmm.' Jodi contemplates this. 'I might join you. But I think my followers would be more interested in something like a luxury helicopter tour.'

'I like the way you think, mate,' says Vincent. 'I'm planning on filming myself jumping into one of the beds,' he continues. 'Then that splices into me jumping off a cliff. I can splice it with a few more jumps, then back into bed . . . that would look very, very cool.'

Who says things like *very, very cool*?

'Anyway –' Vincent waves his hands in the air – 'it's all a bit of fun for us, isn't it, Theo? Something to do until we take our rightful positions in the family business.'

'I won't be taking a position in the family business,' I say grumpily. The moment I've said the words, I realize I've made a huge mistake and said too much. God forbid something like that would make it into the press – my father would eat me alive, or worse, take it out on my mother. I'm not supposed to ever say anything negative about Eau Jeune. He made that very clear as being a term to him continuing to take care of my mother.

'I mean, not anytime soon. I'm not done having fun.' I try to use a light-hearted tone that matches Vincent's but his eyes narrow as if he can see right through it.

'You know, mate –' he pats my shoulder and drawls with his perfect boarding-school diction – '*privilege* wouldn't be called *privilege* if we were meant to be ashamed of it.'

He walks off with a simple '*see you later*' and leaves me seething. Jodi is watching me with mild amusement.

'Maybe he needs help with the cliff-diving,' I say, grumpily stirring my coffee. 'I'll be happy to do the pushing.'

After brunch we make our way to a large conference room. Content creators slowly filter in until we are all at our allotted places. I spot Margot from the corner of my eye. Georgina takes her place at the podium and looks out at us, beaming.

'Good morning, everyone. We hope you have really enjoyed your stay at the Royal Rita resort, part of the Maison Partout rebrand. Thank you so much for taking part in our influencer preview weekend and for all of the amazing content you have already posted and will continue to post. Our engagement is through the roof and we are pleased to say that the Royal Rita is trending.'

At the word trending, the room of content creators breaks into applause and I shrink back in my seat.

'Now, on to the challenge.' The hired videographer comes a little closer to her and she looks into the camera. You have to hand it them: Georgina and Maison Partout know exactly what they are doing here. The entire competition was streamed; people will be invested in the winner from the start.

'Every single entry was mind-blowing,' she continues. 'We stayed up late reviewing them, and the board of directors and myself are deeply impressed. There were a few that stood out, and we will take a moment to watch them now.' The lights dim and the projector comes on.

The German couple's video is first. The girl squeals and her partner squeezes her hand. It's a pretty standard high-quality video of them kissing in last night's rain. Then him stroking her back in one of those flower baths, then, looking out at the forest, he twirls her around in the pool before kissing her. I guess Bali is, at large, a couple's destination. Maybe this is all Maison Partout wanted all along.

I look over to Margot – a tiny smile plays out on her lips. A smug smile. I cock a brow. Does she know her video is better? How much better? She catches me staring and scowls. Message received. Don't look her way. God, what a righteous . . .

Jodi's video is next and I get over my public anxiety to whoop and cheer for my friend. He's made a really nice video of him smoking a cigar, interspersed with him pushing down his fancy glasses and looking out at the view, then in the gym working on his six-pack, then shopping in the gift shop. It's all shot in a whimsical Wes Anderson-style, with the colour popping and a jaunty jazz song in the background. He definitely made the hotel look good. I clap at the end and he seems satisfied with the response. It's a very good entry and makes the hotel seem appealing and luxurious, even if perhaps the nature element was slightly missing.

They show the Estonian girl's video of her meditating underwater, flowers tied to her hair. They show a bizarre entry from the Korean vlogger where his transitions are all tied to coffee grounds, a little too artsy and deconstructed for the posh hotel chain. Vincent's video follows, as high-end as I would expect, with quality shots and perfect editing; it looks more like a grand tour of the facilities, with exhausting slow-motion of his perfect dives. It feels like a commercial for a travel destination that you see on an aeroplane screen. Soulless. Polished. But the final shot makes me choke slightly on my drink. Him being in the pool cuts to him joining a beautiful girl in the pool – he's half out of the water and swims towards her, joining her at the rim of the pool, and the camera pans to the stars. Something in my stomach contracts unpleasantly. Why would Margot *want* to collaborate with an opponent? I don't have to wait long for an answer.

Margot's video is up next. She has done something clever where it's shots of her back home in France and then, when she closes her eyes, she is here in the same dress, doing the same things. The last shot is slightly provocative of her pouring milk across her naked body in one of those tiresome flower baths. She does everything in the same white dress she seems to have been lucky enough to have packed. Then it's her in the dress in the living room of the villa – there's candlelight, and Vincent is twirling her in the dim light. It's the picture-perfect couple. The essence of romance. The succession of both videos makes it seem even more like they are dating. They've joined forces, I realize.

Find home in the escape . . . reads a caption at the end. It's clever to juxtapose our countryside to this. It's also aesthetically beautiful, and the rock–folk-music hybrid she picked is very fitting. But is it too provincial for Maison Partout? The whole room jubilates, clearly enamoured by this fake dating display. I glance from Vincent to Margot – both seem satisfied. I clap lightly because I don't want to seem like I'm bitter.

All right, she clearly went for the give-me-likes-for-being-attractive package, and if the expression Jodi and Vincent are both staring at her with is anything to go by, it clearly works. I look away, irritated. What does pouring milk all over yourself in a bath full of flowers have to do with a holiday destination?

Then, finally, mine, and I shrink further back in my seat. High-res shots of the hotel, drone footage of the beautiful pools, a monkey nursing its young behind my coffee, a screeching boat heading directly towards the camera, the splash of water, shots of the sizzling kitchen cooking away, shots of morning dew, and, my wildcard, scattering frogs gliding across feet and stairway in the nighttime rain. Some applause follows, not nearly as enthusiastic as for Vincent and the romantic entries, though I hear a supportive holler from Jodi.

Two more videos play after mine but I've completely lost my focus.

'We will announce the winners in a few moments,' Georgina says with a wink, fanning the growing excitement in the conference room. The camera operators start to reorganize their equipment so that some of the cameras are facing the room for the big announcement.

It's clear by the reaction of the room my video wasn't a crowd favourite. Was it the monkey? Did I not show enough of the hotel? Self-doubt begins to creep in on me as the rows of people break into gossip and conversation.

Minutes later, Georgina clears her throat by the microphone and taps a glass with a coffee spoon to get everyone's attention. Then she sets both items down and picks up a gold envelope like the ones we received on the second morning.

'Thank you all for your patience ... without further ado –' she opens the envelope theatrically and reads from it – 'the winners are . . .' She pauses again briefly for dramatic effect. My heart sinks a little and I feel my pulse quickening, my body letting me know how much I actually want this.

'MARGOT AND VINCENT!'

A few rows away, Margot screeches and Vincent's expression turns smug as he rights his button down and heads for the stage. He saunters over to the podium to accept the big fake cheque that they've made. It's symbolic and means nothing, not until they finish the brand deal in forty-five days' time and can cash the more pocket-sized versions. But I can't help but look at the giant cheque that Vincent is twirling in his hands like those roadside people dressed like hot dogs. I actually feel a pang of uncharacteristic jealousy as I look at the cheque and see my mum's entire medical expenses on it. I'm surprised when I look at Margot that I feel bad she will be travelling with a guy like that. Jodi puts an arm on my shoulder.

'We'll get them next time, tiger.'

I walk out of the room feeling a little heavier – my mind is racing with figures and plans on how to get that money now that the competition is out of the way. I check my email – I've been offered a deal with the French sailing programme, but I get seasick.

I walk into an adjacent hallway and smack into a group of people surrounding Margot and congratulating her. She whips her hair over her shoulder as the crowd quietens.

'Congratulations on your win,' I say awkwardly. Because we are stuck in this tiny hallway, I need to get past them and I don't want to seem unfriendly or bitter in that way.

'Thanks, and good effort,' she says dryly. I turn to walk away, but with my back turned hear her saying to her audience rather than to me, 'Maybe in the future keep in mind that luxury hotels don't like to advertise that they have frog infestations.'

The crowd of admirers giggle and my shoulders tense. I keep walking. Maybe she's right and it was stupid to include them.

Someone calls after me. For a moment I think it's Margot wanting to apologize but when I turn, it's Georgina.

'Hi, Theo,' she says with a smile, the most perfect corporate smile.

'Hi.' I'm hesitant. Maybe they would like another video from me? My heart leaps a little. I can see Margot watching us. Judging. Georgina holds a card out to me.

'It's a personal card,' she says. 'With my mobile.'

Is she . . . hitting on me? 'Look, I'm flattered but . . .'

'Oh god, no. I'm old enough to be your mother.' She blushes. 'What I wanted to say is that we at Maison Partout would be honoured to host your father at any of our Maison Partout resorts across the world. We have presidential suites which are fully equipped for important visits. I can send you information anytime.'

'Thanks,' I say, making a show of pocketing the card. 'I'll let him know.'

She thanks me profusely as I walk away. It wasn't about my video; it wasn't about working with me. It wasn't even a shoddy attempt at getting together. There is no *me* in this equation. Maybe I was only invited because of my father in the first place. Doubt creeps in as I make my way to the villa.

Of course, that's what it was. It doesn't matter where I try to walk. All roads lead to my father.

CHAPTER 13

MARGOT

The following morning after the competition ends is my most relaxing yet. I stretch my legs out, digging them into the cloud-like duvet. Three months of this, three months of luxury bathrobes and velvety slippers. Three months of cinematic views. Three months of room service at a whim. I walk out to the garden, wrapping my sheet around me like a toga, and take a deep breath. Then I take a photo and post it to my stories. Not too long after, I get a comment from Dimitra. *Missing it already! And you <3*

I start by packing away some of my clothes, then I do what I normally do and put all the amenity bath products from my bathroom into my suitcase. There can never be too much free shampoo.

When my suitcase is half-packed, I go back to checking my socials and descend into a scroll. Videos of cats, videos of cakes shaped like miniature movie sets, videos of police beatings in my home country. I flinch as news of water cannons floods my screen again. I scroll past it, then, wracked with guilt, I go back again.

The footage hurts my heart. But I force myself to watch it a few times. Even though I can't help in any way, it feels like a bigger betrayal to look away. My finger hovers over the send button – I think of sending it to Theo; maybe he should see the type of things his father's greed has led to. I decide against it. I never have to see that boy again, so why make him feel like he can DM back? Since Dimitra has left already, I call the front desk and ask for a solo floating brunch. Soon I'll be on my flight into the future. Forty-five freaking days of adventure.

A new notification pops on my phone about the protests. I'd better call my mum.

It takes a few rings before she picks up and her tired face fills the screen.

'*Maman*,' I coo, mock kissing the air in front of me.

'*Mon amour*,' she coos back. 'Finally, took a break from paradise to call me?'

'Home is paradise too, *Maman*.' I smile at her. *Just one that requires a lot more manual labour*. Her hair is red like mine but curlier and cut short. She is a beautiful woman, even if the imprisonment of my father and all the work that followed have tired her visibly.

'Sure it is.' She rolls her eyes. 'Alexandre is here helping out, by the way.' My cousin's joyful face pops up behind her, smiling wide.

'*Salut*. I heard you moved abroad, got famous and are no longer coming home.'

I roll my eyes at him. But just then my brunch arrives and, after opening the door, I show them the full glory of the floating tray, the pool and the view.

'They keep us well fed,' I say, flipping the camera to front view again.

'Show-off.' Alexandre's gap-toothed smile fills my screen again. It's still bizarre to video call him and see a young man instead of a child. He's only a year younger but I've always felt protective of him, as if I were the older sister.

I love him so much, always have, ever since he was a pudgy toddler waddling around my father's allotment getting his rakes in a row.

'What are you guys up to?'

'I came to fix the chicken coop before class,' he says.

'*Merci.*' I blow him a kiss for the much-needed help. 'And the university applications? How are they going?'

Alexandre raises a brow. 'You can't nag me from a pool, cousin.'

He has already been arrested once for protesting and I worry whether that will affect his applications. He hands my mum the phone back and her face fills the screen again, and we share a knowing look. Neither of us want him to end up like my father. Lost so far in a cause he ends wandering the dark alone.

'I heard that Theodore Delacour is on the brand trip too,' says Alexandre out of shot. 'What's he like?'

I bite into a croissant. 'Awful. But he's lost and gone home now. Good riddance. Don't need a Delacour souring my last day.'

'Oh, come on.' My mother's voice is soft, face creasing as the connection drops ever so slightly. 'Sins of the father and all that.'

My mother has always been the type of person who can find empathy for nearly anyone. Even for my father, who put his obsession with activism above his family, his inn and his farm, leaving us to pick up the pieces. I grin at her, eager to change the subject. 'Guess where I'm flying tonight?'

'Where?'

'Guess!'

'Jamaica!' Alexandre yells out of shot.

'No, silly, Hong Kong!'

'Ooof, that's amazing!' says my mother. She's smiling wide but there's something loaded in her gaze. She keeps looking to where I know Alexandre is, tinkering by the tool cabinet.

'Alexandre is waiting for his friends and they are going to the protest,' she blurts out. 'I saw the signs in his car.'

'Camille, you said you wouldn't say anything,' my cousin laments. His face fills the screen again, sighing. 'Don't worry, Margot. It's just a small one.'

'You can't go!' I exclaim, reaching for words. 'I . . . I forbid it!'

'You forbid it?' He laughs, but the lightness doesn't reach his eyes. 'I have to go now. Love you. Send me photos of Hong Kong.'

'Please, *Maman*, stop him.' My voice is hoarse as her face returns to the screen. 'Delacour is cracking down on the protests – who knows what could happen.'

'As if I could,' my mum says sadly, not looking at me. She's looking at the door. 'I'll call you back after I walk him out.'

I want to vomit. It broils in my belly, mounting to the surface.

'It's just a little protest,' Alexandre shouts, and the call is dropped.

Nothing about the footage I just saw looked *little*. It looked like at least five thousand people. And Delacour has been putting pressure on the local authorities – any hint of a protest and the local police are there within minutes, throwing their weight around. He has connections with all of the local councils and government bodies – it's not in anybody's interests to stand up against him. My heart whispers that there is no winning. He will do what he likes. My cousin is grown up now. I can't stop him from making mistakes, even if it puts his future on the line. I close my eyes and hope that this time there will be no escalation.

CHAPTER 14

THEO

It's my last day in Bali, so I spend the morning bird-watching long after Jodi leaves for his mother's house on the other side of the island. I recall the names of some of the birds, thanks to my teacher – spotted doves and kingfishers – as they land on nearby trees. I watch a monkey for a while, picking nits off his mangey friend.

Over breakfast, I scroll my feed, lingering on footage of the protests back home. I have texts from my mother asking me if I'm okay. I imagine her reading my reply, that I've lost the competition, and going back to her pickling and shows. As if she is addicted to knowing that I'm okay, and once she gets that hit of dopamine she can continue snailing on. She doesn't want to know that I'm well or the details, she just wants to make sure I'm okay because fear dominates her like a lighthouse, guiding her away from jagged shores. It's all she sees. But when I make her better, everything will change.

I soften when I see that she sent me a photo of some embroidery. I love the woman. I just hate that I have two parents and both only really worry about whether I'm alive; the fine print is a footnote. Well, I wouldn't call my father's version of worrying real worry.

I have an email from one of his aides that requests I come to the château upon my return. I don't want to go home. Don't want to leave the peace for the war that is my father.

I continue bird-watching, eyes opening and closing with the sound of rushing water. Inevitably, I think of what I could have done differently to win the competition. I think of Vincent, and of Margot. They deserve each other. Let them dilly-dally across the Maison Partout chain, creating vapid content of breakfast bowls and Vincent's pectorals. Jodi said my video was amazing and that maybe he could send it to his contact at the Bali tourism office so I could do content for them, but that won't pan out anytime soon.

My phone dings and I flip it with irritation. It's either more news, texts from my mother, or from my father, and I'm in the mood for none of it. I need to get up and finish packing and do my usual cleaning-for-the-cleaning-lady routine I've done since I was a tween. But my heart lifts a little when I read the text on the phone. I wasn't prepared for what it says.

A text that changes everything.

CHAPTER 15

MARGOT

I'm sitting cross-legged in the business class lounge. It's my first time and my belly is uncomfortably full. I squeeze in one more raspberry tart for good measure. I've already hit up the Caesar salad stand, where a chef shredded some rotisserie chicken just for me and grated parmesan over my entire plate. I've also had half a fresh-baked pizza, a tiramisu and six pieces of sushi. I wonder if being carted from the lounge to the aeroplane due to overindulgence might be part of the luxury service.

I scroll my phone. There's a message from Dimitra.

Good luck. I hate you. (Kidding – I love you.) Do not under any circumstances fall for that Vincent guy. If you open the dictionary to 'aura farming' his picture is right there.

I text her back. *Can't make any promises.* Even though Vincent is really far from someone I would ever date. I can see that he's arrogant, and privileged and pompous and in many ways similar to someone like Theo. I'm not interested in men who can't hang up a picture to save their life. I check the clock on the wall; he should be arriving any minute.

I check my phone again. Alexandre has texted to say the protests are slowing a little and he's back to work. Relief floods through me.

I pull out a compact from my bag to fix my make-up. Even though Vincent isn't my type, he's very easy on the eyes and I don't want to look like his troll companion.

I'm applying gloss when I see a familiar shape pass me and sit down at the edge of my row. Oh my god, I can't shake this guy. He's probably on his way back home. I check the board and don't see any flights to France.

I walk up to him.

'What are you doing here?'

Theo looks around, as if he's as surprised to see me as I am him.

'I'm catching a flight.'

'Where to?' I look at the board again.

He sits up a little and takes a sip of his cappuccino. 'Hong Kong.'

'Hong Kong? What are you, some stalker or something? That's literally my and Vincent's first Maison Partout stop.'

He contemplates me for a while as if he could read something beneath the surface. It sets my teeth on edge. Then he runs a hand across his buzzcut and readjusts the hood of his hoodie. With his other hand he's holding a book, a battered copy of *Twenty Thousand Leagues Under the Sea*.

'Vincent isn't coming,' he says, cracking open his book.

'What do you mean he's not coming?'

'Injured himself while cliff-diving yesterday.'

The news knocks the wind out of me and I sit down on the leather lounge chair opposite him. We only had one extra day at the Royal Rita and that idiot went bungee jumping? Something more shocking flits into my brain.

'And you're . . .'

'The runner-up,' he says without looking up from his book. I want to rip that book from his hands and fling it onto the tarmac. The entitled brat. I pull my phone out.

'I'm calling Georgina. I'm not going to travel with you. No way, no how.'

This time he looks up but his expression is still full of vague disinterest.

'You can't just call the manager on this. I was runner-up.'

'I can't travel with someone like you.'

His blue eyes flash. 'You're welcome to pull out.'

'You'd like that, wouldn't you.'

'I don't care what you do. Also, you are the last person on this green earth I would ever stalk.'

By the time we are done arguing, it's last call for Cathay Pacific. Theo walks over to the boarding gate and I reluctantly follow him through the narrow bridge and into business class. I smile at the flight attendant who is polished and prim and leads me directly to my seat, a wide cocooned little pod. Theo is seated on the other side of me with a divider in the middle, only I don't quite know how it works.

I can hear his breathing and it irritates me. He orders water but I agree to the champagne and the orange juice. I've never flown in business class but I'm not about to let some posh billionaire's kid know that. Equally, I'm not about to turn down a single amenity that he seems used to.

'Here's your amenity kit,' says our attendant. 'And a menu. Would you like some more champagne? Oh, and here are your pyjamas.'

I nod blankly and zone out from amazement for a second which Theo seems to notice as he tucks his bag away into the overhead compartment, raising a brow. I flash him a finger.

'Very mature,' he grumbles, getting back into his seat. I open the lovely little leather beauty bag that the attendant has given me and unravel its contents like it's a treasure chest. There are ear plugs and an eye mask, but beyond that there is a range of delightful products, from lip balm to eye cream.

I study my menu – even though I'm still full, I'm also curious. Irritation is still growing inside of me, simmering and boiling over.

'Oh no,' I say dramatically, right as an attendant passes Theo. She pauses when she sees my concern.

I look at Theo. 'The menu doesn't feature anything gold-leafed – I'm not sure what you'll have.' He rolls his eyes. 'Perhaps they have goat's blood, or even the blood of a virgin? Sorry, I'm not clear on what food you consume in your ritualistic château sacrifices with Daddy.'

The attendant seems to perk up at the word *château*.

'She's a nervous flyer,' Theo says to her. 'The prescription for it gets to her head.'

The attendant gives him a giant smile, still probably stimulated by the word *château*. Then she gives me a pitying look and moves on.

'How dare you?' I hiss. My fingers are combing the various buttons, trying to pick a film and figure out how to adjust my seat.

His head whips around. 'How dare *I*? You're the one throwing around your weird illuminati jokes, even though . . .'

He keeps ranting but it's too late. I've figured out how to raise the partition and with a quick movement my headphones are in, *Mean Girls* is on, and the partition is quickly going up – shutting out his face which is red with rage.

The contract I signed says I need to do the brand trip with my partner. It never said I had to make it pleasant.

HONG KONG ISLAND, HONG KONG

The Pearl Hotel by Maison Partout

welcomes you to Hong Kong.

During your time here, you will enjoy:

A trip to Victoria Peak

A dinner in the Sky

An invigorating spa experience

Please let us know if we can be of any assistance. The Pearl aims to be a five-star destination for anyone doing business in Hong Kong or for couples seeking an upscale hotel for their time in the city.

CHAPTER 16

THEO

I'm weary by the time Hong Kong airport air-con whiplashes my face with cold. Being hated takes its toll on the body, one way or another. And so does my deep-seated fear of take-offs and landings. I'm not sure if Margot noticed anything as she sporadically shot me mean glances, but I've become pretty good at hiding my fears.

Margot rushes past me and quickly takes her place at the front of the very long passport control line. By the time I approach it, a wave of arriving passengers surges from both sides and I end up a couple of hundred people behind her. She looks back at me and smiles smugly, arching one perfectly plucked brow. I was going to patiently wait my turn but her constant righteousness is getting to me. I take a U-turn.

By the time she arrives at baggage claim, I'm already drinking an iced Americano, my coat and camera bag slung over my collected luggage.

'How did you beat me here?' she demands, as if I cheated in some imaginary race. I sip my Americano.

'There was a priority line for my tier.'

My father's never-ending first-class flights put the family in a gold tier in multiple airline unions. Meaning that if I keep my eyes peeled, I can usually find a priority line that cuts through. This is one of the few perks of being my father's son that I'm happy to use since there's no way he can know I've used it. Margot could have cut as well because she flew business class but I bet she doesn't know that.

She mumbles something about Daddy's money and silver spoons. I ignore her.

Her pink suitcase arrives and I reach for it when I see her struggling, but she yanks it back, which causes me to lose my balance and lurch forward onto the luggage belt. I brush myself off and see her flash me an infuriating smirk as she walks past me towards the *nothing to declare* channel. This is going to be a really long trip.

'Your royal highness,' she says, bowing low in front of the taxi driver by the kerb and gesturing for me to sit. I suppress a growl and smile at the cab driver sheepishly, pretending I'm in on the joke.

'I'm sick of your little prince jokes. They're cliché,' I tell her in the car. She's in the backseat. My eyes narrow on her in the mirror – how is her hair still so perfectly styled when I'm sweating like a chimney sweep? I offered her the front but she ignored me, lifted her giant suitcase into the boot, despite the driver's protests, and took the back.

'You don't know the first thing about me,' I add. And it's true. She would be shocked to know I live in a two-bedroom with my mother, who doesn't leave the house. But I'm not going to give her the satisfaction of telling her. My mother still needs my father for survival, and those strings come laced with a gagging order. The last thing I need is the queen of likes filming me admitting something about my dad and posting it to the internet. Not worth the risk.

'Clichés are clichés for a reason.' She puts her bulky headphones on, and with that the conversation has come to a grinding halt.

So many retorts build on my tongue but I fidget with the zip of my jacket instead, letting the scenes of Hong Kong wash over me. I take in the sea on one side, an unnatural cerulean blue speckled with unceremonious container ships piled high like floating Jenga towers, while green hills loom before us looking out of place in such a sprawling metropolis. It's as if a child has made the entire landscape out of Lego.

Our speed drastically diminishes, and in the overhead mirror I can see that Margot is wide-eyed. She's taken her headphones off and is watching the fleet of neon signs, fruit vendors, racks of shoes, and window displays of glazed duck fly by. I stare too as the city becomes a technicolour swirl of sights and sounds I want to explore further – a blood-red flash of a temple peeking between skyscrapers, urban playgrounds, laundry on balconies, all of which are towered over by imposing glass and metal. The old merges into the new in a chaotic yet seamless way, as if history is being absorbed by the metal and re-formed. The driver points out the peak but it's too late to see it. I focus on the harbour, my eyes narrowing on the junk boats with their wine-coloured sails, like pirate toys bobbing in a bathtub.

My father always liked Hong Kong. When I was younger, he'd tell me stories of this place, explaining that it was where the old lives harmoniously next to the new. Hong Kong has been on my bucket list for years, although when I tell people that they are often surprised I haven't been there, or to other famous locations, assuming my father would take us with him on all his business trips. But he preferred to travel in the comfort of strangers and associates.

'My job is no place for children,' he used to say. What he meant was that his family was a distraction from the things that really mattered to him. He doesn't like to mix business with pleasure; he often said that in order to succeed in life you can't let people get in the way. I don't like thinking about what my father said. I like it even less that I agree with him completely.

CHAPTER 17

MARGOT

Ever since we got off the aeroplane my body has been seething at the sight of him. The nonchalance with business class, not even being impressed by the free one hundred per cent cotton pyjamas and toiletry bag. And how could he say no to all those desserts? Even the divine chocolate mousse, and the complimentary Lindor truffles, and the morning smoothie? He barely ate. Probably saving himself for some keto nonsense. He barely filmed anything either. He either thought he was too cool for it, or all that luxury was so everyday for him he didn't even notice it. Didn't even care to savour it.

I send my mother a photo of the view from the plane and tell her I've landed. Dimitra has sent me photos of herself back in Athens and all-caps reactions on my new travel partner.

WHAAAT????

ABSOLUTELY NO WAY!

At least he's easy on the eyes, she writes. *Vincent had a real* American Psycho *polished look to him that made me worried for your safety.*

I don't care if Theo is easy on the eyes. If I had to think of one thing that could ruin this perfect opportunity it would be doing it with him.

I'm a little sad I spent half the flight worried that Theo would see how excited I was, and the other half making sure to film everything I possibly could: from the tiny little face mists they provided to the edible flowers on the langoustine salad. Luxury airline content is so aspirational, I'd be crazy not to include it. Not only do my followers love stuff like that, but a part of me also wants my friends to see how far I've come. For my mum to be proud of me. For all I know, we might be in economy for the rest of the tour and this was just a special treat for the start. I even filmed a *Get Ready with Me* in the giant toilet, complete with shower demonstration. To which Alexandre promptly commented *I'm not one bit jealous.*

I had no idea first and business class had such large toilets. But then, of course, Theo had to see me in my Korean sheet mask, taking pictures of my slippers and smoothie as he walked by my seat, and I could feel the heat rising through the slimy paper on my cheeks. I swear I heard him laugh under his breath.

I bet he thinks he's too good for all of this. Too cultured. When all he really is is too spoiled to enjoy something magical like being 30,000 feet in the air with custom-made juice freshly squeezed from whatever fruit you like.

I don't let him catch my excitement about how breathtaking the jungle-cradled Hong Kong skyline is either, the way the river is surrounded by what looks like a thousand skyscrapers which are then surrounded by lush misty foliage, the city made up of blue, grey and green stripes. Once in the car I leash the excitement inside of me as it continues to brew, covering it up with a scowl which I treat Theo to every time he looks at me in the rearview mirror.

The Pearl Hong Kong hotel, just like the skyline and the flight, is a dream – everything from its opulent marble lobby with its bright pink velvet couch in the shape of lips, to the sparkling chandeliers hanging above our heads. From the corner of my eye, I spot that there's even a macaron stand, a shop selling nothing but fancy teddy bears, and a stand full of matcha drinks. It's so whimsical and adorable my hand is already itching towards my phone. I hold back as a swarm of hotel staff flutters over to greet us. Three women and a man, all in sharply ironed, crisp white shirts beneath perfectly fitted black blazers.

A young woman with jet-black hair pulled back in a tight bun held in place by a butterfly-shaped clip steps forward and shakes my hand. She introduces herself as Xiu and tells us she's the manager of the hotel. She then hands us a crisp business card, the rest of her entourage following suit – Head of Bookings, Manager, Restaurant Manager, Marketing – until I'm left holding four business cards like an idiot.

Theo introduces himself and hands over his own business card. *Of course* he walks around with business cards. What do they say? *Hello, I'm Theo, son of a corrupt billionaire.* He looks over at me and raises one eyebrow. Am I meant to be impressed? I bite back all the comments bubbling away in my mind and smile at Xiu as she explains that we will start with a tour of the hotel and hands us both info packs.

'It is late now so we will leave you to rest. But for tomorrow we have booked a sightseeing tour of the city in the morning, an array of treatments in the spa at four p.m., then a dinner for you both in our sky garden at seven p.m. There is also a night garden on the twenty-first floor if you want complimentary high tea.'

'Please split up all the activities and meals,' I say quietly, my voice wavering a little. 'We won't be taking them together.'

Xiu stops walking, as do the rest of the staff, and we grind to a halt. Theo doesn't say a word and simply stares at his five-hundred-dollar trainers as we all block the corridor. The manager of the hotel stares at me blankly. She blinks once, then twice, as if I have more to add to my comment. I don't.

'But we also booked a tour and excursion to Victoria Peak, and a private breakfast on departure day with the chef,' she says eventually.

'I'm just saying, *we* . . .' I gesture to Theo. 'We don't work together. We don't even know one another that well. I'm sure the meal reservations can be booked separately, you know, double the content!' I give a nervous laugh.

Xiu's knowing eyes are narrowing with every word I utter, while Theo just looks embarrassed by what I'm saying.

'This is how the head office scheduled it – this is what they requested,' the manager says, the tone of her voice getting higher and higher with fear as if she's talking about some ominous controlling entity somewhere. The three other members of staff steal nervous glances at one another as they shuffle from foot to foot.

'Oh, well, I just meant that, you know, we don't have to do any of it together . . .' My voice starts to shake and falter and dip, making the tension in the air grow even thicker.

'Very professional start . . .' Theo says under his breath, although I'm sure the entire team has heard him.

'I *am* very professional,' I snap. 'A profession that I do alone with nothing but my phone and a tripod. Not with a team of people and editors.'

Theo swallows, his jaw tightening and twitching. The awkwardness I've created permeates every inch around us, growing as heavy as the fog I saw from the taxi earlier.

'We will stick to the schedule. It's a nice schedule,' Xiu says with a strict finality as she nods in our direction and hands us our room keys. 'We hope you enjoy your stay with us. Maison Partout is so happy to have you. There are some fruit bowls in your rooms. *Georgina sent us your specifications*,' she says in Theo's direction.

Who has specifications for fruit? I roll my eyes so hard I'm at risk of dislocating an eyeball, making Theo fidget uncomfortably. I stifle a yawn and I realize I have no idea what the time is. It's dark outside but I'm so tired I don't know whether I should be eating, sleeping or making content right now.

Xiu must sense how exhausted I feel. 'Your rooms are the first two to the left on our skydeck floor,' the manager says, pressing the elevator button. 'Please take note that room service is available at all times. The restaurant closes at eleven, and we are two streets away from a famous night market.'

I think the hotel staff would have normally walked us to our doors but they all look like they can't wait to get away from us. The elevator pings, the golden doors open, and with a final 'goodnight' from Xiu, Theo and I are left alone in the gilded elevator.

'I don't have a team of people,' he says under his breath as the doors slide closed.

As if! I roll my eyes again, noting with satisfaction that it makes him grit his teeth harder.

‘You sound like one of those people who says *I’m self-made – all it took was a lot of hard work and my father’s million-dollar loan*.’

He stays silent and it feels like a victory. The elevator isn’t small and we left our luggage with the concierge downstairs, yet it still feels cramped in here and I’m eager to get some distance between us. I keep catching wafts of Theo’s aftershave mixed with the musty scent of our damp skin. I catch sight of myself in the mirror and want to tidy up my hair that has grown frizzy from the humidity, but his gaze catches mine in the reflection and I lower my hand. I’m not going to give him the satisfaction of thinking I’m vain and vacuous.

The lift finally opens to a beautifully carpeted hallway and a gust of welcoming AC. Theo still hasn’t taken the bait or retaliated; he just swipes his key card on the leftmost door and disappears into his room, leaving me alone on the plush carpet. I can’t decide if what I’m feeling is seething rage or something a whole lot emptier.

CHAPTER 18

THEO

The opulent fruit bowl in the corner of my suite mocks me. I move it three times before realizing I can see the generous kaleidoscope stack of dragon fruit from any vantage point. The dragon fruit feels metaphorical: beautiful, yet void of substance. Just like Margot. Her accusatory tone rings through my mind like a train line announcement. *Me and my father's million-dollar loan* . . . I won't give her the satisfaction of knowing that I don't have a good enough relationship with my father for him to pay for my mother's medical bills, let alone give me a million-dollar loan for a business venture. I can understand how she might have the wrong end of the stick; paparazzi have always favoured photos of my family on holiday. If all you had access to were aerial shots of me and my father on his yacht in Monaco or outside our chalet skiing, then you might think we get along swimmingly. But I don't owe other people the burden of clarifying their misconceptions. Not when they are this rude about it. Not when they are so volatile and unpredictable in public and always armed with a phone. I think about how frank she was in front of the flight attendant, and again now in front of Partout staff. I can't trust her. Her lack of professionalism makes my blood boil.

I open the sliding doors leading to the balcony. The air is so hot and humid you can practically chew on it. I breathe in deeply as I take in the sweeping Hong Kong skyline, inch by inch. I take the opportunity to send my mother a photo. Her reply is fast and predictable.

Be careful over there, I saw a terrible video . . .

She goes on to describe every possible natural, and unnatural, disaster that has ever happened in Hong Kong. A few minutes pass before she tracks down the terrible videos in question and sends them to me. I scroll through. Some aren't even about Hong Kong, but all contain scary predictions and overall danger and gloom.

I'm in a luxurious suite where the most dangerous thing is the welcome basket of Asian sweets they left me. I rip open a packet of flavoured seaweed, chew on it, and wander back to the window to take in the rest of the skyline. There's so much colour, so much movement and sound, yet all is silent and still up here. My father would love this suite, the penthouse that might bring him closer to God. Personally, I've always loved a good ground floor, close to the earth. Less trapped.

It's past eleven, which means the restaurant has closed. I browse the late-night room-service menu – burgers, club sandwiches, schnitzel. Everything designed to cater to the Western visitor. I'll be damned if I spend my first night in Hong Kong eating schnitzel. Margot's judgmental gaze or not, I'm leaving to find something interesting. I'm sure she's photographing the spa anyway, based on her content.

I track down a pair of shorts and head out into the humid streets.

The rattle of nighttime Hong Kong is like music to my ears. The flickering neon of fruit vendors, the slice of a knife as someone decapitates a fish on a white, bloodied surface. Arguments erupt, or what seem to be arguments to me but might be loud banter. Voices come from all over, calling and pinging off dark alleys, pots simmer violently in the back of food stalls. I follow the directions the front desk gave me, trusting my internal compass which has always been excellent. The city is so alive – everyone is bustling, eating, hacking and coughing, laughing, hurrying somewhere even though it's late. A lot of cities like to say they never sleep but for most it's a lie; in Hong Kong's case it's the very obvious truth.

The smells hit me one by one: fruit, fish, meat, smoke. Each one more potent than the last. The city is overwhelming, in the best possible way, washing over me and waltzing with my senses in tandem. Which means I can't even think of anything else. Not even my mum, or dad, or Margot's hate.

I focus on getting through the foot traffic, feet light, becoming one with the flow. The neon light pulls me like bait on a fishing rod, until a moment later I'm in the half-orange darkness of a dim alley and then spat out again into the light of a Seven Eleven. Inside, the air conditioning washes over me like a sheet of frost and I get myself an ice-cold lychee drink. Sweat beads across my brow as I allow my body to focus on its rising hunger. My heart is pounding, but in a pleasant way, the way it does when I know adventure is just around the corner. These are the highs that I live for.

I find the night market easily enough. Rows and rows of temporary stands are flooded with white light as they showcase their delicacies and wares. Haphazard scatters of shiny luxury fakes, bulbous Hello Kitty backpacks, stalls of those irritating dancing toys my mum would bring me every Christmas, like a ferret chasing a ball in a circle or a dog on a lead mechanically hopping away. Stalls with sugar-cane juice and phone chargers, and then finally, rows and rows of steaming food.

I start to salivate as my senses are assaulted with the sights, sounds and aromas of all these interesting dishes. I start with a custard bun, even though I didn't want to start with sweet, but the food vendor was persuasive and I made eye contact for too long. Then I have two beef skewers in a spicy bean sauce, then a rice noodle roll with shrimp and sesame, and lastly, a black-milk brown-sugar bubble tea. I sip on my icy cold drink, which offers a little respite from the humidity, and I decide to save some room for dinner while I browse the market stalls.

I look at phone cases, because mine is rubbing off at the edges, then move on to the Marvel figurines, elaborate chopstick sets, and I examine a travel chess set. The dealer convinces me it's hand-carved, which I doubt because his whole stand is littered with them. I buy it anyway, in the hope that I might come across someone on this journey who might want to play with me. Chess club was one of the few weekend activities I was constantly signed up for that I didn't hate. We were taught by a Grandmaster. And though they would probably balk at the non-traditional design of these pinkie-sized figurines, I feel like having this in my back pocket brings me closer to the memories of when things sucked a little less. Before my father left my mother and the whole province hated him.

I remember halfway through the market to get some footage of the sizzling woks, the thick crowd and the vendors' handing out tasting samples, so as to add some culture and flair into my Maison Partout videos. We've got to film the parts of the itinerary according to the theme of the hotel, as well as all the amenities, bringing everything back to *Home Is Where Your Heart Beats*.

But on the phone, when she told me I was the runner-up, Georgina said we were expected to make no less than three pieces of video content of each hotel, multiple carousels, daily stories, and were encouraged to make reels about the destinations in general as well. That's on top of complying with each hotel's requests. There's not really any time to waste, I think to myself as I examine a few more phone cases at a stall. As my gaze travels deeper towards the hole-in-the-wall accessories shops that line the market on both sides, I spot Margot a few feet away from me.

Her head snaps up and she swings around to look behind her, almost like she can feel my eyes on her. She's sitting on a stool, taking photos of the sparkly sandals on her feet. I watch as she turns her head this way and that, her bright red hair shining beneath the neon lights of the stall.

I cock a brow at her, closing the distance between us and leaning against the doorway of the shop. 'When Maison Partout asked for engaging daily stories, I don't think they meant feet pics. Nice as your feet may be.'

'For your information,' she says icily, gesturing to the shopkeeper and paying her, 'I'm getting some shoes for my mum and was sending her choices.'

I stare at the shelves, wondering whether my own mother would also like a pair of glittery butterfly sandals. But I immediately know the answer, and I'm surprised to feel a tinge of jealousy at Margot's simple relationship with her mother where she can buy her souvenirs and keepsakes.

She points at another pair and recounts her money. 'I'll take them in pink, and blue, and the frilly ones.'

'You'll run out of luggage space by our first destination.'

‘I’ll just buy another suitcase then,’ she replies, gesturing with disinterest at the large luggage shop next door. That’s the fifth luggage store I’ve seen since I got here. Clearly running out of space is a problem shared by many who visit Hong Kong. Margot collects her bags and walks towards the back of the phone case stall, examining a gaudy bedazzled Sailor Moon case. Then, without so much as thinking about it, she buys that too. Then snaps a photo of it.

‘So, what? You, like, followed me?’ she asks, without turning, and I get whiplash from her suddenly switching into French now that we are alone, her sarcastic tone stronger in our shared language. She then walks onwards, out of the phone case tent towards the steaming-food stalls. As if I’d let her just leave that accusation hanging between us.

I follow her past another bubble tea stand and into the market, acting like the creep she just accused me of being. ‘Do you always accuse people of stalking you? Even when they’re travelling with you?’

‘If the sparkly shoe fits.’

‘Hey!’ I plant myself in front of her so she has to gaze up at me, although my bravado fades a little when I see the ice in her eyes. The look of cold disdain on her petite face is such a contrast to the silly, sparkling pink sunglasses on her head, which she also seems to have purchased tonight.

‘For the record,’ I say, as sternly as I can muster, ‘there’s no one I would rather not run into at this night market than you.’

‘That’s a double negative.’

‘It’s true.’

But as soon as I utter that last line, something in the snakelike swarm of marketgoers catches my eye. Just a flash. A face.

Something that proves my former statement isn't true. There actually *is* someone I would rather not run into at this market, someone a lot worse than Margot. And his brutal blue eyes are now trained directly on me. My heart begins to thunder so loudly it drowns out the hustle and bustle of the market, beads of sweat collecting on my top lip and under my arms. This can't be happening. I'm imagining things. I crane my neck, searching the crowds for the all-too-familiar face, but he's disappeared. He's melted back into the throng. I grab Margot's hand and hold it tightly as she tries to yank it away.

'Hey,' I hiss. 'When I say *run*, you run!'

CHAPTER 19

MARGOT

'Run,' Theo spits as we spin around the corner, his clammy hand grasping mine so tightly I've lost feeling in my fingers. Before long, my sandals are flapping against the pavement of an alleyway, then he's leading me down one street, and another, rounding through a wholesale fruit market where shoppers yelp and jump out of our way as we barge past them, then into another side street under a construction trestle. Theo keeps to the shadows, his eyes darting side to side then glancing behind us.

'What the hell are you doing?' I shout out, but either he doesn't hear me or he doesn't care because he doesn't slow down.

I thought I'd be scared, but I'm not. I also don't know why I'm trusting him like this, but I do. I guess with my dad's past disorderly conduct and endless arrests, I was raised to believe that when someone says 'run' . . . you don't stop to ask questions. As my heart pounds, I'm brought right back to when my father vandalized an Eau Jeune truck while we were out together. He just threw a brick through the windscreen and told me to run.

We start to slow down, and my heart rate begins to ease too. Theo also appears to be a little more relaxed now, having gone from a sprint to a fast walk.

Was someone following us? I couldn't see anyone, but it certainly felt that way.

My thighs start to ache just as Theo grasps my hand tighter and leads us through a dark doorway into an empty temple. The incense hits me as his grip finally loosens and I yank my hand out of his before doubling over, hands on my knees, and taking large gulping breaths. Maybe I shouldn't have eaten three bean-curd buns at the market just now.

'Eww, your hand is sweaty,' I hiss, wiping my hand on my trousers.

'Well, it's like jungle heat out there,' Theo replies casually. He appears to be less out of breath than me, which is irritating. Drops of sweat are trickling down his forehead. He breathes out hard, running a hand across his face and over his short hair, coming to rest at the nape of his neck. With his other hand he absentmindedly taps away on his phone, as if searching for something.

'Why did you drag me in here?' I ask.

'It's safer.'

'Safer than what?'

'Than staying in the market. Trust me.'

My eyes widen, my heart rate rising again.

'What do you mean? Was there, like, a bomb threat or something?' I ask.

He narrows his eyes, his brow creased with confusion. 'A what? A bomb threat? No.' He shakes his head as if I'm the one being ridiculous, even though he's just made me run across the whole of Hong Kong for no good reason. 'How would I know if there was a bomb threat? I'm not Nostradamus.'

'Who?'

'A famous psychic. You know what? Never mind. It was for the best. A few more minutes in here then you're free to go.'

'You still haven't explained why you've dragged me here.'

But Theo ignores me and walks off towards some steps leading up to what appears to be an altar of some kind, and, as my eyes adjust to the low light, I can finally see how beautiful our surroundings are. Every wall is lined with red hanging lanterns, and at the base of the stairs is a giant golden bowl. I wish Xiu was with us so I had a local to tell me what I'm looking at.

But my wonder is quickly replaced with indignant rage. What the hell did Theo think he was doing dragging me around the city like I was nothing but a ragdoll? Seething, I follow him up the steps to the altar. He's already made his donation, and when I reach him he hands me a few candle offerings. I don't want anything from him, but equally it feels rude to not accept a symbol of peace in a place of worship. I nod my thanks. Through the flickering light I watch Theo, head bowed, eyes lowered, as he lights candle after candle while muttering things under his breath.

Is it weird to think about what your enemy prays for? I light my own candles and ask the god whose name I don't yet know to help my dad recover from his issues. And to keep my cousin safe at the protests – safe from following my dad's path.

'We're okay to go.' Theo breaks me out of my temple trance a few minutes later, his voice sounding far too loud for this sacred, empty place. I get up from my knees but my legs have gone numb and I stumble a little, the ache of the hard-stone floor and our spontaneous sprint getting the better of me.

Theo catches me as I fall forward and find my balance.

'Easy,' he says.

'I'm fine,' I mutter, shaking him off. Neither of us say a word as I follow him out of the temple and across a few streets, assuming his sense of direction is better than my abysmal one. But as soon as the hotel appears into view, I round on him.

'I didn't even get to eat my fill at the night market because of you!'

He looks over my shoulder at something behind me. 'That place is still open. The woman at reception said it was famous, remember?'

I turn around and see the dim sum place he's looking at. Fine. My grumbling stomach agrees that yes, it's more than fine. Wordlessly, I head towards it, but I'm not alone. He's right behind me. I spin around and fix him with a glare.

'What?' He shrugs his shoulders. 'I haven't had my fill either. Let me treat you to dumplings as a thank you.'

'A thank you for what?'

'Running when I said so. And running faster than your abilities.'

Faster than my abilities? I'm going to murder this boy.

'I can buy my own dumplings,' I hiss. But he's already entered the restaurant and is gesturing to the waiter. Inside it's crowded, which I guess is a good sign, but not all the tables are taken. Reluctantly, I follow Theo inside but I choose a separate table. He can thank me from a distance; I've had enough of his company for one night.

CHAPTER 20

THEO

The siu mai pork dumplings are so divine that I barely feel Margot's hateful glare trained on me in the small dim sum restaurant. We are sitting at different tables but within speaking distance, which I'm finding hilarious. She might be one of the most stubborn people I've ever met.

'So, you're *still* not going to tell me why we had to run the Hong Kong half-marathon?' she says through a mouthful of duck bao bun. I dip my shrimp dim sum in my beef broth and pop it in my mouth before answering her. The chopsticks slip out of my fingers and fall to the table with a clatter. I readjust them, silently sighing under my breath as they keep crossing over like dowsing rods. My father ate sushi my entire childhood and insisted I ate it too, the correct way. Then he would get frustrated because I could never get the hang of the chopsticks. I still can't. I curse as they slip out of my hold again and fall into my soup, splattering me with broth. Margot snickers, clearly delighted at my ineptitude.

'I saw someone I know from home,' I say quietly, although loud enough for her to hear. 'Someone complicated. I know they would make our time here unnecessarily difficult.'

Margot pops another dumpling in her mouth before removing

the wooden top off a tray that's just arrived, pulling a steaming mushroom out of it.

'What? Like an assassin?' she says, far too casually.

'No, not really. An old friend.'

'Because if he was there to kill you, I would have run towards him, not away.'

I'm not sure I believe that she really wants me dead. Someone enjoying a char siu to that extent doesn't seem like the murderous type to me. But who knows? Judging by the latest comments on my Instagram, she's not the only one who wants me dead.

Nepo Baby.

Son of a killer.

Why aren't you speaking out for everyone that got sick?

Even though it's gone midnight, more people keep entering the bustling restaurant. When the waitress notices us speaking to one another she, to my great amusement, forcefully makes Margot move to my table.

'*You sit with friend*,' she keeps repeating. '*One table only!*'

Margot balks at the grumpy older lady and wordlessly changes places, sitting opposite me as the waitress clears room for her new customers.

'Is that all you're going to tell me about the person you were running away from?' she mumbles. 'Okay, stay mysterious then.'

She probably thinks it was an ex-girlfriend, which is fine by me. Safer that way. Another steaming circular box arrives and she films the act of opening it, almost in a panicked way, like she forgot she was meant to be creating content.

'Do you think . . . that Maison Partout expects us to be on each other's socials, like, to collaborate?' she says quietly.

She's acting nonchalant about it but her cheeks are pinking and she's fiddling with her napkin. After her obvious disdain towards me, I'm glad she has the grace to feel a little shy about the situation with the hotel staff. But clearly, she doesn't want to disappoint Maison Partout head office either.

'I think it could be beneficial to us both if we have a temporary truce and collaborate sometimes.' I voice what I've been thinking about for the better part of the last few hours. Margot and Vincent likely won because they were in each other's videos, bouncing off each other; there's no way Maison Partout isn't hoping for a little bit of that.

She arches a brow, her face nearing something like disgust. 'Why?'

I fight the indignant heat rise in my face. 'I have a strong feeling that it's what Partout wants – for us to be in each other's videos the way you and Vincent were, especially with the whole *Home Is Where Your Heart Beats* theme. The brief even said they are pitching themselves as the new destination for *couples* and young professionals. It will be very hard for either of us to bring that across without helping one another.'

'Sorry, are you suggesting we fake being a couple on Instagram?' She scrunches up her face like I've served her a bowl of live crickets. I scoff and wave my hand. The idea of me dating her is beyond preposterous.

'No. Fake dating someone like you would be as negative for my brand as it would be for yours. I'm just saying, it wouldn't kill us to meet them halfway. This might be a surprise for you but I kind of need this brand deal too.'

She arches her brow even further, probably wondering why I could possibly need Maison Partout, or why I said *someone like you*, but she doesn't ask. Out of pride or disinterest or something else entirely. I only said it because of the face she was making, like I was a gargoyle made flesh. She continues to say nothing, watching me with her fox eyes. She eats a dumpling instead.

'Making videos with the sons of corrupt billionaires doesn't bode well for my personal brand,' she says, blowing into her tea.

What an absolutely infuriating girl. '*Vincent* is the son of a corrupt billionaire too,' I say through gritted teeth.

She leans in. 'So, you agree? You think you're the son of a corrupt billionaire?'

'Back off, Regina George,' I say, fully clocking the reference and turning my attention back to my food.

'It's not the worst idea, in regard to Maison Partout . . .' she says finally. 'But it's not just about my audience – my friends wouldn't understand what I was doing with you. Not with them being at the protests and all.'

So, her friends would hate her even being near me. Interesting. They are still bound to piece it together on socials, once they see us posting about the same experiences, but I guess she can say she avoided me as best she could. Which she has done.

'Dessert?' asks the waitress.

I point at something on the menu. 'Is there any citrus in this?' But the lady doesn't understand me. 'Lemons? Oranges?' I continue. I try with Google translate. She shakes her head.

Margot orders some yuzu cake creation but I stay away from it.

'This is delicious,' she says, nearly moaning into her dessert. 'Try some.'

'No, thanks.'

'Oh, come on, stop being so freaking precious. First the fruit bowl, now this.'

I tense, my father's words ringing through my mind – *Never show weakness* – but before I know what I'm doing, the truth escapes my lips.

'I have a few allergies,' I explain. 'Two of them quite severe.'

Why did I just give her my perfect kryptonite? *A weapon that doesn't even require spilled blood*, my father would say.

'I, ugh . . .' she hesitates a little. 'I didn't know. Sorry, I guess.'

She bristles as she speaks, as if I'm still the one at fault somehow.

'It's not public knowledge,' I reply.

Her eyes flicker a little and I notice that they are both green and brown, depending on the light. And yet they were emerald in the sun. Her plump mouth forms a perfect round 'O' as realization dawns on her that the information I've given her is quite valuable. I force my attention back to my complimentary tea.

I instantly feel regret at letting my guard down, but equally I'm tired of being treated as infallible. I'd rather she think I'm allergic than precious. It's the truth, after all.

But then again, now she knows I'm allergic to citrus, she could drop something in one of my water bottles and I'd drop dead and she could celebrate with her friends. I haven't always been this paranoid, but ever since the lawsuits against my father started, security in my family has become a bigger issue. Last year, someone broke into my father's yacht in Monaco, making our little security issue international instead of local.

'Relax,' she says, noticing the fear in my eyes. 'I won't murder you with a clementine.'

My shoulders sag a little in relief and she laughs into her dumpling.

An hour later, and full of dim sum, I walk Margot to her room.

'Goodnight,' she says dryly, as if we haven't just had a really bizarre night together. I'm a little taken aback – the jokes, her laughter over the dim sum. I straighten up, dropping any sign of a smile, and nod.

'Don't forget to look over the itinerary and be on time tomorrow.'

And with that, she slams the door in my face, leaving me standing in the corridor. She just couldn't make it to the end of the night without a reprimand.

I walk into my room, shut the door behind me, and stretch my arms towards the ceiling. I'm exhausted; it has to be nearly two in the morning by now. Suddenly, the hairs on the back of my neck stand on end and a familiar sensation spreads in my chest. I switch the light on.

'Good evening, Yuri,' I say to the bald, blue-eyed man in my armchair. 'Nice to see you again.'

CHAPTER 21

THEO

I'm so exhausted I can barely focus on my bodyguard's lecture. I throw myself onto my bed, cross my arms and petulantly turn away from him.

'That running away stunt was unnecessary,' Yuri says. 'I don't need to engage with you, or whoever you are with, I just need eyes on you to keep you safe.'

'Safe from a night market?'

'Safe from the perils of being *you*.'

I turn to face him.

'It's a tricky time,' he adds. 'The new class action lawsuit is gaining traction and the extra security might be needed.'

I can't stay mad at him. Despite his ogre-like physique and brutal glare, Yuri has always been there for me. From stupid parties to serious functions, always facilitating my early exits, always making sure the paparazzi don't get any photos of me, always checking in on me. In some ways, he's more present than my father. But that's a thought hole I don't need to go down tonight.

'I'll stay under the radar, *Theo the escape artist*.' His use of my childhood nickname makes me squirm a little and his lip curls at the edge into the faintest smile the brute can muster. When I was little, I used to run away from him at father's château, which borders a large pine forest, and chuck all my SIM cards away so they couldn't track me. I hid in a bog once, playing with my toys.

'I'm tired,' I tell him, making my way to the door.

I check the hallway before opening it fully and gesture politely for him to leave.

'All right, but no more running,' he says on his way out. I put a hand out to stop him.

'I just . . .' I start awkwardly. 'I'm not trying to make your job harder, I just don't want the other influencer I'm travelling with to know I have a security detail,' I say feebly.

It's not that I am ashamed of Yuri; a number of rich people's kids that I've met have had bodyguards, especially with travelling abroad and having a target on your back for kidnappings. In my father's case, a lot of people hate him and want retribution. So yes, I do think Yuri is a necessity sometimes.

It's just, Margot will never ever let me live it down. She only just agreed to be civil and not stand in each other's way. If she finds out I have security, that might be a massive step back because it will remind her exactly why I need it in the first place.

'Understood.' Yuri nods his head in a way that brings us both to the fact that he is sort of my employee. A realization that always hits like a ton of bricks, like drinking tea with your beloved nanny and then suddenly realizing that beneath that smile she's paid to be there.

'Margot Baré, just turned eighteen last year,' Yuri says in a hushed, relaxed tone. 'Born and raised in Puyfleur. Her father served a sentence for arson on city hall, and vandalism on an Eau

Jeune site and other municipal buildings. Then he went back to prison on a charge for aggravated assault. The family appealed for early release due to poor health.'

'Cancer?' The question is near automatic when it escapes my lips but my voice is low. A deep fear tangles through me, tightening. If my father's venture was responsible for Margot's father being sick, I will never be able to look her in the eyes again.

'No.' Yuri shakes his head. 'Diabetes – the appeal was denied. Her family business is an inn with a small farm. It was heavily affected by the *situation*.'

The situation. A thinly veiled reference to my father's scandal. Yuri is always careful how he speaks in unfamiliar environments. I'm assuming he means the water affected the livestock and the farm operations, a reason why most farmers in the region hate us. The fact that it's an inn is worse; tourism and occupancy across our province dropped significantly after the scandal broke. No one wants to stay somewhere known for its cancerous water.

'But my sources report Matthieu Baré ran it further into the ground with gambling debts, then he got involved in Yellow Vest activities. Margot's cousin is in the Yellow Vests too – minor infractions, mostly pranks, and attends the protests. One arrest.'

I nod pensively. From rising farm taxes to government regulations to the Eau Jeune water scandal, the Yellow Vests are a group of working-class and farmer protesters that take matters into their own hands – from blocking roads to covering government buildings with manure. They might be the only thing my father has ever feared. Well, maybe *fear* is the wrong word, but he's found them highly inconvenient. And it seems like I'm travelling with the daughter of the revolution.

'Either way, your father is very displeased with this,' says Yuri, catching on to my train of thought. 'I've assured him that we've looked into the girl's media usage and it seems she is safe. Mostly reposts in her stories, it's not had much traction. Messages came back clean too.'

Media usage. The fact that they can look at her platforms and personal messages makes my skin crawl, even though I'm so used to it. People like to ask influencers if the loss of privacy affects them, but I've only ever read about privacy in books. From early childhood it was a distant concept to me, never anything I experienced first-hand. Knowing all my communications could be read, my whereabouts tracked, my companions' backgrounds checked was the norm as far back as I can remember.

Although, what Yuri just said about Margot's father sheds some light on things. It definitely explains her hatred of me a little better.

I yawn. 'Night, Yuri.'

'Night, sir,' he replies, resuming formality as he walks stealthily into the hall. The more intimate tone and relationship was confined to the space of my room, and now we are back to business. I don't bother wondering if Yuri has secured a place to sleep, or where his stuff is, or how exactly he tracked me to the night market.

My bodyguard is like a cat, always landing on his feet. Well, that and the access to my father's funds, which means he probably has a room in the same hotel.

Maybe it's all that running, or all the eating, I did tonight but it doesn't take me long to drift off into a quick and heavy sleep. My dreams are peppered with bulbous dim sum and flashes of Margot's face, full of disappointment.

CHAPTER 22

MARGOT

Even Theo's brooding, grumpy presence can't ruin the perfect itinerary of the next day. It's like last night never happened as we expertly ignore one another. Online, it's been a relatively slow morning with the protests due to the time difference, and my timeline has briefly returned to cats and cooking videos. Which meant I was able to relax at breakfast, despite filming every second of it, and I can now enjoy my first full day in beautiful Hong Kong.

'We are heading up to the famous Victoria Peak,' Susan, our guide, says, breaking me out of my thoughts, as we ride in a very sharply inclined but adorable tram. I grab onto the rail as the sharp slope becomes uncomfortable. We squeeze past high-rise buildings, then forested hills, until finally, with a gentle yank, we pull into the funicular station and disembark.

The views from the top are truly mesmerizing, and, as Susan dishes out a good ten minutes' worth of history, both Theo and I stare, mouths ajar. From the coastline to the harbour, the epic skyscrapers, the seemingly endless greenery, the fog that swallows parts of the view and spreads over the city, making us feel like we are in the clouds. No wonder it's a world-famous view. I have to remind myself to get my camera out.

After our tour ends, Susan leaves us to explore Peak Tower, a complex of shops, and we get coffees without speaking to one another. I sip an amazing latte I got from a café while taking in the view at the Sky Terrace, watching the harbour boats in the distance. I look at the green mountains and then browse the souvenir shops, buying a tiny pram keychain because I can't stop myself. Somewhere between shops, I lose Theo and his tiresome equipment because he pompously says he needs to go and get some 'real footage'. As if what I do is fake and vain. Eventually, I wander towards the Peak Circle Walk. Butterflies fly past me, and I see colonial-era mansions and the banyan trees that Susan mentioned.

I wander off the beaten track, exploring the side of the peak. The city below me is shrouded in fog again, with a smattering of skyscrapers peeking out like toes from a woollen blanket. I stare in wonder at the beauty of it all, the way nature and innovation mix so effortlessly here to create an unexpectedly harmonious city, meditative in its chaos.

There's a rustling behind me and Theo steps into my shot with his mass of camera equipment.

'This place is occupied for filming,' I say, keeping my face as still as possible. I need him to take me seriously and understand I mean business. This is my job and I'm not messing around.

He waves his hand at me like he's swatting away flies. 'The light is fading so I have to hurry. I can't wait for you to be done with your selfies.'

The way he says the word *selfies* makes me want to push him over the edge of the cliff.

I watch him work for a little while, curious, despite myself, about his process.

'I was just wondering . . .' I say, toeing some gravel. 'You really have a thing for nature content, huh?'

He turns and looks at me suspiciously, aware I'm not just engaging in fun chit-chat.

'And?'

'Don't you find it ironic?'

He turns back to the view. 'Find what ironic.'

'That you love something your father is destroying,' I say. I'm not sure if I'm trying to trigger him or make him feel bad, but there's something about being around him that makes me want to dig deeper and pick at the scabs. Maybe if I peel back enough layers, I'll find more information.

He turns and stares down at me, leaning into the imbalance of our heights. Some red hair whips across my face but I don't give him the satisfaction of looking away.

'Why are you trying so hard to catch me in a lie?'

'I'm trying to catch you in a truth, Theo.'

'Truth is subjective,' he says, camera clicking.

I run my hand across a nearby leaf. 'Yeah, well, nature isn't.'

Contaminated water isn't subjective is what I want to say. And I hate that he would even suggest that there's some fluidity to all of this. 'Over a hundred people getting cancer isn't subjective,' I add. He has the good sense to look away now.

There's a flash of movement in a tree to his right, and again, lower on the stone railing that separates us from the cliff's edge. I take a panicked step back.

Theo is staring at me. 'So, what? I make you physically recoil now?'

'No! Well,' *yes.*' I right my clothes and shoot him a look. 'But mainly *that* makes me recoil.'

He turns around and sees the ginormous macaque sitting in the far-off branch. Two friends join it, tails swinging about. I take another step back and whimper.

'Are you afraid of monkeys?' He laughs.

'I'm not afraid.' *I'm petrified.* 'But it's their fingers and tails and those pointy teeth. They put me on edge. And they're too clever.' I'm still slowly inching backwards.

Another monkey joins the group and my heart starts to pound. 'I wish they would just put them somewhere else.'

'The monkeys were here before the people,' Theo mutters, before starting to photograph them. One begins to move towards him. Great. Now they've taken an interest in us.

'Stop photographing them,' I hiss.

'Hmm, no. I need the perfect shot,' he says, his camera clicking away wildly.

Who needs this many photos of freaking macaques?

'Enough,' I say. The monkeys are taking way too much interest in us – more have joined, their beady eyes darting from me to Theo, probably wondering which one will be easier to take down. I make a squealing sound, which amuses Theo as he continues with his incessant clicking.

'That's me, remember? I like to take pictures of the pests.' He smiles, referring to my dig about the frogs in Bali.

A monkey jumps a branch and I yelp.

'That's it, I'm out of here!' I cry.

I hear him laugh as I flip him the finger and walk off shakily, back to the tram.

That evening, I decompress in the art-deco-inspired spa, complete with white and gold tiles and a large water feature jutting out of one wall. It took me hours to film everything after the sightseeing, including a *Get Ready with Me for a Fancy Evening in Hong Kong* TikTok in the foggy mirror afterwards. I took great care styling my new floral dress from one of the stalls at Kowloon market. It's covered in large orchids and pairs so well with Hong Kong, even if it's slightly sexier than I like to show in my feed. I try to reconnect with my cottage core roots by filming a beautiful teapot and flower tea, blooming from the spa.

I post my pretty spa video and let the staff escort me to the fancy dinner. Just before we reach the elevator, my phone pings. It's my cousin and he's sent me a bunch of articles.

One is about the Yellow Vests forming a blockade to the water plant.

We ride at dawn. He sends me a photo where he's sporting a freshly shaved mohawk and a yellow vest. *We are trying to prove that the water plant still has contamination protocols in place. But they have crazy security and the police are here. We've barricaded the entrance.* His expression is playful and light but there's a hardness there. Resolution. And anger. A quiet anger, so very much like my cousin. Even though I admire his bravery, a ping of nerves hits my guts and guilt coils in my stomach, making my dress suddenly feel impossibly tight.

And what will that get you? If you're able to prove there are still protocols? I write back.

It proves he lied in court yesterday.

Please be careful, I write back.

I feel like I should be there – I don't want my cousin risking his future prospects, getting a record like my dad, or being gravely disappointed when none of this pans out. I watched my father for years, obsessed with trying to set the farmland injustices right, and it didn't lead to anything but him wasting his time and now being in prison. I walk along the sky bridge that leads to the restaurant, suspended a thousand feet in the air, caught between guilt and grief and regret.

All the relaxation from the sauna has evaporated from my body.

CHAPTER 23

THEO

I'm seated opposite Margot, but this time she doesn't say anything about being placed at the same table. I go to make a joke about the monkeys but instead of her usual scowl, tonight she looks pensive and maybe even . . . scared?

She's clearly tried hard with how she's dressed, her hair piled on top of her head, secured in place by a fresh orchid that matches the pattern on her black dress. I wonder who she's trying to impress – Maison Partout? Should I say something nice to break the ice? I remind myself that she hates my guts and thinks I'm the devil; a compliment on her dress or hair won't change anything. It might just make things more awkward.

I look away, unwilling to let her catch me staring. She fits in the restaurant better than I do. I spent far too long shooting the mountain with my drone and editing footage that I missed out on the spa, and just about had time to throw on some linen trousers and a blue shirt.

'That's a nice dress,' I say to her, despite my internal monologue. If I don't say anything, the silence will drag on for an unnatural amount of time. She looks up like she's only just noticed me. I wait for her to say something about my crumpled outfit or the fact that

I haven't had time to shave, my buzzcut is slowly growing out, but she stays silent. The compliment seems to have disarmed her. Her voice is small.

'Thank you.'

The waiter comes to our table and explains the luxurious specials, something the hotel has purposely chosen for us – lobster rice rolls, baked goose puffs, and something called abalone that even I'm unfamiliar with, among others. The waiter places some white ceramic chopsticks before us and two tiny porcelain bowls, before wheeling a trolley over with wicker baskets of dim sum to start.

I really want to ask for a knife and fork, but Margot has already started to pull the dough from the platter onto her plate using her chopsticks.

'Can I get you anything else?' the waiter asks.

I smile and shake my head, too ashamed to ask for a fork like a common tourist or toddler. I wait until Margot isn't looking before placing the chopsticks in my right hand and attempting to make them work. One slides onto the table so I use my fingers to pick up a dumpling and pop it in my mouth.

She looks up and I smile. She doesn't. I try my chopsticks again, this time dropping them both onto my plate with a clatter of ceramic against ceramic.

Margot sighs and moves her chair closer to mine.

'You're starting to frustrate me with that,' she says, reaching out and correcting my fingers around the chopsticks. 'Doesn't the chef at your château make sashimi every day?'

She's drawls like I'm a spoiled prince who can't use basic cutlery. I stay silent as her fingers move over mine. My cheeks are warming up.

'Yup,' I mumble. 'But I never got the hang of these things.'

'I bet. Try now.'

I move my fingers, copying her demonstration, and tentatively try to pick up some shredded duck from one of the baskets. I don't lose the meat or the chopsticks, keeping them steady as I place the food in my mouth. I try not to show how pleased with myself I am because she looks like she's searching for an insult. Instead, she says, 'So, what's it like then, growing up in a palace?'

She makes a little pancake with the pinch of her hands while I think of an appropriate response.

'I grew up in a château, not a palace.'

'*Oh, excusez moi!*' she drawls in mock apology.

I swallow my roll and take a deep breath.

'My father's house is luxurious, and lonely, and grand.'

'Why is it lonely? Aren't there other kids?'

'No. It's lonely because you can't go out when you want.'

She frowns.

'I heard you have your own McDonalds.'

'Rumour.'

'Crocodile pond?'

I choke on my food. 'Definitely a rumour.'

'What's *he* like then?' She glances at her phone as she speaks, like she doesn't actually care, and it dawns on me how powerful my dad is – even though she hates him, she still wants to know what makes him tick.

I shouldn't tell her anything. It's wrong. Dangerous, even. But tonight, she's being kind of civil, and helpful. It would be great to continue in this vein for the rest of the trip. Not as friends, but as co-workers.

I lower my voice, though Yuri isn't anywhere near us. 'My father is intimidating.'

She seems temporarily satisfied with that basic response.

'The protesters –' she moves some food around her plate, all gaiety and lightness gone – 'they've chained themselves to the southern water plant. They were hoping to storm it but got stopped.'

I don't know why she's telling me this when I have clearly seen it on my FYP. Maybe she's gauging my reaction. I put a poker face on. I don't particularly have any feelings about the Yellow Vests as a whole. I think they have every right to protest my father's companies. Not only did he cover up water contamination in his plants which led to people getting sick, he also bought up a lot of farmland in our area and drove the prices up. I understand why people protest, and I understand why they hate him. But I draw the line at violence, and I can still remember what it felt like to have our house vandalized. My mother paranoid in the night, my father making use of his never-before-touched panic room. I understand why they hate him but I don't understand why that hate extends to my mother and me. And I'll never forgive what that drove her to. Yes, the divorce made her like this, and the tabloids, but the Yellow Vests that broke into our house drove her over the edge. That's where the fear was truly born.

Either way, I doubt there will be a desired effect. I toured the plant when I was young, but have no idea if everything is above board there now. But one thing is for certain, my father cares little about protests or people chained to trees. He's too big a fish. Too vicious a fish. It's all just a minor inconvenience to him. Flies landing on a giant's nose.

'Do you go to the protests?' I ask her.

She continues eating. 'Not as much as I should. My father went a lot, so does my cousin, but I'm always busy making content.'

I feel like she's trying to explain it more to herself than to me.

'I'm sorry about your father, by the way.' I sip on the iced tea the waiter just brought me but when I look up, I immediately know I've said something very wrong.

Her green eyes flicker with predatory precision. There's a taut silence that stretches a little too long and I set my chopsticks down.

'How did you know my dad's in prison?'

I fiddle lightly with my hands. 'I saw when you posted about it.'

'No. You didn't.' Then, after a pause, 'You've had me background checked?' she says.

'What? No?' I splutter, but it comes out as a question instead of a sure statement. My voice wavers, I leash my nerves. 'You've mentioned it on your channel. Or something.'

She wipes her mouth and puts her napkin down. 'I have never, ever, mentioned my father and what happened to him on my channels.'

'You must have.'

Her eyes have a glazed look to them. She rises and stares down at me. Righting her dress into place with a stoniness that puts me on edge.

'If you're going to invade my privacy, at least don't try to gaslight me into thinking I spoke about something I would never speak about.'

I watch her turn and leave. Understanding the weight of the invasion she feels doesn't make it any better.

CHAPTER 24

THEO

Mercifully, the protests go by peacefully and with little violence. I'm surprised. My father has every local businessman, councillor and politician in his pocket – and his tolerance for the protestors is low. Maybe he managed to get away to Monaco this weekend in between hearings. But it's a new week now and that means it will be a few more days before everyone gathers again effectively. People will be pulled in different directions with university studies and jobs and farming and Monday-type needs. Protest might be a privilege Mondays can't afford.

It's been a few days since I last saw Margot - she's been keeping out of my way and I can't say I blame her, but this morning I find myself looking for her at breakfast. Perhaps the peaceful passing of the protests has improved my travel partner's mood. I locate her at breakfast, filming her brioche French toast.

'Good morning,' I say, a little too formally. 'I apologize for the breach of your privacy. To be honest, it's standard operation. The people that take care of me, they –' I scratch my head, thinking how to word it delicately – 'background check people. But I know how bad it feels, and I'm sorry.'

She nods. I don't want her to know that the 'my people' bit is the large bald man currently pretending to mind his business six or so tables away.

'Just because something is standard, doesn't make it okay,' she says, her voice icy.

'Agreed.' There's a long silence that stretches before us.

'I've never been background checked before,' she says.

'That you know of.'

Her eyes snap to mine with a degree of violence.

'Even someone like Maison Partout management could have run background checks. What if you had like a murderous history?'

'*Hmmppf*, sounds familiar,' she scoffs dramatically.

Fair enough. 'Can we start over from now?' I reach my hand out to her. She shakes it.

'Sure.'

I get changed after breakfast and hurry down to the lobby where Xiu tells me that Margot has already left.

'She took the car service,' Xiu explains. She's holding a suspicious clipboard in her hands.

'She said you would both split up today and that you wanted to spend some time with me filming the administrative facilities?'

The administrative facilities? Like the business centre?

Freaking Margot. I curse in my head, but muster a fake smile and nod. I'm not about to get on the wrong side of the Maison Partout management. Not if I can help it.

'And where has Margot gone?' I ask Xiu as I trail her to the elevator.

'Disneyland.'

Of course she has. I resist the urge to kick a nearby bin. She's gone to meet Asian Mickey and signed me up to photograph photocopy machines.

'After you,' I say with a smile at Xiu.

After an hour and a half of cursing Margot's name and filming the excessive business facilities inside the Hong Kong Maison Partout branch, and listening to Xiu go on and on about capacities and which crypto launches they have hosted and whether or not I would like to have some pictures of the corporate canapés they offer, I finally wrangle myself free. I save the footage. Margot thinks she threw me under the bus, but I know from experience I can take the footage and sell it back to Maison Partout as a cool edit of the corporate offerings at a later date. I've done it before. With these clients, you provide some videos at first, then later, when the contract runs out, you offer them more footage.

It's our last night in Hong Kong so I head off to explore, but I'm going to take it easy as I need my rest for the next destination. I eat pork bao buns and explore a beautiful temple dedicated to the god of literature. Then I visit Hong Kong Park and the aviary, followed by ramen and a visit to another night market. This time I eat my fill, almost in revenge.

Back in my room I scroll my phone. Beneath footage of the last protest from the weekend are Margot's photo carousels from the day. I scroll past images of her at Disneyland, biting into a giant Mickey donut, snacking on grilled squid, eating dumplings shaped like *Toy Story* aliens. A victorious giant smile on her face, a half heart formed with her hand.

The comments are positive.

I guess we weren't on any kind of equal footing. And we are not getting a fresh start. I had imagined it all. No wonder she tricked me and left me behind.

After all, why would you take someone who makes you so unhappy to the happiest place on earth?

KYOTO, JAPAN

The ENA Hotel by Maison Partout

welcomes you to the city of Kyoto,
a city both ancient and serene.

During your time here, you will enjoy:
An exploration of the ancient shopping street of Sannenzaka
A bicycle ride in the park
A dinner cooked exclusively with ingredients from our gardens
A hot sand treatment
A visit to the city of deer

Theme: Modernity meets tradition. An ancient place made modern.

CHAPTER 25

MARGOT

We are over here fighting for something that matters and you're in Disneyland with that monster's son. Bitch.

My finger hovers up and down the DM I got from a former classmate whose mother got sick from the water in our province. I don't blame her for the hate. It's like they say – hurt people hurt people. And that's especially true for the internet. But I guess me hoping to keep my brand trip around the world separate from Theo's in people's minds was impossible. Everyone from our province knows who Theo Delacour is. There's no escaping people that *will* know we are travelling together. One of my DMs is a stranger asking me if we are '*together, together*'. I scroll. Another asks if he's as hot in person as he is on screen. I balk. People really think they can say anything to strangers online.

I hug my giant plush Piglet I just acquired and rock back and forth on my heels in the Osaka immigration line. I text my cousin Alexandre, *I'm sorry I was at Disneyland while you were chaining yourself to a pillar.* I finish with eyebrow sweat emojis.

That's okay. I'm happy for you. You've wanted to go for ever, he writes.

Of course, he means Disneyland Paris which is so much closer than Hong Kong, but I've never been invited to a brand deal in Paris. With everything my family has gone through in the past five years, Paris and Disneyland have felt out of reach. I even feel a little guilty I didn't mention that the hotel had dropped *two* complimentary passes to Disneyland before Theo came down to breakfast yesterday. But, whatever. I bet his father hired Disneyland for his birthday when he was a child. It's his penance for invading my privacy. He'll survive.

Alexandre's name flashes on my screen again.

PS: You better have bought me something from Lilo and Stitch, you raging capitalist.

I have, I reply. There's a keychain of Stitch in my bag with his name on it. His favourite character when we were little – we would watch the film for hours in the lobby of my parent's inn, La Voile Rouge. We would racketeer the kitchen for the long straw-like chocolate sticks we knew they kept in the pantry and then stuff them into fresh-out-of-the-oven baguettes meant for breakfast, thereby making our own gooey pain au chocolat.

Guilt wraps its black, lacy edges around me and the anxiety starts to roil in my gut. Should I delete my post? I've dreamed about going to Disneyland, any Disneyland, since I was little. I couldn't just skip my chance to go to the one in Hong Kong; I might never get this chance again. I guess I could have just not filmed it. Dimitra's voice rings in my head – *if an influencer fell in the forest but didn't film it, did they still fall?* Would I have enjoyed myself any less if I hadn't shared my day? Maybe if I hadn't been alone, but I wanted to spite Theo and leave him behind when I went to the magic kingdom. Maybe this is my karma. I scroll the comments – someone asks me where my flowy white dress is from. I tag the dressmaker in my answer, happy to receive a non-Theo-related question. My mother has left her comment consisting of heart emojis and *Ma belle fille* – my beautiful daughter.

I look around for my travel companion. I don't see his smug face in the sea of weary travellers and wheelie carry-ons, and realize he's probably beaten me to the conveyor belt again.

I find him by baggage reclaim and stand next to him, hands crossed over my body, not saying a word as the suitcases begin to slide onto the carousel. There's an airport employee whose job it is to correct the course of the bags on the conveyor belt, preventing them from falling off. So considerate. So very peak Japanese. I feel something nudge my leg and whip around.

'Excuse you,' I snap. Then I realize Theo is a few feet away and I am staring at nothing but thin air. Then I feel the nudge again, look down, and come face to face with an adorable beagle. The dog handler hovering over him, wearing an official uniform, says something to me in Japanese but I don't understand.

'He's saying *Sumimasen*,' Theo explains. 'It means *excuse me*.'

'No one asked you, Theo *the polyglot*.'

I bend to stroke the beagle's ear but he retreats, returns and signals adamantly at my hand luggage. Oh, the dog works here too. I'm too tired for this and I try to shoo him away. It's not like I have anything on me.

The man gestures for me to follow him and my stomach clenches. I haven't picked up my suitcase yet. What does he want from me? Am I in trouble? I don't want to ask Theo how to say 'I'm innocent' ... but I am. There's nothing of interest in my bag, unless beagles are big fans of Lilo and Stitch.

I trail the uniformed dog handler to a counter where a woman shows me photos of fruits, vegetables and seeds. I think she's asking me if I've brought any of these into the country, like I'm some kind of farming smuggler.

'I don't have any of these on me,' I keep saying, shaking my head with every image she points at.

Irritation is mounting in my chest from lack of sleep. With every shake of my head my stiff neck twinges. She's so polite, but so persistent. I feel like crying.

'I don't have any cash on me, or alcohol, or anything,' I say, my hands held up for assurance. I haven't even picked up my luggage yet. A wave of exhaustion washes over me. Then panic. I just want to get my suitcase, have a double shot of coffee, and go to my hotel.

'*Paaan*,' the woman says, flashing me a picture of a yellow blob. '*Paaan!*'

I squint sideways at the paper full of pictures she's holding but can't quite make out the yellow thing she's showing me. The dog is still signalling at me, nudging his little snout at my rucksack. This is all too much. I want to scream.

Theo materializes behind me, the handle of my suitcase in his hand, fuelling my irritation further. This is the kind of stuff he does, acting all valiant when it's just a point-scoring exercise. No one asked him to do that. I'm not some incapable little princess that needs to be rescued. All of his 'helpfulness' is just an opportunity for him to show off his superiority. None of it is genuine.

'*Bread*,' he says into my shoulder, I can feel his breath on my neck. He's too close to me. Why is he always hovering?

'Are you brain dead or something?' I gesture at the woman. 'We can eat a snack when I'm done here.'

Theo rolls his eyes. 'They're saying *you* have bread on you.'

I'm still for a moment. 'I don't have any bread on me.'

But when I turn and look at the blank-faced lady who is still pointing at a laminated piece of paper, a faint memory from the flight barges into my brain. I reach into the front pocket of my bag and pull out a round parcel wrapped in napkins, plonking it on the table. The lady chucks the bread in the bin, and the beagle, satisfied and victorious, wanders off with his handler.

I put it off for as long as I can, but when I eventually turn to face Theo his expression is so unbearably self-satisfied I want to ninja kick him.

'Hoarding bread, are we?'

'It was a pineapple bun from the plane,' I correct him.

He doesn't respond, instead turning to the lady at the counter.

'*Arigato-gozai-mashta*,' he says, smugness coating him the way cologne coats a Duty-Free hall, plentiful and asphyxiating.

I yank my suitcase handle from his hands. 'Let me guess, daddy bought you fancy Japanese lessons?'

He snickers. 'No, I watch a lot of anime with subtitles.'

'Right.'

I want to make a joke at his expense but nothing is coming into my blank travel-weary mind. I know next to nothing about anime. We walk through the *nothing to declare* line, breadless and full of shame.

'It's not my fault you're smuggling bread like you're a sailor starving at sea,' says Theo once we've crossed the threshold of declaration. I think he's trying to lighten the situation but my nerves are already at their limit.

I whip around on him. 'My grandma literally starved as a child and taught me never to throw away bread.'

This quietens him. I don't care if I'm shutting him up. I search the faces of all the waiting drivers holding up handwritten or printed-out signs, looking for the familiar Maison Partout welcome. Theo looks perturbed. *Good.*

'I didn't mean it like that,' he says softly. 'I was teasing.'

There's something sincere in his voice that makes me pause for a second, an earnestness I didn't expect, but I'm too tired to think about that right now.

'It's fine. Let's get our taxi and get out of here.'

CHAPTER 26

THEO

Margot has this rare talent to turn even the most comical situation into a socio-political issue. Something funny, like her slamming that darn pineapple bun on the counter as the beagle breathed out a sigh of relief, has now become a *Theo is the villain situation*, yet again. Fine, maybe I shouldn't have made a joke about starvation. It's true, I don't know anything about food scarcity, but it doesn't matter what I say I'll always be her designated villain.

Maybe I can ask Yuri about whether she really did grow up *that* poor, or if she's exaggerating to make me feel bad. But then again, doing that would probably make me exactly the type of person she's accusing me of being. Exactly the type of person she hates. Someone who is entitled to someone else's story.

We're met by the single most polite driver in the world and ushered over highways in the direction of Kyoto. The drive is little over an hour, and I spend the majority of it on my phone, connecting through a cheap online SIM company that once offered me a brand deal. I go and name drop them with a screenshot and my promo code in my stories. It's easier to keep on working than to bask in the awkwardness that Margot perpetuates in the small Suzuki taxi. She is not any keener than I am to talk and spends the majority of her time editing photos of Hong Kong on her phone. I'm excited to visit Japan but I don't see much out the window except the expanse of the expressways, the crisscrossing of long bridges, followed by dense atypical suburbs. It's only when we are close to Kyoto that I start to see the roofs of temples and a hint at the nature that gets me excited – maple, cedar, cherry tree. The glimpses of the soft, serene nature I recognize from films makes my heart race. I've spent my life travelling but I can't actually believe I'm here.

By the time we arrive at the Maison Partout Kyoto branch it's late evening. I'm not hungry, I ate my fill on the plane, but now I'm wondering if Margot needs to eat. I know she ate what constitutes as three dinners on the plane but who knows with that girl. I hate that she has me thinking about her hunger levels now. The hotel is a modern mid-rise and beautifully lit, with stone walls and clean minimalistic lanterns. It's called the ENA Hotel. The Maison Partout signs we saw in Hong Kong have not been added yet, which might mean it's a newer acquisition.

I take a few exterior shots and send a couple to Jodi and one to my mum. Next to me, Margot is doing the same. Our eyes meet and we both put our phones away, like two cowboys tucking their pistols back in their holsters. Despite being an influencer, technically, I always feel so ridiculous reaching for my phone.

We're welcomed into a spacious lobby and served tea with tiny red bean cakes. Everything in the hotel is sleek and textured, from the fabric-lined walls to the floors and curtains; the black, grey and maroon patterns blend beautifully. It may not be regal like the Bali location, or grand and commercial like it was in its Hong Kong skyscraper sister hotel, but it's so beautifully designed and small it's still somehow delightful.

We're checked in and welcomed by the main manager, Kenta, who walks us through some filming needs they have. We are to capture the food, the accessibility to the Kyoto temples, and focus on 'modernity meets tradition'.

He gifts us scarlet-red fans, massive paper cranes with the hotel logo on them, and a mochi gift set. I look at Margot, thinking we may share a glance at the gifts, but she continues to avoid eye contact with me.

In my small suite, I'm surprised to see that rooms in Japan come with way more than even the nice hotel rooms I'm used to. There are skincare kits with serums and rice-water creams, wooden slippers, a tea set with designer chocolates shaped like cats. In the closet, I find the softest dimpled honeysuckle pyjama set I have ever seen. One set is labelled as *indoor* and one as *outdoor*. A pamphlet explains that there is a late-night buffet and guests are welcome to use their outdoor pyjamas to explore the perimeter and relax.

There's also a laminated schedule for our three-day itinerary in Kyoto, and for the one-day excursion to nearby Nara, the city of deer. I change into my indoor pyjamas and catch my reflection in the large mirror in the hall. I balk. I'm used to seeing a scowling face staring back, brow furrowed. But here in Japan, I'm pink-faced, grinning so wide I feel an ache building in my cheeks. I've dreamed of this place since I was little and here I finally am.

The itinerary for the next day promises a tour of the shopping street, then a visit to a temple the following day. I wonder if all the locations we visit will have religious places on the itinerary. Should I always pray for the same thing, for my mother's health? I shake my head. Maybe I should pray for the protesters. Maybe I should pray for myself.

I check my phone out of habit, thinking of getting some footage of the amenities in the room, when my father's face fills my screen. Unwanted, as it usually is. People are posting pictures and articles about him all over social media due to the new trial. His expression is cold and stern, the one I recognize from fragments of my childhood. He looks angry. Outraged. But all of it is leashed beneath the surface. Bubbling, almost imperceptible, like the soft birth of a geyser. He's so masterful at it that an unknowing onlooker might think he's aloof, composed. But I know better. I know to see the storm beneath the calm. The signs of incoming danger. In the past, it was a sign that my mother was about to cry.

Whatever is happening with his lawsuit, he is not pleased.

In a video someone has posted I watch my father as his mouth moves and turn the sound up.

He is disputing all the allegations of there still being contamination at one of his plants. The southern one closest to Margot's home. I wonder if she's watching this video too. The interviewer argues that he hasn't granted anyone access to the water plant. My father deflects masterfully.

Hours later, I wake up with a start to the sound of his voice, instinctively making my heart jackhammer against my ribcage. It's okay, he's not in the room with me. The video on my phone must have kept looping as I fell into a heavy slumber. It's 4 a.m. but I'm too awake to sleep now, so I distract myself editing. Creating an elaborate compilation of the amenities in the room. I've always loved editing and filming because it gave me control. Everything about the life of being my father's son was curated. The food, the opinions, the narrative. But once I got hold of the camera, it was *my* narrative. And no one could stop me. Yes, he controls my life in more than one way still. My mother's house, her bills, and other invisible threads of power that keep me dependent. But he does not control my own story, or how I express it. If I want to post a six-minute video about birds, no one can stop me. He can make me take things down but it's always too late at that point – thousands of people have already seen it and I've still exercised my freedom in whatever small way. It still feels significant.

Social media meant I could suddenly have my own story, even when living in the pages of someone else's.

CHAPTER 27

MARGOT

I'm standing in the courtyard when Theo arrives. There's something different about him today – he almost looks giddy with joy.

I woke up early and had my breakfast alone. They let you pick between Japanese or Western, as they call it (eggs, bacon and so on). I opted for Japanese, which means tiny bowl portions of rice, fish, pickles, a rolled omelette, seaweed and a small bowl of miso soup. It doesn't sound as appetizing as the eggs Benedict I see carried past me but once I start combing the ingredients I wonder why I've never had rice for breakfast before. It really hits the spot and pairs well with the eggs and pickled toppings. I might have to buy a rice cooker and continue this tradition at home.

I've been waiting for Theo for twenty minutes now. I could have left without him again as the first point of the itinerary is self-guided, but something made me wait in the lobby. Maybe leftover guilt from Disneyland. I've spent the whole time staring at thc bcautiful fountain beside me, observing the wisps of steam coming from it. Is it very warm? Who has a warm fountain in an indoor courtyard?

'You look different,' I blurt out as Theo approaches me. He's wearing a hoodie and wide jeans, his buzzed hair is beginning to grow out, and there's a sparkle in his bright blue eyes. There's a pink tinge to his cheeks, making him look younger yet calmer. This close, he's almost pore-less, and his facial structure is kind of perfect. He looks like a Renaissance painting that decided to make a rap album. The combination of angelic and brooding is unnerving.

'Different how?' he asks.

'Less ... serious.' I stare up at him for a little too long. '*Ahem*, less murderous,' I add, clearing my throat.

'I'm just happy to be in Japan,' he says, smoothing his hoodie down. 'Thank you for waiting for me. I meant it, you know – back in Hong Kong. About us starting from scratch. We can still be professional.' But before I can respond, he carries on talking. 'We should go. Our shuttle to the shopping street leaves in ten.'

I roll my eyes at his urgency. I chose to wear my cute butterfly sandals again even though my feet still ache from all the walking in Hong Kong. I scrunch up my toes, and wince.

'I'm sorry about the comments people are leaving on your post,' he says. I nod – I stayed up late deleting all the heinous comments people left about my trip to Disneyland during the protests. To start, there were my diehard fans sending hearts and positive vibes. My mum was of course the first to comment – she has post notifications on – but then the horrible ones started slipping through. Some even going as far as comparing me to Disney villains.

Read the room, Cruella.

I blink the tiredness of screen time from my eyes and Theo catches my gaze.

'They don't understand how this is our job, and just because you're having fun doesn't mean you don't care about what's happening back home.' I try not to make a face at the news that he's been monitoring my posts. But at the same time, it's kind of nice he's noticed because the comments *are* getting to me . . . just when I think I've figured this boy out, he surprises me with yet another sign of being human.

I look up at him. 'I guess you're used to negative comments, huh?'

He nods. 'Maybe fewer people calling me a cartoon villain, but I get other stuff.'

'And how do you deal with it?'

I spent so much time checking my phone I made my thumb seize up, so now my feet and hands both hurt. This whole experience is making me feel hollow. I've had hate messages before, but never so many in such a small space of time and such vitriolic ones. As if all the online hatred were an ice scooper scraping out bits of my soul. Anyone else could just delete their posts or not look, but being online is my job. It's everything. I can't look away.

I contemplate explaining all of this to Theo but I'm not sure he would understand. One thing I've learned about rich people is they're a lot less concerned with being liked; it's probably how they get to do whatever they want unencumbered and guilt-free. People liking you isn't power, not really, it just feels like it is. It's embarrassing to admit, but it feels good to be admired. I feel pathetic just thinking it, so I'm definitely not going to say it out loud.

'You learn to ignore it. People hiding behind screens wouldn't say half of this to your face.'

'Saying half of this would still be a lot,' I say melancholically.

'I get half a dozen death threats a week – doesn't mean anyone is coming for me. The internet isn't a real reflection of the world.'

'Death threats?' My eyes widen. I mean, I knew he was well

liked in some circles and that he also had haters, but threats of death is a lot for anyone to handle. He nods subtly but looks like he doesn't want my pity.

'So just ignore them – enjoy the moment that you're in right now. *The moment is all we have.*' He scratches his head. 'I read that somewhere. Anyway, now five minutes to shuttle,' he says, as if the shuttle booked expressly for us is going to leave without us. He's a master at changing the subject.

'How are *you* being in the moment if you're counting down minutes till the shuttle? Chill out.' These butterfly sandals are doing nothing for my feet that are now pulsing in pain, so I take off my shoes and head barefoot to the steaming fountain.

'What are you doing?' he says. 'Come on, you can't get in. The Japanese are very strict here with their rules.'

I dip one foot in the water and then the other. It's blissful. Then I stand in the fountain. 'I'm being in the moment. The moment is all we have,' I parrot him and his cheeks go pink.

'Still. You can't just get into fountains in the middle of a hotel! This is ridiculous,' he says, running a hand across his head. He keeps looking around as if the fountain police are going to get us. I kind of like watching him squirm. I bite my lip and lean back, enjoying the sensation of the flowing warmth.

'It's warm because you're *meant* to get in. I've been wondering about it all morning.'

He stares at me and then does a double-take. 'What, like an *onsen*?'

'Oh, you're suddenly interested now?'

He takes off his socks and shoes and rolls up his trousers, before going to read a small placard on the ground. 'An *onsen* is a hot spring, very popular in Japan,' he says. 'So, you *are* right, you are meant to get in. But we are officially late for the shuttle.'

'Shhh, we'll get the next one – enjoy your foot bath.'

'Foot *onsen*,' he corrects me.

'Do you have an *off-sen* button?'

He rolls his eyes, and I focus on the delightful heat beneath my feet. But I can see him smiling as he steps in. I'm surprised he can enjoy something so simple and whimsical. He looks giddy, even, and I don't think I've seen him like this in any of his videos or any paparazzi photos. He always looks stern and serious, guarded, but here, miles away from home, he looks like a different person entirely. I guess Japan brings out the joy in people.

We walk along the tight, ancient shopping street of Sannenzaka. Up towards a pagoda, and then down again as we loop past the prettiest Starbucks I've ever seen. We stop for something called *dango*, then local mochi wrapped in leaves, then I buy a drink with pink jelly bits in the shape of hearts. Theo buys a pickle, and just stands there holding it like a baby bird.

'You are really into gelatinous things,' he says, watching me consume some cream-filled mochi like purple cloud that came on top of my matcha latte. I nod through a mouthful and then pull the mochi from my mouth, creating a strand-like texture.

'I like the way it pulls. The gooier the better.'

'How bizarre.'

'Says the boy with the single pickle.'

'It's a special pickle.'

I laugh despite myself. 'Sure it is.'

I can't explain the fascination I have with gelatinous food.

When I was a kid, I would love the jelly cups at school. In two shades at the time, forest green and blood red. The wiggle of a good blancmange, a panna-cotta-type dish. The fruit jellies – *pâte des fruits* – my mum would get at the market that would stick to my teeth.

The Japanese seem to share my fascination except it's all in shades of pink and matcha, with glitter, which makes it even better.

'I never want to leave,' I say, more to my ball of mochi than to anyone in particular.

'Me neither.' Theo is eating a sesame yakitori stick he just purchased, and he hands me the second one. I take it, watching him cautiously. It's the first time we've agreed on something. I can't help but notice again how different he seems today. Maybe he was serious about a fresh start. But there's something more – I always thought someone with his background wouldn't be so curious. Eager. Surprised. Impressed. It's the same feeling I get when I travel. I don't know. I shake my head, trying to free my mind of these thoughts, as we tackle another incline.

By the time I have a blue bubble tea full of Pokémon characters, I'm clutching my stomach. 'If I keep eating, I'm going to vomit,' I say, putting a hand against the wall of a shop and taking deep breaths.

Theo is eating a sakura soft serve and appears to be unbothered by this possibility.

'If you do,' he says, 'will it come out like jelly?'

'Shut up.' I clutch my stomach. 'Or I'll aim right at you.'

But Theo isn't listening any more. He's spotted an arcade-like building full of vending machines. He chucks his cone and strolls forward like a zombie propelled by neon signage.

CHAPTER 28

THEO

If my father could see me right now, he would hate the very sight of me. Although it wouldn't be the first time. I'm at a neon arcade full of rows and rows of bulbous white dispensers.

My heart is racing as I listen to the metallic clang of the gears when I twist the steel knob into place. The metal grinds and a plastic capsule tumbles to the lower level. Gingerly, I pop the teal pod open and observe its contents.

It's a koala reading a newspaper. It's not the exact one I wanted, but it was in my top three. I debate having another go on the machine but decide against it. I recycle my capsule and move on to a *Naruto* one in the corner, when Margot's annoying voice interrupts me.

'You're a massive nerd, you know that?'

'Yes,' I say, turning another lever. 'I read real books and get my news outside of TikTok. It must be appalling to you.'

'Don't flatter yourself. I'm talking about the toys. *This* . . .' She holds up a figurine of a hippo before me.

'That's not a toy.' I bristle. 'It's a *gachapon*.'

'It's a hippo in a wetsuit and I got it from one of these –' she waves her hands around – 'supermarket rubber-ball dispenser things you seem to be obsessed with. Just because you give it a fancy Japanese name does not make it less childish.'

I turn back to the gacha in front of me. 'Tell me you don't understand subculture without telling me you don't understand subculture.'

'*Ooh la la.*' She openly mocks me. 'I'm so sorry. I didn't realize that vending machines are the height of culture.'

'Are you keeping that hippo?'

'Yes,' she says, clutching it to her chest. 'It's cute.'

I sigh, leaning back against the large claw machine behind me. 'Look, there are four more floors of this. You're welcome to do your own thing.'

'Four more floors?' She looks around, shocked. 'What the hell?'

'Well, not just of *this*. There are all sorts of other stuff. But you can go to a Japanese beauty shop down the street or something,' I say dismissively.

'*Excuse me!*'

Her eyes narrow at me angrily. I'm surprised she's stuck around for so long – maybe she's finally happy to start afresh.

But I know I'm obsessing and would rather do it in peace. Again, thoughts of my father enter my head, as loud as his helicopter.

'So, are you staying or going? Decide, because that Mickey Mouse keychain shaped like a cup of bubble tea over there is calling my name.'

She looks around a little nervously.

'Okay, okay, when else will I get the chance to explore Japanese subculture and enjoy people *nerdgasming* all over the place?' She follows me as I head into the basement, trailing a steady flow of people and more neon and cartoon-sounding songs.

'I would prefer a different terminology, but okay.'

Downstairs, we discover rows upon rows of claw machines and games. The main difference being that the claw machines back home (and I assume around the world) are impossible to win, just cons that make you overspend and doubt your sanity. But here in Japan, they are fair. And we spot people winning all around us so I tell Margot as much.

'Okay, anime boy, how do you play one of these things?'

I look at her, but she seems genuine, so I start talking her through how the claw machine works.

'It's straightforward, of course, but there's a little trick with getting the grip on what you want.'

Margot nods, and then she picks out her target – a pink teddy in the corner. I drift away to another machine until suddenly Margot yelps next to me, grabbing my arm.

'Theo, I won, I actually won a freaking claw machine! I thought that was impossible. Eight-year-old Margot would be so proud right now.' She holds up a pink teddy triumphantly and I can't help but smile at her.

'Why are you looking at me like that?' she asks, realizing her hand is still on my arm, warm through the sleeve of my hoodie. She quickly drops it.

I make a face as if to say she's imagining things, but the truth is I've never seen her like this. Margot's anger is always just under the surface whenever we spend any time together, but right now she's giddy like a kid. I kind of like seeing her like this. Shaking the thought away, we move on from the claw machines to a racing arcade game but the constant light and sound gives both of us a headache and we wander out into the afternoon air.

CHAPTER 29

MARGOT

As much as I was determined *not* to spend time with Theo today, he's not been completely insufferable. I can almost see him as a boy I'm supposed to do a brand deal with. Plus, when I'm alone, I find myself itching for my phone but when I'm with someone else, even Theo, I don't.

The next planned activity is dinner at the Maison Partout hotel, so we choose to explore Gion. We gaze upon a wooden tatsumi bridge and wander the small side streets. Each time we ask if we can attend a real-life tea ceremony hosted by a geisha, we're denied because they're fully booked months in advance.

It starts to rain. Deflated, I follow Theo out of the quaint little district. We saw glimpses of a few trainee geishas across traffic, hurrying through the drizzle, but I didn't get a good look.

I send my mum a photo of a beautiful street and explore a shop full of Moomins. One day, maybe we can travel together – once the inn is back up and running. For now, she's happy to see the most personal parts of my trips, the stuff that won't get likes and fuel the algorithm but things that feel special to me. Then Theo and I set off on the journey back home, tummies rumbling again.

The rain intensifies and as I'm entering a crosswalk my sandal slips out and my feet hit the large puddle by the pavement. I'm soaked.

'Great!' I try rolling up my wet jeans as Theo reaches down to offer me a hand and another taxi pulls up to the light and splashes me again. 'Ugh!'

'Maybe get out of the intersection,' says Theo. I ignore his hand, wishing I still had my corn dog from earlier so I could throw it at him. I haven't yet had a chance to move as a third car pulls up. I look up angrily before bouncing up on the pavement. I come face to face with the passenger in the back.

Her hair is jet black, arranged in a bulbous fashion, shaped like a beetroot. Perfectly slicked back into a complex silhouette and adorned with pearl embellishments. Her kimono is peach and teal and emblazoned with a cylindrical pattern. Her lips are red, and skin whiter than I could have ever imagined. She spots me, eyes locking in. She smiles a coy smile, flings open a teal fan and covers her mouth. Then her eyes flick upwards, and down again. The square vintage taxi pulls away and the rain starts to pelt harder.

'*That* ... that was a geisha,' I say breathlessly to Theo, finally climbing onto my feet.

'Yes, I could see that,' he says, perplexed by my expression. 'That's who we were looking for before.'

'No, you don't get it.' I stare at the spot where the car was moments ago. 'The geisha and I ... we had a moment.'

'A moment?'

'She looked me up and down, coquettish. Like she could see right through me.' The rain is cascading down my face now but I can't stop smiling. My cheeks burn from the giant grin on my face. A geisha. Like the ones I read about. Real and stunning and mythical somehow.

'We shared a moment,' I repeat, and Theo chuckles. I shove him.

'Okay, okay, you shared a moment with a beautiful geisha.'

'She *was* beautiful, wasn't she?' I'm still staring at the space where the taxi was when Theo steers my elbow. I don't notice when another car comes around the bend and Theo pulls me back just in time, out of the way before it splashes me. I collide against his chest and for the briefest moment his arms close around me, tugging me away from the gush of water. I'm breathless and soaked and when I look up, he's too close for comfort. I can smell the cedar in his aftershave. Theo releases me just as quickly and I take a step back, breathless.

He shrugs. 'Didn't want you to get even more soaked. I'm starving. So, could we go eat, please? When you're done fangirling.'

'Whatever,' I say, ignoring whatever *that* was and focusing on the geisha again. 'An actual geisha smiled at ME. Nothing can ruin that moment.' I point at my chest like he wasn't there to witness it.

CHAPTER 30

THEO

'I'm happy for you that you got to fulfil your wish of meeting a geisha; now can we please fulfil my wish of eating some Kobe beef. The hotel recommended *this* place.' I flash her my phone, knowing full well there's no reason for us to continue the day together. 'It's on me,' I add. The Maison Partout chain continued their generous stipend of 250 dollars a day for both of us throughout the brand deal, so she doesn't need my offer, but I'm hoping it makes it more enticing. I don't really want to eat a beautiful dinner on a beautiful canal in Japan alone.

'I assumed Kobe beef is what you have at all of your family barbecues,' she says, eyes sparkling.

I look down at her. 'Margot, it's enough now,' I say quietly.

'Sorry,' she mumbles. 'Habit.'

'That's all right,' I say, leading the way past small restaurants with swaying lanterns outside, 'our family barbecues were mostly pheasant and other game from that week's hunt.'

She looks at me, wide-eyed, unsure if I'm joking. Then she laughs when she has decided I am. I let her believe it.

Hunting, *la chasse*, was very common practice and a big deal at my father's estate, and the game caught was often served, especially if he had guests. I only joined on the line-fishing outings, or offered to take care of the hunting dogs. The rest was too macabre for me.

I lead Margot down a sparkling canal as sakura petals fall elegantly onto the water. I look out at the many alleyway ramen places that have neon signs and paper lanterns strung out front. I have to stop and steady my breath for a moment, and I'm acutely aware of Margot standing next to me doing the same. It's far too beautiful here.

We watch as tourist couples, clad in rental kimonos, take pictures on the canal bridges. Then we head to a small barbecue place off the main street.

After some fiddling with the menu and trying to understand what I'm ordering, I'm brought beautifully marbled meat cut in perfect squares and I start to cook them studiously on the small grill placed before us. I wasn't given any advice on how to do it just right. But we are brought sauces and vegetables and mushrooms and sake.

'This meat is so fatty because it's massaged and fed more beer over a period of time, apparently,' I say.

'That's a misconception,' she counters. 'The marbling comes from the breed of cow.'

I cock a brow. 'Hmm . . . and you were accusing *me* of being posh and eating Kobe beef all the time? You seem to know a lot about it.'

'My dad is a dairy farmer . . . was,' she corrects herself, 'before all the stuff that happened . . .'

I don't say anything. Then, after a beat, the eureka moment slithers into my brain just as she confirms it.

'The cows got sick,' she explains. 'And because tourism had

dried up since the water poisoning was made public, we had no guests at the inn. We couldn't afford new ones.'

'I'm sorry that happened,' I say. Sometimes the best thing you can say is that you're sorry something happened. Not be defensive or deflect. But she looks at me with suspicion.

'What?' I say, placing another piece of beef on the hot plate. 'You think I'm the type of guy that is happy people and animals get sick?'

She flips her vegetable. 'No, I'm just very surprised you're admitting that people even got sick in the first place.'

I swallow. Admitting any wrongdoing on behalf of my father and his assets goes against all the media training I've had. But something makes me want to prove to Margot that I'm not an idiot. I know people have got sick, and I know my father isn't innocent.

Like an olive branch of sorts, a line of trust. If she wanted to, she could take this to the tabloids and there would be a headline tomorrow accusing me of betraying my father. But I'm hoping that she doesn't.

'But maybe if you were to speak out, then ...' She pushes around her food and my phone vibrates in my pocket. Probably another notification to remind me that we're not here alone, that back home the protests are brewing, escalating, gaining speed in the background of our Kobe beef dinner.

'My father isn't the type to indulge push-back from me.'

This admission feels way more intense than the last. Something like recognition flickers across her gaze. She seems to realize the meat on our mini barbecue is the last of it and scrabbles for her phone, in a bid to film the rest of the Kobe beef before we eat it all. I scroll through my phone – I haven't done that well with footage either. But then I put my phone away completely. Screw it.

‘Do you think I should have filmed the geisha?’ she says, looking a little sad. ‘I didn’t even think to pull out my phone.’

I pick up the second to last piece of meat and pop it in my mouth, gesturing for her to have the last one.

‘I didn’t film the Kobe beef either.’ My eyes lock on hers. ‘Some moments are just for us. And that’s okay.’

For the two days that follow, we visit all the temples that Kyoto has to offer and plunge ourselves into our work, making sure to illustrate the theme of *ancient meets modern* as outlined in our welcome brief. We visit Kiyomizu-dera Temple, Kodaiji Temple and Yasaka Shrine. Stopping for convenience snacks, like spicy fried chicken and glazed *dango*, and decked-out soft serves, each one more opulent than the last. Every temple seems well catered for by a food market and competing Lawsons and Seven Elevens. We buy handrolls and spicy fried chicken and more *dango* and *daifuku*.

That night we're at Yasaka Shrine. Margot bought four kimonos earlier that day. She’s wearing one now, the red of the silk making her own hair look even more vibrant in the glow of the lanterns surrounding the temple as we walk by it.

‘But why would you possibly *need* so many kimonos?’

‘Theo, you don’t understand a damn thing about life,’ she replies before surveying the temple.

And maybe I don’t. But I know enough to know that Japan is one of the most amazing places on earth, and the thought of leaving depresses me before we are even halfway through the trip. She stops, having found the perfect spot for a photo opportunity. She’s pulling her tripod out of her bag, adjusting, before docking her phone. She has a little clicker in her hand to take the photo remotely and moves over to pose in front of the temple. I've got used to this little routine as we've been working together. She comes over to check the photo and I look over her shoulder.

'You've completely cut the roof off,' I point out.

'Yes, I can see that,' she says, annoyed.

I put my hand out to her and she looks at me, guarded.

'I know how to take a photo, Margot, and I'm taller than that tripod. Let me take the shot.'

We've been working parallel to one another for a couple of days now. Though we're obviously not posting any videos together. She does her job, I do mine. It's purely professional. But this is the first time I'm offering to take a photo of her, which admittedly blurs the lines a bit.

She hesitates, but looks back at the temple and seems to make a decision.

'Okay, give it your best shot.'

She walks back to her spot and looks up at the closest lantern, her face lifted at the perfect angle, her hair and dress bright red in the night. I frame the photo immediately but can't help my finger lingering for a moment before taking the photo.

'Done,' I say, walking over, handing back the phone. Margot smiles in a way that makes me feel like maybe I do know something about the world after all.

The next morning, I eat my breakfast alone. I've opted for the Western version today, after trying the Japanese one the day before. The eggs are silky and perfect with white squares of toast and the most perfect two pieces of bacon. I take a photo and send it to Jodi.

Breakfast the way it was meant to look. No teddy-bear shapes in sight.

Jeez, you even know how to take the fun out of Japan, he writes back. I briefly wonder where he is and how come he's awake.

Then I retreat to the courtyard with my Americano. I get a look at the sandpit outside that our guide had pointed out to us previously – it's a sort of hot tub full of sand covered in a tent. I'm starting to think the Japanese place a lot of value on warmed feet.

I watch a family – mother, father and a toddler with a bowl cut – play in the courtyard. The son squeals with glee as he chases a chicken. The hotel boasts that they have their own organic eggs and grow their own vegetables. Chickens might seem out of place at a fancy hotel in the West but it somehow blends here seamlessly. The luxury and the nature.

I catch myself thinking I wish I could tell my dad how they do things here. The emergency packs they have in the elevators – with stools to sit on and dominoes and food in case the elevator breaks. The special vending machines that can serve drinks hot or cold. The umbrella holders outside hotels that dry your umbrella off. And that's only scratching the surface of their ingenuity, their practical approach to the everyday. I feel he would find it interesting.

But I can hear his voice now. The leashed drawl. Never a raised voice but always in full unyielding control of the narrative. *When are you done travelling? It's time to do something serious. This influencing thing has lasted long enough.*

I spot Margot before she spots me. She's almost comical bustling through the entrance of the courtyard with a multitude of shopping bags first thing in the morning. She clocks me and comes over, bobbing excitedly, much like the chickens.

'Taxi for Nara is here,' she says, dropping the bags at my feet. An attendant promptly appears and asks if they can take her bags to her room. The service here is unparalleled.

'You skipped breakfast.' I gesture.

'I know. I found a place that does croissants the size of my head.' She looks down at me over her nose, cheeks pink. 'Come on! Hurry up. Let's go.'

I'm not really used to this side of her that's been coming out since we got to Japan, the side that actively wants my company.

'You want *me* to come?'

'Well, yeah, they sent a shuttle for *both* of us, and they asked us to film ourselves cycling through the deer park.' She squeals a tiny bit with glee at the word *deer* but then steadies herself. 'Which I literally can't do without your help.'

Flustered, I hurry and follow her into the van waiting for us outside.

It's a one-hour drive to Nara, and the hotel told us they want us to feature Nara on our channels as they are planning on opening a second location there – this way we can plant the seeds for both hotels, the existing and the future.

After an hour, we arrive at a charming little lake dappled with rays of sunlight, and meandering ducks. We disembark, and just as I'm longingly staring at the Seven Eleven I hear Margot squealing. I turn twenty degrees and am faced with three giant and rather regal deer. Sitting in the middle of a small patch of grass, mere feet from me, they look like ancient and mystical creatures. It's a misty mid-morning and I feel like I just walked into a Disney movie. Even though I had read about Nara and expected to see deer – it's known as the city of free-roaming deer after all – I didn't expect them to be this brave and wander into the actual city centre. I thought they would be in the park mainly. Also, I didn't think they would be so big and impressive.

Deer are animals I'm used to catching fleeting glimpses of as they scatter from you across the château grounds or near a forested road. When you are facing them from a few feet away, it feels weird. There is a small crowd gathered, taking turns to be photographed next to them. Even petting them.

'Check this out,' Margot calls to me, one foot away from another regal deer. She splits open a paper packet of something. Then she bows to the large deer before her, and to my astonishment he bows back. She hands him what looks like a biscuit. *Where have I landed?*

'I feel like I'm in some fairy tale,' I say to Margot as we head towards the bike rental nearby.

'Enjoy it,' she says, flashing me one of her rare smiles, making me grin back at her. Or at least, it's rare for me to be on the receiving end. She hands me a biscuit and I bow to the deer as he bows back, feeling silly but very much alive. Next to me, Margot laughs as a deer shoves her lightly, eager for his biscuit. I doll out my cookies in a marvelling state. I could get used to this.

CHAPTER 31

MARGOT

As per the hotel's advice, we spend the day cycling through the park. Theo cycles close on my tail, helping me with some filming, and I don't mind his presence for once. I need the footage and he's become somewhat tolerable. Maybe because he showed me his dorky side and it's hard to continue violently hating someone who geeks with you over snacks and tiny toys from vending machines. We pass hordes of deer, hundreds of them, and gaggles of gathered tourists, both Japanese and foreign. We make stops and bow to deer and treat them to the round papery cookies, each one emblazoned with a cute deer symbol. The whole time I feel like I'm in another world. We eat peach soft-serve ice creams with little deer antlers made of chocolate sticking out of them, we buy berries and browse the kitschy souvenir market full of talking deer toys and fluffy white-and-brown ears. Again and again, we stop to feed more deer.

We stop for a little too long and suddenly the deer swarm Theo. He flinches and throws the cookies a few feet away so that they let up.

'Jeez, they can be quite rough, huh?' he says, brushing himself off and cursing in French under his breath.

I bow to a large deer opposite me. 'You know, you love nature, frogs and monkeys and all that, but you have no idea how to actually interact with wildlife.' Expertly I feed another deer and take a moment to pet his neck.

'I didn't have any animals growing up,' he says.

'Not even dogs?' I gawk.

He shakes his head. 'Well, only the hunting ones. They lived outside.'

'God, you imagine this billionaire life as all fun and puppies and yachts and . . .' I pause, looking him over. 'No offence, but your childhood sounds so dry.'

He tries to pet a deer but then pulls away as soon as the deer moves towards him.

'You have no idea,' he says. 'All yachts, no puppies.'

I chuckle, then realize I've run out of cookies but a few persistent deer keep following me.

'I don't have any more,' I say, as one head butts me in my side. Another one juts its antlers into me and I yelp. 'What the hell? Violence isn't the answer!'

I can hear Theo snickering as I speed up, but they follow me. Shoving into me from each side. Like a deer ambush. I'm not going to lie, it's starting to feel a little bit intimidating.

'This is bullying,' I declare as Theo's snickering turns into full-on laughter.

A large deer rams into my side and I actually feel teeth next to the back pocket of my jeans. I reach and feel a lump, then I pull out a batch of cookies and throw them away into the grass, squealing as the deer try to swarm me further. My eyes lock on Theo's as he tries to hide his laughter behind the hood of his oversized hoodie.

‘Very funny,’ I say, finally free from the deer as they’ve scattered towards the cookies on the ground. The cookies Theo managed to slip into my back pocket for this big joke. He reaches out to borrow my Instax and I let him snap a Polaroid of me with the few remaining deer.

Theo is still laughing. I flip him off but crack a smile despite my best efforts not to.

That afternoon, we see a large bronze buddha in a temple and overhear a guide tell a crowd that the Nara deer were considered messengers of the gods according to local tradition. Hurting them was harshly punished. I can’t imagine anyone hurting these majestic bowing animals. Though that makes me a hypocrite: I know people eat venison both here and abroad, and I’ve eaten it too, plenty of times at our inn. My father would cook a *ragoût de cerf* that was divine. I repress the thought as we pass another cluster of the regal animals.

We cycle back to the small town centre and park our bikes outside a shopping complex before heading to a neon-lit sushi place for which the hotel gave us some vouchers. We marvel at the fact that no one seems to be chaining their bikes up; in fact, the hotel didn’t even give us locks. My province isn’t exactly crime ridden, but in the nearest larger town you wouldn’t be caught dead leaving your bike unlocked for everyone to see.

Thc chcfs ycll out a greeting, *Irasshaimase!*, as we enter and take our place by the conveyor belt. I pour myself some complimentary green tea from the tiny tap before me and resist the urge to start grabbing the moving plates straight away. We browse the laminated menus instead, pretending to be civil instead of ravenous. I let Theo take the lead on ordering and begin to pick out my tiny colourful plates from the belt.

We eat fatty tuna and three types of sashimi and watch the selection as it keeps rolling on past us like a never-ending river of perfectly cut fish. Our plates begin to pile up into rainbow towers as we sip on miso soup, blowing into the steam. Slurping on the silken tofu.

My phone beeps with a few notifications and Theo catches me staring at it.

'My cousin has been at the protests every day,' I say through a mouthful of tofu. It's been playing on my mind these past few days. I've been thinking of my cousin, in particular since I saw his Instagram story this morning, a placard in his hand. I reposted to my stories and it got a ton of engagement. Now that Theo has been showing himself to be a bit closer to being human, maybe it's worth talking to him about it.

He frowns. 'Are you guys close?'

'Grew up on opposite ends of one street.'

'That sounds really nice.'

'On a muddy country road.' I laugh. 'Nothing like your château.'

'Yeah, but I would trade it for a dirt road with friends.'

I cock a brow at him. 'So, I grew up poor. And you grew up lonely. Well, at least we've established that both suck.'

There's a twinkle in his eye. 'And which one is worse?'

I think about this for a moment. 'Poor, definitely poor.' There's a moment of taut silence. 'My cousin's mum, *Tante Francoise*, my mother's sister, used to feed me when we didn't have a lot, when my father was in jail the first time. She worked in a shop so she could give us a little extra. But sometimes I felt really bad that it meant we were taking from her and my cousin – she's a single mum. Alexandre is like a little brother to me. I know it's wrong, but I kind of hate the idea of him going to these protests. Risking arrest, a record, unemployability, his whole future.'

There's a long weary silence. 'I guess he's brave,' Theo offers.

I nod.

'Brave and stupid share the same grave,' I say.

'Did you just make that up?' He watches me over his tower of empty plates.

'Yup. Thought it had a nice ring to it . . .'

Theo pauses, thinking about something. 'Why did your father become so obsessed? I mean, not that it's not valid . . . just. Was it the effect on the livestock, or the occupancy drop, did he know someone who got sick?'

I'm taken aback by his candour, and the way he has opened up, using words like *sick.* No doubt he's been taught not to say these kinds of things. I sigh. 'After they found traces of the special plastic in the water, the carcinogens,' I say, and he nods, leaning back in his chair. 'The animals were sick first and then my mum had a health scare.'

'Is she . . .' His expression is one of pure terror.

'She's okay. She's okay,' I say, putting my hands up. No reason to torture the guy. 'But it all made my father very angry, and he was responsible for a lot of vandalism. He was let off the hook twice but on the third time he got a sentence – one year. The animals were getting sick and my mother was still recovering, and with Father gone it wasn't possible to maintain the farm or the inn attached. She closed it and got a normal job at a shop. But my grandmother lives with us. We struggled to make ends meet until . . .'

'Until you started your channel,' he fills in knowingly. I nod. Something passes between us now that he knows the truth. Like an open current. He doesn't avert his gaze or change the topic; he just continues to gaze at me in the dim lanterned light. Curious, and maybe a little sad.

'My channel afforded us a way out, and I was able to support my mum till Dad returned. But he continued to be on the front line of the protests so . . . I don't know, to answer your question, I don't know what made him so dedicated. I just know he chose it over us. He's serving three years now for aggravated assault of a cop.'

I can see that Theo is processing this new information, that my father came back but didn't continue to care for us.

'I'm sorry,' he says simply. What more can he really say when I admit my dad is in prison for a long time?

I'm the one eager to change the subject now, even though I feel guilty for changing it. Theo's gaze is intense and unwavering. And I want to be in this moment, not dipping my toes into the icy pools of the past.

'What was your first ever post online?' I ask.

He grimaces awkwardly. 'I had, *uummm* . . . a chess-centred YouTube channel when I was a kid and . . . hey, don't you dare look it up!'

He tries to snatch my phone but it's too late. The screen fills with an eight-year-old Theo playing chess against himself and explaining the different moves in a squeaky voice.

I giggle. 'It really was lonely in the château, wasn't it?'

'Shut up,' he grumbles, plucking at the final plate he's picked – assembled fruit. Though I can tell he's amused. 'Or I'll fill your hotel room with cookies while you sleep and lead the deer there.'

The lighter conversation continues as we compare our online trajectories, talk about the times we both went viral.

'I once pretended my bra was a Covid mask – I was standing outside a shop and I was quite young and didn't have a mask so peeled off my training bra expertly and put it over my nose. I filmed myself doing it. One point four million views.'

Theo laughs. 'I went viral in Covid for ranting about two different types of pastas. Someone was trying to say they were the same.'

'Which pastas?'

He laughs. 'Fettucine and linguine.'

'You could have been cancelled for that.'

'I nearly was cancelled once,' he says. 'For being on a yacht with a bunch of government people that were meant to be passing a new bill instead of sunbathing in the south of France. I was only a kid then with a grainy Instagram.'

'Oh my gosh, I remember that!' I say, recalling some paparazzi shots of his family on a yacht on the cover of some gossip magazine in the village salon. 'I nearly got cancelled when I shared some political meme I didn't understand.'

'That's why I stay out of politics,' he says.

'I'd like to stay out of politics, but it's impossible when politics affects you. Affects your family.'

He doesn't say anything then. We keep doing this, tiptoeing around the hot cores of conversations, leaving them unfinished.

We leave the sushi place satiated and barely able to mount our bikes so we decide to walk it off a little. I still magically find room in my stomach to buy more mochi from a stand that boasts that they have original mochi-pounding sessions in the mornings. We browse the fluorescent shopping galleries. Theo tries his luck at yet another claw machine, winning a capybara plushie on the first round. He hands it to me and I just stare at it like he's trying to give me a stick of dynamite.

'Why are you giving this to me?'

'I don't have anyone else to give it to.' It feels odd to have dropped the pretence, both his and mine. My childhood was poor, his was lonely. We have a lot that divides us, but we are slowly finding out we have a lot in common too. I take the toy, but awkwardly, not sure I'm ready for any gifts from someone like him. Wondering whether I've opened up too much.

'Don't you have a girlfriend or something?'

'No,' he says, but my mind goes back to the girls I've seen him photographed with – models and heiresses – even a few weeks ago.

'Well, a cousin? Your mum?'

'I don't have any cousins. And my mum, she's funny about gifts.'

'What, like she only likes nice things? Birkins etc.? I don't mean it in an offensive way,' I hurry to say. 'I just mean, does she only like luxurious gifts, and maybe doesn't see any use in things like this?'

'It's okay, you don't have to explain,' he says, picking a stray crumb off the plushie I suddenly realize I'm holding pressed to myself.

'My mum isn't weird about presents because of luxury; she has other reasons.'

'Like?'

He searches my eyes as if looking for something. Judgement? Curiosity? Wondering if I'm being genuine?

'Mothers are a whole other conversation, Margot.' There's a

twinkle in his eye, but also a little sadness. 'Perhaps sometime when I haven't eaten my body weight in sushi. But you know what I really want right about now?'

'What?'

'I never thought I'd say this, but I think the best way to end this evening is some hot sand.'

CHAPTER 32

THEO

I switch into my *outdoor pyjamas* back at the hotel in Kyoto. I head out to the sandpit and Margot is already there. It's not that I don't want to tell her about my mother; it's that I don't really trust anyone with that information. And it's not the easiest thing to convey. There's so much nuance there. My mum is a former shadow of herself. And all I want to do is save her. It's not a conversation that pairs with claw machines and sushi and strangers.

I sit down at the rim of the sandpit and peel off my slippers, looking at it curiously. I've been to many spas around the world, but I've never encountered a hot tub of sand. Margot looks hesitant too.

'Ready?' She slips out of her house shoes to reveal a teal pedicure and eases her feet into the sand. I follow suit.

It's a warm, gooey feeling as your feet plunge in and settle somewhere towards the bottom where there's a strong soothing source of heat. Strange indeed, but very enjoyable. And Margot agrees by the sound of her deep sigh and the way her shoulders sag.

She clears her throat.

'So, earlier,' she ventures, 'I got this feeling you don't like your dad as much as I might have thought.'

My phone is in my pocket and I'm no stranger to being recorded.

'He's fine,' I say, trying to reach it.

'That's not what you said earlier.'

'Well, it's what I'm saying now.'

Finally, I manage to pull my phone out and switch it off. I gesture for her to do the same. She photographs the sandpit and switches the phone off, quickly catching on.

'Sorry,' she mumbles.

'I'm not sure discussing it changes anything. But yeah, you're right, I'm not his number one fan.'

'Because of his ethics? Or the second marriage? Or other family stuff?'

I swallow hard. I didn't expect her to be so frank, and I didn't expect to be grilled with my feet tucked in hot sand. 'All of the above, I guess.'

I've said too much and I'm instantly full of regret. 'Look, talking about it won't change anything. He's not going to change. And I'm not sure protests are going to change anything either.'

'What's so great about believing nothing can change? Where's the hope in that?'

'I didn't say it's great. But rooting for change is hopeless.'

'So what my cousin and friends are doing is hopeless?'

The anger in her voice is rising and it seems too late to stop. She switches her phone back on, scrolls a little and puts an article with my father's face before me.

'He's denying everything at the trial and countersuing – he won't even admit to any wrongdoing.'

I don't look at the phone in her hands.

'Can't you talk to him?' I look at her and her gaze is pleading. But there's nothing I can do. The man is an infallible institution. I don't know what she wants from me and, frankly, I'm tired of her expectations of someone she barely knows. I can't even get my father to care for my mother and she thinks I can get him to turn on twenty years worth of a career.

'I'm not your solution, Margot.'

Her eyes widen. 'So, this is my problem, not yours? That's what you're saying? An entire province is getting sick. It's a joint problem.'

'A hundred people got sick, not an entire province, Margot.'

'Oh wow, so they're just numbers.'

'You were the one who started with numbers. I'm correcting you.'

'Human beings are not collateral damage to business ventures.'

I sigh, exasperated, and the next words leave my mouth before I have a chance to control them.

'You sound naïve and stupid.'

She doesn't move, and for a blissful moment I think maybe she hasn't heard me and I can still take the words back. A soft wind blows, causing the sakura above us to blow into the courtyard and rain a faint shower of pink. Some buds land in the sand.

'I'm sorry for that,' I say, but it's too late.

She leaves me alone, looking stupid with my feet in the sand.

I head to bed, tired again, only to find Yuri sitting in the corner of my room, sipping on a green tea from a cast-iron pot. A second pot next to it is waiting for me.

'This is a small hotel to hide in,' I say. 'How are you holding up?'

'Today I was attacked by a deer. That's a first in my line of work.'

I stifle a laugh, careful to not be loud, then join him at the small retractable table and the floormats.

'Look, I'm not really in the mood for chit-chat, so what is it?' I'm still haunted by the hatred and disappointment on Margot's face, and the fact that I called her stupid. And I know enough about my bodyguard to know he's here for a reason.

'I've been asked to bring you home.'

My answering tone is icy. 'Not going to happen.'

'I've talked him out of it by convincing him abroad is safer at this time . . .' he continues. 'But there are stipulations.'

Of course, there always are when it comes to my father.

'What?'

'The girl needs to post less. And less protest stuff. Media is starting to pay attention to the fact you're travelling with her. The optics aren't good for him.'

'How the hell am I supposed to do that?' I push my tea away. 'I can't get her to stop insulting me, let alone get her to change her socials.'

Yuri sets his tea down and puts his jacket on. 'You'll have to figure it out, boss. I'm down the hall if you need me,' he says.

Absolutely freaking great. Not sure how I landed in a position where Margot thinks I can control my father and my father thinks I can control her, when they are both uncontrollable. How am I supposed to do any of that? I don't have to think for long because when I open the door for Yuri, I come face to face with my travel companion.

Margot's eyes narrow on Yuri who towers behind me and then her cheeks turn pink as if she has interrupted something important. I have seconds to save this and I think quickly on my feet.

'You, umm, still have my camera from earlier,' she says, referring to her Instax I borrowed for a picture of the deer. My brain races but I school my face into calm and relaxed.

'Sure, I'll go get it in a second.' I turn to Yuri. 'Thanks for everything. Margot, this is Sasha, my father's lawyer; he was in Osaka on business and had to bring some urgent documents for me to sign regarding my trust.'

She cocks a brow. Her expression grows colder the moment she realizes he's someone who works for my father.

'Nice to meet you.'

'Pleasure,' says Yuri with a casual smile he's a little too good at pulling off for someone who was in the special forces for fifteen years.

'I'll courier over anything else if needed before my flight back,' he adds in my direction. Yuri knows a layered lie is sweeter.

I wave him off and busy myself fetching her camera. I break out in a sweat and I hope she doesn't realize that Yuri left with no documents. And that he's built like the terminator.

'I'm not stupid,' she says as I hand her the camera. I'm convinced she's about to say *I know that's a bodyguard* but instead she says, 'I might not know about fancy documents, and big business, but I'm not stupid. You called me stupid earlier . . .'

I don't say anything, waiting for her to finish.

Her voice comes out a little sad. 'If you call me stupid again, I won't speak to you the rest of the trip.'

And I believe her.

'I won't,' I say. 'I promise.'

And I don't apologize, because I know she values actions over words.

'And you know, if you had a boyfriend or if you swung that way – I'm not someone you need to hide that from. I'm cool with it.'

Huh? Boyfriend?

Her eyes dart down the hallway where Yuri has disappeared. *Oh!*

'My father's lawyer is not my type. We just signed stuff in my room for privacy – it's common practice for families that get photographed a lot.'

'Okay. But just know I accept you either way,' she says as she begins to retreat down the hall. 'Maybe someone closer to your age though . . .'

'Thanks,' I say through gritted teeth. 'That means a lot. But there's nothing to accept.'

'*But* if there was, I would.'

She winks at me infuriatingly. *He's my bodyguard*, I want to shout. *And if there was anything to accept, I wouldn't keep it a secret and I don't need your approval because you are not the almighty morality police and you don't even like me!*

But I say nothing and she gets the last word.

I throw myself onto the bed, wondering how I'm going to convince her to tone down her socials. This oasis of a hotel has turned out to be more stress than relaxation.

RISHIKESH, INDIA

The Grand Rishikesh by Maison Partout

welcomes you to Rishikesh,

the yoga capital of the world.

During your time here, you will enjoy:

Unlimited yoga in our striking studio

A ceremony by the Ganges

A tour of an ashram

Theme: Nature and nurture – an oasis of recovery.

CHAPTER 33

THEO

It's a long flight from Osaka to Delhi, with a brief stopover in Singapore. I can feel Margot's judging eyes on me, singeing imaginary holes into the back of my head, cratering me like a planet with her unbridled hate. She's been seated in the row behind me this time. I tinker with my phone, trying to not let fear show. Especially when we hit turbulence.

I should be watching a sitcom or something to calm down; instead I've downloaded my father's latest trial recap and I've watched it twice. But something tells me Margot has watched it too: her expression has been grumpy most of the flight, only smiling briefly when she was brought chicken curry.

I press play again on the video as we taxi into place. I watch him speak a third time, almost like picking at a scab, listening to him claim he was not aware of any water contamination. Not aware of the high concentration of for-ever chemicals in the water he was not only not warning people about but also bottling and selling. He wasn't aware of the use of illegal water treatments being done. Not aware of anything really. Ready for middle management to take the fall.

I watch his lips move as he claims his hands were, and are, clean and everything was an accident, the camera switching, once in a while, to the most expensive Parisian legal counsel money can buy. I know it's all lies. I remember the hushed arguments he and my mother had at night. Long before rumours of people getting sick began. There was time to warn people.

But what am I supposed to do? The damage is done. I don't owe it to Margot to hate myself or to throw my mother under the bus by speaking out. What if she gets dragged into it again? What if she's guilty by association? My mother can barely leave the house as it is. By some miracle, I managed to get her out of speaking at the trial with the referral of a psychologist who cost a fortune.

I look back at her. Margot is still frowning at something. I roll my neck in an attempt to relieve the flight kinks, promising myself I don't care what she thinks. Humans were not supposed to be stuck in a tiny metal pod thousands of feet in the air for hours at a time. So what if my dad was on television delivering some inorganic speech after his trial? That's what he does half the time. That's his biggest talent. She thought I could change something and now I'm at fault because I can't? That's not how the world works.

It's a longer drive from the airport this time and right away I can tell that we are somewhere drastically different. Rickshaws cut us off from traffic and we regularly go from barrelling down a small street to driving at a crawl. Vendors, with their makeshift stalls and mismatched clothes, watching us go by. We pass hordes of backpackers, carrying their belongings like tortoise shells, chatting excitedly to one another dressed in trinkets and t-shirts purchased to prove to their friends back home that they lived the full traveller experience. A truck overtakes us – in the back is a mass of copper pots. The air is thick with humidity, peppered with cumin, incense and the scent of jasmine.

We swerve through the dusty streets lined with ramshackle houses, some so close to the bustling road that I wonder how long they will survive. Every gap between buildings has been turned into a home with corrugated roofs and simple walls made of blankets and cardboard. We swerve to avoid giant potholes baked into the clay earth, mounds of rubble, and stray dogs and playing children. My seatbelt is so loose I doubt it would do much to prevent me flying through the windscreen if we were to brake suddenly.

In the backseat, I hear Margot cough and then gag ever so slightly. I turn around to look at her. Her face is tinged green.

'Are you going to be carsick?'

'No. I can make it.'

'It would help if you open your window,' I tell her. She shakes her head. When I intercept her gaze, I can see what she's looking at. I was so busy looking at ground level that I failed to notice the families of large macaque monkeys migrating from telephone pole to telephone pole above us. Who knew that a fear of monkeys would be such a large problem across such a wide selection of countries? Though the monkeys of Victoria Peak were some distance away, and the monkeys of Bali's Ubud were cute and on the small side; both comparisons make these large macaques look scarier than they probably are.

'They aren't going to jump into the car,' I say, but she ignores me.

We make it to the stunning Grand Rishikesh hotel by Maison Partout, by far the most rural, nature-surrounded resort we've been to. It's a sandstone building straight out of a Wes Anderson film, surrounded by distant jungle and with carved wooden statues guarding the ornate front doors. Our bags are swiftly collected, Margot's so overstuffed I'm afraid it might burst as the porters carry it away.

I feel Margot's presence closer than it normally is and blink as I take her in, nearly sandwiched to me.

'The monkeys,' she says. 'Will they be here at all times?'

I fight the urge to say some smart quip, only because I can see a tremor in her hands and feel bad for her.

'Well, they are not birds, so I don't expect them to migrate. But I'm sure they won't bother you.'

We're welcomed by a large pink-cheeked manager who eagerly introduces himself as Ranjit. Margot repeats her question about the monkeys. The manager looks around as if he's forgotten the animals are there. There's a giant grey one, nearly half the size of Margot, nursing her young only a few feet away. I know Margot will hate me for this but I reach for my camera.

'Seriously?' she snaps at me.

'Yes, ma'am,' the man says to her previous question, shaking his head as we would shake to say *no*, but it's an Indian sign for agreement.

'Wait. Yes, ma'am, which part? Yes, they will be here, or yes, this is a temporary thing,' she presses.

'Don't worry,' I say. Snapping my first photo. 'They are harmless.'

She relaxes a little, but then the manager behind us chuckles. 'They are not all harmless, ma'am – these are langurs. Large monkeys that the other monkeys are afraid of. But their tails are very strong. They are not harmless; in fact, they are very, *very* dangerous. You must exercise caution. And the macaques, you must not look them in the eye or they will attack.'

I give him a quelling look but he continues his monkey speech all the way into the marble lobby.

CHAPTER 34

MARGOT

'Are you afraid of monkeys, ma'am?' says the nice manager, who has just given me a twenty-minute lecture on how incredibly dangerous they are.

'I wouldn't say "afraid",' I reply, clutching my bag tighter to my chest as I keep walking, sandals slapping against the marble of the lobby.

'More like terrified,' says Theo. I want to flip him off but I'm holding too tightly onto my bag. The hotel is stunning but all I can see is its open air, without proper windows, and the sprawling veranda has about three of those langur families. Why are there so many? And why is my whole body shaking? I didn't even know I had a monkey phobia until I set off on this journey we're on.

We had a business class flight to Delhi. Nine hours in total. Which was heaven, with the four-course meals and cheesecake and even a snack buffet you could visit anytime. But the last leg was a local flight that caused a crick in my neck. Theo was editing the entire time, and I can see he will have another billion hours of footage to edit if he keeps filming every damn monkey family we see.

'Remember, visitors don't want to see that hotels are covered in pests,' I tell him, recallingwhen I mocked him at the Balinese hotel when he filmed all those frogs.

'They are not pests,' he says. 'It's nature.'

We emerge into another open-air hallway and I hear the rush of running water. I peek through the glassless window and see the mad emerald rush of the Ganges beneath us.

'Hah! If they aren't pests then how come this sign says *don't leave food lying around because pests will come in*.' I point victoriously at the sign on the wall which has a cartoon monkey on it.

'Well, the monkeys just get *curious*,' he says, and bursts out laughing.

I watch him laugh at his own joke and raise a brow.

'What is actually wrong with you?'

'Curious,' he says, sobering and pointing at the makeshift sign. 'Like *Curious George*.'

'Excuse me?'

'It's a children's book. About a monkey. *Georges, le petit singe.* I loved it when I was little.'

On closer inspection, I can see the cartoon monkey on the sign. They must have googled monkeys and just copied whatever image they could find.

'Never heard of it,' I say.

'Best kids' cartoon of all time.' He traces the outline of the monkey. 'You should check it out.'

'Cartoons aren't for adults,' I grumble. I'm vaguely aware I'm being unpleasant but the last thing I watched on the flight was his father's stupid speech about how he's supposedly so innocent, and I'm hungry and tired and I've seen enough monkeys to last me a lifetime.

'Your loss,' he says.

‘I’m not going to watch your weird monkey cartoon, Theo,’ I snap under my breath. God, why is this man-child so incredibly infuriating?

The manager and porters politely pretend not to hear our monkey debacle as they lead us down two more open-air hallways, filled with the rush of water, and to a hallway that has two adjoining Ganges-view suites.

The manager opens my door and I thank him, before calling out to Theo, ‘You know what? I might be a little afraid of monkeys, but you are unhealthily obsessed with them!’ Then I disappear inside.

On the bed, I unzip my luggage and it bursts open like an overstuffed sausage. Silk spills onto my large four-poster bed. My luggage barely closed when I zipped it up back in Kyoto. Between the macaron-shaped hair accessories, bows, deer paraphernalia, four vintage kimonos that were a complete steal, and a wooden picture collection of cute animals eating mochi, I’m not sure I can buy anything else in India. Money-wise I can, what with the generous Maison Partout daily stipend. But I have officially run out of luggage real estate.

I sigh as I stare at the pile I’ve just created on the bed. Maybe I can fit a little more? India is literally the best place for buying stuff. I take a moment to take in my suite in its tones of peach, gold and coral. The bed is ornately carved, and the mini bar stocked with interesting snacks I don’t recognize. I breathe in that intoxicating smell of being somewhere new and unfamiliar.

My phone vibrates madly in my palm as I log into the hotel Wi-Fi. Notifications ping in like tiny bullets, reminding me I have bigger things to worry about than how I will fit my new saris in a suitcase stuffed with kimonos. I track down Alexandre's name in my contacts, asking him to confirm he got home okay, for the third time, after the latest protest where they took over an intersection. Then I check the French news sites. The protest ran almost parallel to our long flight.

Three people seriously injured after Yellow Vests clash with law enforcement.

I reread it with relief. Injuries, but none dead. Mercifully. And that's what I need to cling to in order to calm my nervous system. I let my mother know where I am. She texts me back that she has had a word with Alexandre about curbing his attendance as they undoubtedly become more violent. *He's got a bright future*, she writes. *It's time he focuses on that.*

The class action lawsuit isn't going well. Public consensus is that Pierre Delacour is a liar. That's another win, I guess. And I can see a big creator from Paris has reposted my story. It's becoming bigger and bigger. More drops of good news in what feels like an ocean of bad. I scroll my phone mindlessly on the balcony, the Ganges river rushing below, eleven or more storeys down, creating a meditative soundtrack to my scrolling.

The algorithm has, as always, seemingly read my mind against my consent. It serves me video after video of the protests. I feel nervous; what if the class action fails? None of those people will be compensated, everything will have been for nothing. Will the protests erupt in earnest, this time more violent? And what if the class action is won? Will Theo's father go to prison?

I don't know how Theo stays calm and continues working efficiently knowing his father is essentially on trial for murder. Or maybe not murder, but being at fault for dozens of people getting cancer and dying. Does Theo care? That boy is a mystery to me. I look up Theo Delacour. The first page of results shows me an article on his father with some blurry pictures of him getting into a car a few years ago; the next is just his name on some fancy private-school website as a member of the chess club, and then an online tabloid saying he was spotted 'looking cosy' with an heiress named Ginevra Calinessa and an even blurrier photo of what could be Theo and a gorgeous Italian model on a beach somewhere. I click on his profile and scroll. He so rarely shows himself; it's mostly the expanse of nature. Drone footage of hard-to-access places. Little challenges he sets for himself. But so rarely his face. Though with that face, he would get even more traction by showing it. The same way his friend Jodi shows off his body every time he gets a chance. I think of what it would look like if Theo made videos like Jodi, standing shirtless in a waterfall.

Then I quickly exit his profile, appalled at my thoughts.

I keep scrolling but it does little to ease my anxieties – a rising smog inside me. I call for room service; I can't brave the night in Rishikesh right now. Or the noise of the rickshaws or Theo's face.

I try a breathing exercise on the balcony. Then I call down to book a morning yoga session. Maybe that will calm me down. An hour later, when a text arrives from Alexandre confirming he hasn't been to any protests because he has too much homework, I can finally ease into my chair on the balcony.

I swat away a few mosquitoes and try to lean all the way back. Dad was always a drinker, or off getting in trouble, and I learned to breathe through the nighttime anxiety – how to breathe deeply when you feel that something bad is coming. With the ongoing trial, there have been more first-hand accounts of the victims of the water contamination. I watch a few of them, mostly out of guilt because I feel that we were spared. Even though our lives also fell apart after the contamination, my mother wasn't sick in the end. And some of these stories are so sad. I force myself through a few, feeling like it's my civic duty, and then I switch off my phone.

There's something so acidic about watching people suffer through your screen – it's like being suffocated, because you feel the pain in their voices and instantly you feel their pain beneath your skin. Involuntarily, almost like a compulsion, you imagine that happening to you and your loved ones. You can't help yourself. And it all becomes real then – you are no longer watching something that happened to someone you don't know. That very thing feels like it's happening to you at that moment. Like your nerves are exposed, singed by a live wire. I feel helpless, like there's nothing I can do, and yet, I'm changed after every piece of footage that I watch, unable to just put the phone down and keep going about my day but forced to anyway. *Water is everything. Water is life. And when someone compromises that, the consequences will be felt by generations.* Words of my father echo in my brain. I do feel grief at not speaking to him, even though it's my choice, but it's that rare kind of grief that is sugared with a layer of relief. A relief that if you aren't speaking to someone they can't disappoint you any more.

I hear Theo's relaxing music through his open balcony door. Then I see him emerge onto his balcony next to mine. For a moment, I just watch him. There's the glint of moonlight. He's not wearing a shirt, and I don't know if he was just doing push-ups to his Latin music inside but his muscles are tense and flexed. He's wearing white linen yoga trousers that look like he got them in Bali. He takes a few steadying breaths before his head turns to mine, and his eyes adjust to the dark of my balcony. He doesn't startle upon seeing me there, just takes a laboured breath. I try not to look at the dip of his abdomen, the shadows of his abs. Slightly like what I imagined earlier, except surprisingly more defined. But when my gaze snaps up, it meets his eyes, and I find him focused and intense. He looks as sad and exhausted as I do, and the vitriol I felt earlier evaporates a little. He keeps staring at me.

'Can't sleep?'

I shake my head.

'Me neither.'

'I've watched too much of the trial,' I say.

He nods. 'Me too.'

It makes me feel better to know he's seen some of the same stuff and feels the heaviness weigh on him in the same way. We share the dense silence, cut through with the rush of water below. *Water* ... the be-all and end-all in this case. The thing that keeps you alive and the thing that could have killed us.

'Do you think it's safe to drink?' I say.

He looks down at the rushing water. 'I've read up on it. It's actually full of this stuff called bacteriophages, like a virus that feeds off bacteria, so essentially the Ganges is one of the cleanest rivers in the world.'

'*But* does that make it drinkable?'

'Umm, no. It's also full of industrial waste like clothing dye and sewage and run-off.'

'So how is it clean?'

He stares down at it. 'A paradox, I guess.'

'A paradox,' I repeat. Staring at the shirtless boy who is kind of a paradox himself.

'And what are your thoughts about the trial?' I ask. He looks at me with that brooding stare that puts me on edge, like he can see right through me, and sighs.

'I think that what happened to those people is extremely sad.'

'What was *done* to those people,' I correct. He looks at me again.

'What was done to those people,' he echoes. My heart gives a little lurch. Is he agreeing with me?

I don't dare press any further. Scared it was a fluke, that if he dismisses what the victims have been through I might never be able to look at him again. And I'm starting to enjoy looking at him. Even though he's smug and full of boring facts.

'It's going to end soon, the trial,' he says quietly, 'and there will hopefully be closure for people when all is said and done.' Whether he's telling me or himself, I can't tell. For the short moment though, it's enough for me that he seems to care. Or at least, seems encumbered by all of this. Not defensive and arrogant like his father.

'Try to get some sleep,' he tells me. 'You'll need your strength for the tour of the monkey temple.'

I flip him off and hear a rumbling chuckle from the dark as I make my way inside. But I hurry over to the laminated Maison Partout itinerary, relieved to find there's no monkey temple on it, just yoga, and a tour of an ashram. *That* I can deal with.

CHAPTER 35

THEO

The Maison Partout hotel in Rishikesh is truly amazing. My hand hovers over the send button to share my photos of the Ganges river and the stone cliffs, thinking for a minute to share them with my father, and then my mother, but then deciding on neither and sending them to Jodi instead. My father will say I'm wasting my life travelling, and if my mother was scared for me in Hong Kong, then she'll be terrified on my behalf in vibrant India.

I do send my mother a brief check-in and my location, but all I get in response is a YouTube video about the dangers of conmen in India.

Our spa hotel is entirely open air, laced with pillars and gold paint and hovering over the Ganges below as if floating mid-air. I've had a decent night's sleep but I can't help but stretch as the jet lag stalls me, making me slow and sleepy.

I make my way to the opulent dining hall. The Indian Maison Partout branch seems to have a focus on luxury and natural beauty. I remind myself of the brief and film some of the nature, making sure to upload stories as I go.

I dig into my delicious dosa, a thin chickpea-flour pancake full of spiced potatoes served with sweet sauces in tiny tins – coconut chutney, mint chutney and dark tamarind. I chase it down with the most flavourful milky chai I've ever had. I chose to sit out the Ayurvedic yoga this morning but judging by Margot's smug expression as she joins me at breakfast, she hasn't.

'How are you?'

'Invigorated,' she says, but I can see lines of worry on her face. Probably because of our friends with opposable thumbs. I have already spotted no less than six monkeys on the balcony alone – but I never imagined that there would be monkeys *inside* the hotel too. Ranjit, the manager, dressed today in a stunning purple kameez, comes to greet us.

I feel weary as I try to focus on him laying out our four-day itinerary.

'You will visit The Beatles Ashram,' he says, and I perk up. I've only read a little bit about the time The Beatles spent in this town and how transformative it was for them.

'Sorry to interrupt, and I don't mean to be rude,' says Margot, snapping me out of my Beatles stupor. 'But those monkeys, the very large ones, are they here all the time?'

'The langurs?' he interjects. 'They are our protectors. We use them to protect us from the more aggressive macaques.'

'Do they come into the actual hotel? Like, would they come in here?'

'Yes, ma'am, they wander freely.'

Margot sinks a little into her seat, all the smugness from the yoga gone.

Ranjit tells us about the festival out on the Ganges, then explains what the hotel would like us to focus on. They would like Margot to do some spa footage and wellness aspects, and for me to really focus on the surrounding nature. I promise to secure great aerial shots. They also want people to know about their range of retreats and classes. I try to weasel my way out of the afternoon cooking class on offer but Ranjit tries to insist we both have to attend as it's very popular with couples.

'We are not a couple,' Margot corrects. Ranjit eyes us both warily.

'Couples are a target audience for the Maison Partout brand,' he says. 'That's what head office said. I'm so sorry, ma'am.'

This shuts her up. Ranjit goes through the rest of the programme.

'You were fine pretending to be romantic with Vincent Coles,' I say, as Ranjit leaves us to our breakfast.

She scoffs. 'No, I wasn't.'

'You were practically kissing in your Bali video. Probably part of the reason you both won. And now you're surprised they want more of that from you.'

I'm surprised to find my voice has gone up a decibel.

'I'm not going to film anything lovey-dovey with you, Theodore.'

Her use of my full name does something funny to me. Then I bristle.

'Literally no one asked that; they just said couples are their target audience.'

I don't know why it bothers me that she was perfectly fine suspending her ethical code for that Vincent dude, but then I'm like the anti-Christ. I try to refocus on my work; she has this magical ability to knock me off-piste.

'We should go film while the light is optimal,' I say, exasperated.

She sighs into her chai, and dimples form as she takes her first taste of the milky spiced liquid.

'Sometimes I forget this is my job,' says Margot in contemplation. It's true, it's easy to forget that in the midst of this beauty and time changes we are expected to produce specific top-quality content. That's what we are getting paid for, after all. I barely notice a langur monkey wandering nearer to our table until I feel Margot's entire frame tense.

'Maybe some content creation will help distract you from your fear?' I say, conscious that time is slipping through our fingers.

The animal comes closer, entirely undeterred by our presence, so close I can see its fangs. It stops, as if goading us, sitting up straight to show us its size and strength, sharp eyes trained directly onto ours. Margot begins to shake and closes her eyes. I know what that fear is like, the same fear I have at take-off, and though I don't get it about the monkeys, I know how she feels. I reach out and put my hand on hers. She tenses further, but then turns her palm upwards and grabs my hand desperately. Like someone on a turbulent flight might grab onto the passenger next to them. Something I've never been brave enough to do.

'It's okay. I've got you,' I say quietly.

We stay like that, still and silent, hand in hand as the monkey watches us for what feels like an eternity. It nears and she holds my hand tighter, trying to quell the tremor. She rises with a quiet squeal as the monkey goes under our table, its tail rubbing across her leg. Her eyes still closed, I gently guide her towards me. Slowly, I step in front of her, her left shoulder behind my right one, her quick breaths on the back of my neck, my hand never letting go. The langur reaches past us and casually helps itself to a bread roll before strolling away as if we never existed. Whoever said lions were the kings of the jungle had never met a monkey.

'He's gone,' I say gently.

Without a word, Margot drops my hand.

CHAPTER 36

MARGOT

I ditch Theo for a bit of shopping. Just as I predicted, shopping quickly takes my mind off the news cycle and the constant looming presence of the monkeys. Which, if it weren't for beautiful cotton dresses for a fraction of the price back home, would send my nervous system into a tailspin. I never used to shop. It took at least two years of producing content and being able to help my family get back on their feet before I allowed myself some clothes that were sent to me for free by a brand. And even now, I only shop cheap. But it's impossible to resist the cotton calls of Asia. Everywhere I look I catch the rainbow glimmer of beads, the interwoven embroidery, dresses flowing on hangers. I try to prioritize buying artisanal products and stop at every stall selling handmade goods. Of which there are plenty.

I buy silver and gold twisted hoops from a small shop, a beaded watermelon purse, and then stop to drink a mango lassi by the river, filming my outing as I go. Though I encounter lots of tourists, I still get my fair share of stares. Some shops I avoid because they are flanked by langurs. The chaotic nature of the streets is a good distraction too – there are speeding painted rickshaws, endless motor bikes and stuffy internet cafés that I thought had died out. There's the ring of chai carts and the smell of frying oil and little girls selling ceremonial flowers. It's a beautiful assault on the senses, full of flavour and colour, and noise, especially after the quiet serenity of Japan. I buy incense and incense holders, a handwoven straw purse and cloth elephants on a chain. After a while I have to give myself the *there's no room in your luggage* talk to stop myself splashing out on spices. I force myself to imagine Theo's look of judgement as he lifts my suitcase off the luggage belt and it bursts, a sea of silk and spice covering the floor, Theo's hands covered in turmeric, and laugh to myself.

I make my way to the famous suspension bridge and find Theo there with his drone. The pedestrian Laxman Jhula bridge sprawls like a floating road behind him, held up by ropes and cables over the rustle of the Ganges below. I falter, feet skidding on the ground, as I realize that both sides of the bridge are entirely flanked by macaques. *Great.* I'm starting to feel a little bit the way I did when I got stuck in a funhouse of mirrors at a fair when I was little and couldn't get out, glass walls everywhere I turned. Monkeys everywhere, no matter where I look.

'Hi,' I say to Theo.

He turns around, the expression of concentration on his face melting into something softer when he sees me. It's the first time his face has shifted this way, morphing to a half smile, lip tugging at one corner. It's different from the usual scowl I'm treated to. As I look over his shoulder, I try and steady the adrenaline shaking in my hands and fail. He follows my gaze to the bridge full of monkeys.

'I can't do it,' I say.

'We have no choice. We have to cross the bridge to get to the next activity, that ceremony by the river,' Theo says, his eyes full of empathy. 'I know there's a lot of them, but if you close your eyes I'll lead you again.'

I frown at him. The only thing worse than being led over a suspension bridge framed by monkey families is doing it blindly.

'Come on.' He reaches his hand out to me. 'Have a little faith.'

His hand slips into mine and instantly I can breathe again. Theo is infuriating, and smug, and annoying as hell ... yet his presence makes me feel safe, and the fact that it makes me feel safe also makes me feel angry. I squash down that feeling and grasp his hand tighter, because right now all I can think about is getting to the other side of that bridge.

My heart is beating so loudly I'm certain he can hear it. Like at breakfast, Theo walks one step in front of me, telling me to keep close and not to open my eyes. I can smell his aftershave again, clove and sandalwood.

'Did you change your aftershave?' I blurt out.

His walk stalls a little, whether because of my question or because there are tourists in our way.

'Yeah, I bought one from a local perfume producer. Does it smell bad?'

'No, it smells ... nice. Like sandalwood.'

'A compliment? From Margot?' he coos.

'It's a compliment to the craftsman. It's covering up your musk of superiority.'

I smile but then I hear the screech of a monkey and my breathing hitches. I hear a mild chuckle from Theo, but he's taking this seriously. He's next to me now and his hand is gentle on the small of my back as he nudges me forward.

'I've got you,' he says again, causing my heartbeat to slow down from a thundering train to a soft beat thrumming in my ears. I focus on my breathing, the touch of his hand in mine, taking one hesitant step in front of the other, telling myself it's just a stroll on the beach and not a treacherous walk over a raging river surrounded by highly intuitive primates. Someone shoulder checks me and I stumble.

'Look where you're going,' I hear Theo say in a colder voice. It would make me smile if I wasn't so terrified.

'We're here,' Theo says. 'You can open your eyes.'

I look around me, blinking into the sun, his silhouette slowly turning solid. He's smiling.

'You okay?' he asks.

I nod, all too aware of how sweaty my hand is in his. I let go and surreptitiously wipe it on my trousers.

'Thank you,' I mutter.

'It was nothing.'

Except it was.

We don't say another word as we follow the river to where the evening ceremony is going to take place. It's easy to find: we just follow the ebb and flow of locals, tourists, and kids selling ceremonial flower offerings.

Theo walks ahead and I watch as two girls, aged around seven or eight, stop him. He buys flowers off them as they examine the bracelets on his arms that he bought in Bali.

'Very pretty,' they both say.

Something tightens in my chest as I watch him take off the bracelets and give them one each.

He keeps walking as if it were nothing. It's rare for an influencer to do a good deed without sharing it with the world, but Theo isn't like that, which only makes the pain in my chest grow stronger.

We find space to stand on the large wide steps in front of the river, thankful that the crowds have scared away any more monkeys. What I believe to be priests already line the shore, holding large brass lamps. Theo gives me a solitary glance, but one that seems packed with something like anticipation as these men line up in careful rows. They start to sing rhythmic mantras, bells chiming and drums banging in unison. There's a heavy smell of incense and something else – ghee? A feeling of eternity and solitude washes over me, like I'm one with nature. And I know it's cheesy, but it all really takes your breath away as the sun starts to set and dip over the Himalayas in the distance and the chanting begins.

I watch the flames waltz on the dark water as the sun sets fully, thinking about how it's possible to find peace on the other side of the world. People say peace is found at home but sometimes home is a state of mind. Sometimes home is a moment in time in which you feel safe.

Theo buys us two tiny boats made of leaves, cradling marigolds and a tiny oil lamp inside. I cradle mine between my palms, marvelling at it.

A chill comes over me and I pull out one of my new purchases – an embroidered shawl – over my head, grateful I couldn't resist picking it up at a local stall. Its silvery and teal and flaps in the wind over my head as we both release our boats into the inky water along with the rest of the crowd. I say a tiny prayer for my family: for my mother, my father and Alexandre, though I'm not sure that's what I'm meant to be doing at this ceremony. No one explained anything and it's pure vibes, but it's so stunning we just go with the flow and try to not be in the way. I spot the expression on Theo's face and can tell he feels the same.

'Dinner?' he says after a while of watching the tiny boats drift away. I nod and follow him.

We end the day with a vegetarian thali in a local riverside café, too tired and hungry to walk back to the hotel to eat, and too entranced to leave this side of the Ganges. A kind waiter explains that the northern Indian style of plates is an Ayurvedic experience with a focus on health-enriching foods. He brings us a giant metal tray covered in small metal bowls, that jangle against each other, each one with a generous serving of rice and bread in the middle. There are dark lentils, colourful vegetable curries and a fluffy chapati which I tear into quarters, inhaling the smell of nuttiness and oil. Indian food isn't very popular in our province so I haven't had it that often. I watch Theo, who has clearly had every cuisine under the sun and plenty of it, use his bread to dip into his creamy dhal and then pinch bits of curry and rice into his chapati with his bare hands and I emulate him. It's an explosion of flavour, until the heat of the unfamiliar spices takes over and I fan myself with the laminated menu, eagerly swallowing a large dollop of the yoghurt-and-cucumber raita to try and calm the heat down. I top everything off with spoonfuls of mango chutney and don't stop until the metal pots are wiped clean. I never thought eating vegetarian could taste this good.

Theo asks for more lime pickle and replaces the empty pot. For dessert we are brought gulab jamun – honey-soaked dough balls that are divine but a little too sweet for me. Theo and I both take pictures but less than I would have if I were alone. When my hands itch for the phone to check on the trial and the protests – I fight that urge too.

Some moments are just for us. Theo's words in Japan come back to me. Even though it's my job to document what I'm experiencing, it takes away a little from the moment each time I pull out my phone. And each time I pull out my phone I don't just film, I scroll and read and consume and let the bad things in the world take me away from the beauty of the now.

I push my phone away, eyes locking on Theo right as he finishes the last bit of gulab jamun. He licks a bit of honey from his thumb and I turn my attention back to my chai, feeling a flush rush into my cheeks.

'I've decided something,' I announce. 'I'm going to disable my news notifications. To be more present in this once-in-a-lifetime trip.'

In an effort to be less obsessive than my dad. I don't say that last part. I show him my screen instead, as proof. No more trial news. No more doom and gloom.

He raises his steaming post-meal chai in the air. 'I'll do you one better and I'll turn my socials notifications off entirely.' Demonstratively he pushes a few buttons on his phone and shows me his screen too. 'There. Done.'

I cringe. 'That might be a step too far. *We* still rely on engagement. For us, and . . . for Maison Partout.' *I* rely on constant engagement, which I've already told him. It's my lifeline for brand deals and for my family. I don't have a trust fund to fall back on. I can't just go dormant. But we've been having to post so much more on a daily basis since this trip began, it's beginning to burn me out.

'Okay, that makes sense.' Theo nods, looking a little awkward, and he runs his hand across his buzzcut, something I've noticed he does every time he's thinking. 'You know what we need? We need fewer posts but with bigger impact.' There's a mischievous twinkle in his eye that I don't quite trust. 'There is *one* thing that I've been thinking about that would make a big impact.'

'I don't like seeing you excited. It's unnerving.'

Theo pays and gestures for me to get up.

'As you maybe have already guessed, I'm suggesting we partner up for a video. Maison Partout will be pleased. And that's double the exposure with half of the labour and more time to enjoy ourselves. I have the perfect idea.'

Oh no. I shake my head but his determination is infectious and I'm curious about what he has thought up. We thank the restaurant for a wonderful meal, and, feeling full to bursting, I follow him across the bridge, which mercifully is near deserted after sunset, and up the hill. The Rishikesh Maison Partout branch is stunning at night; heavily dotted with chandeliers in its open-air spaces, it glows in levels of tiered dancing light, like birthday candles on a cake. We arrive breathless and, after a brief rest, Theo leads me through the lobby and then to a set of large doors that I don't recognize.

'Let's blindfold you with the scarf,' he says, one hand on the door handle.

'Excuse me?'

'Just trust me, okay? I haven't betrayed you yet.'

I sigh. 'Run me through the concept then.'

'You're blindfolded and I dance with you in this ballroom of sorts. You just follow my lead and I will likely dip you once at the end. If that's all right? It's kind of like a trust fall exercise but it will look very cinematic.'

'Who is that meant to appeal to?' I frown up at him.

'It's part of a story, a narrative I cooked up.'

'Well, how come it's *you* that gets to cook up the narrative?'

He rolls his eyes at me and gently pulls the teal scarf from my neck. 'You like my content, right? Like, not me as a person, whom you actively despise, but the content I produce. Do you like it?'

I stare at the pink doors. He cocks his head and catches my gaze.

'Margot?'

I frown at him. The truth is, his content has always been innovative and high-end. He once filmed a video of a donkey giving birth, paired over an orchestral symphony, and it nearly made me cry. But trust? That's a big one.

'Fine. We film one video with your idea. And one with mine.'

'Deal,' he says, fully pulling the scarf away and fixing the blindfold into place.

'I'll come get you after the camera is set up.' He enters the ballroom and I hear some rustling behind the closed door where I assume he is popping up a camera on his ever-present tripod. After a few minutes, I hear the door open. Theo takes my hand and leads me in.

I sense an odd rustling around as I follow him to what feels like the centre of a large breezy space. Another rustle, and then shuffling echoes somewhere, followed by a cold whip of air that raises goose bumps on my forearms.

'Open-air ballroom?'

'Sort of.' His voice is low as he places a hand under my left shoulder and starts to ease me into a slow waltz. I follow, trying hard to not step on his feet. His other hand is closed around mine. He makes a steady lead. There's no music, just an empty eerie silence peppered by the whoosh of something brittle, or soft, like … leaves? Despite the silence, I can tell Theo is following a specific beat in his head, and humming it lightly to remain in step.

'Just another minute,' he says quietly, twirling me around once. It's quite a slow dance and I'm hyper aware of his breathing. He can always speed the tempo up for the video if necessary and so I follow his steps carefully, sure and measured. We glide across what feels like a stone floor. There's still distance between us but it feels like it's shrinking. The rustling sound returns, growing slightly, and for a second I think I feel Theo tense up, but it's quickly leashed. I can still smell his new aftershave, clove and sandalwood and cardamom, blending with the earthy smell of the room. Another familiar smell. I think I hear a sound, like a kitten meowing, and Theo coughs, speeding up his pace. What an odd video this will make.

We do another round, and another twirl. His hand firm on my back, he glides me through a few more steps before he pauses.

My breath hitches when he dips me, lodging itself in my chest.

He pulls me back up and I'm a little breathless, cheeks flushing with embarrassment. I can feel the heat of his breath on my face, and suddenly the blindfold feels like too much of a vulnerability. It feels like my senses are too heightened. As if on cue, Theo gently pulls the knot loose and the fabric away from my eyes.

'Now don't freak out,' he whispers.

I look up. He's inches from me and my eyes lock on his cold blue gaze. His lips are inches from mine. I look down at them, plump, with a Cupid's bow, and set in a determined line. Then something moves behind Theo's head and my gaze readjusts, realizing we aren't alone. I release a squeal but Theo's palm cups my mouth just in time. When he's certain I'm done shrieking he releases me.

I take a careful step back and with a tremor glance at the twenty or so langurs in various stages of sleep or cuddling, a few of them wide awake and staring at us with mild curiosity. On instinct, Isnap my gaze to the floor. Then I smack Theo's arm.

He has the good grace to look a little guilty, if not amused.

'You absolute prick,' I whisper through gritted teeth. 'Get me out of here *now*.'

As I head to the door on tiptoes, flanked by Theo, I suddenly realize that I'm not that terrified anymore. I mean, I still absolutely don't want to get close to any of the monkeys but that inner terror has lifted a little. Like exposure therapy. My rage towards Theo, however, has not lifted one bit, and I vow to take my vengeance.

'See, I helped you combat your fear of monkeys,' he says. 'And you will go viral as a bonus.'

Viral? God, he's arrogant.

'So, you knew they slept there?'

'Yeah, it's the second yoga studio and they use it at night,' he says as he opens the door for me. With relief, I step over the threshold and wait for Theo to close the door, separating us from the monkeys, or at least creating the illusion of separation. They still roam through the hotel hallways like some waking nightmare.

'This better be an amazing post,' I tell him, still keeping my voice low. 'Or I'm going to throw you in the Ganges. And no number of biophages will save you.'

'Well, that can be *your* video,' he says, suppressing a smile. 'But I promise mine will get more views.'

CHAPTER 37

MARGOT

Theo was absolutely right. The internet explodes after he posts the video of us dancing against the backdrop of a langur colony.

Are they a couple?

May this love find me and
punch me in the face.

I want it like this or not at all <3 <3 <3

The comments are pouring in: 8245 comments and counting. I scroll through them and rewatch our video for what feels like the fiftieth time. He's intercut it with drone footage of the bridge, and a sneaky video he took of himself holding my hand walking me down the bridge with my eyes closed. The video says *Leave Fear at the Door* and promotes the hotel and Rishikesh. And though there is no indication of us being romantic, people in the comments have made their own assumptions. Which I guess we've made easy, what with the dancing and all.

I can't believe they are together. Didn't
his dad like poison her whole town?

I hover over the negative comment but a moment later it isn't there any more. Is Theo deleting all the negative comments? Is it for my benefit, or his? The numbers rise as Theo delivers on his promise and the video goes viral. Guess people love monkeys and romance. Then comes a message from Dimitra.

Oh my god, how did this happen? I need all the tea.

There is no tea. He tricked me into the video and I guess people love it or something, I type quickly.

There's no text from my cousin or my mum, who have undoubtedly both seen it. My mum has commented under it – *what beautiful scenery.* And I have absolutely no idea how to feel about the whole thing.

'Maison Partout management is extremely impressed with your new video,' Ranjit tells us with a huge smile over breakfast. He places a giant fruit platter on our table, burgeoning chunks of mango, glistening papaya, rings of pineapples and fresh mint.

'We've booked you a couple's yoga session after your ashram tour.'

'Not a couple,' I remind him.

I roll my eyes at Theo and he conceals a laugh. This video is now going to mean Maison Partout will be asking a lot more of this from us. But I'm in too much of a good mood to complain. We finish our breakfast and head off to our ashram tour.

I'm so drained after the tour of the ashram on our final day, I decide to take a nap and skip the yoga the hotel offered us. India is breathtaking but the fatigue of constant ashram walks and the hustle and bustle are taking its toll on my body. I decide to do some yoga in the room instead, unfolding the scarlet mat they've left for me and marvelling at how they seem to have thought of everything.

Not even bothering to change out of my flimsy nightdress, I start off slowly, sitting cross-legged on the mat, focusing on my breaths. India has been such an assault on the senses, and, coupled with everything happening back home and the strange truce Theo and I have reached, my mind has felt so crowded that I had trouble sleeping last night. Half an hour of yoga should help. Eyes closed, I count my blessings, mutter a mantra about gratitude, then ease into some sun salutations.

It feels good to stretch and move, breathing in the misty scent of the afternoon, the pungent scent of the earth outside, wafts of peanut oil and cardamom from the kitchens below, and the sweet scent of the jasmine plant on my balcony. A light breeze winds its way in from the open balcony door, cooling my skin and reminding me just how lucky I am to be in a luxury hotel in such a beautiful part of the world.

I can already feel my mind clearing and my joints easing up as I stretch the backs of my legs and move into downward dog, my hair falling over my face. I probably should have changed out of my pyjamas, but it's not like anyone can see me. I keep my eyes closed as I breathe in deeply and let the air back out in a guttural sigh.

When I open my eyes, I find myself staring into a pair of black ones.

I collapse onto my mat and let out a shriek, skittering backwards until my back is flat against my bedroom wall. All the zen has left my body as adrenaline courses through my veins, my heart racing, every inch of me clammy with sweat.

A monkey is perched on the edge of my balcony, staring in

with decided curiosity. Gingerly, I get to my feet and tiptoe to the door, maintaining eye contact the whole time, but not enough to challenge him. I then slide the door closed as fast as I can and snap the lock into place.

'You can't be trusted,' I say to the macaque.

Just look at him. The full opposable thumbs, monkeys freak me out. Not to mention the fangs and the large male appendage. With a deep breath I walk back to my mat, telling myself that I have nothing to fear and should continue my routine when I hear an audible *click* and gasp. When I turn around the macaque has already opened the lock and is pulling the balcony door open. I let loose an ear-splitting scream.

CHAPTER 38

THEO

Though the video is objectively a raging success, I have my hands full deleting negative comments. My followers don't tend to tie me to my dad that often. Some follow me because of the wealth, and many, I'd hope, for the nature content. But now that I have collaborated on a post with Margot, lots of her followers from France are on my back. Writing vile things about what they perceive to be our romance. I meant for the video to be a little suggestive, just like Maison Partout wanted, just how Margot had done it with Vincent, but I didn't quite fathom how it would be perceived. This huge and very personal interest in *us*. And there is no us. I definitely feel at fault for whatever shitstorm is unfolding across my screen.

I sit back on my bed, a towel around my waist, to see that more notifications have come through in the time it took me to take a shower. I don't want Margot to see them so I'm heavy on the delete button. I never normally delete anything, and I welcome the clapback that will undoubtedly come from my father for my collaborating with a daughter of the Yellow Vests. But these petty comments? I'd rather wipe them from the face of the internet and run my finger hot on the block button.

Margot has posted a new story and it's an update on the trial, featuring a negative article about my dad. I wouldn't call her outwardly political, but every now and then she's there, posting and supporting. This is likely to upset my father a lot more than any monkey dancing video. I think back to Yuri's warning. I like pissing off my father but his threats do have to be taken seriously. He's not one to bluff.

'THEO!' I hear my name echo through the wall, followed by a scream.

The first scream is disorienting, but by the second one my instincts kick in.

I look around to grab something to wear, but her screams are intensifying so I don't think about changing. What if she's being attacked? I follow her cries outside to the balcony and, without thinking, I hike a leg up and climb over the small barricade that splits her room from mine.

I'm expecting to see blood, or an attacker, or I don't know what. Instead, I find myself face to face with a huge monkey. He's inside her room, the balcony door open, the monkey inside and me outside on the balcony. And now I'm blocking his only exit. As soon as the monkey becomes distracted by me, Margot quickly scrambles to her feet and rushes to the bathroom. The bathroom has a glass door so she can still see me. She turns the lock, mouthing the word *sorry.*

'Seriously?' I call out.

'What was it you said? They're harmless!' Her call is muted through the glass. Great, this is payback for the blindfolded dance.

I turn and face the monkey. *He's not dangerous*, I tell myself. *I'm bigger and stronger and smarter*. But, also, all I'm wearing is a towel which I'm holding on to tightly, so I only have one good hand, whereas he has massive fangs. *Fake it till you make it*, I guess.

In a quick succession of movements, I kick out and roar, trying to ninja kick outwards while entering the hotel room at the same time. Which is not easy when I'm trying to keep my towel from dropping. I fall backwards on the bed and jump back to my feet. He snarls at me but is momentarily confused by the commotion and ninja-kicking. I use what I learned about bears and make myself as large as possible while snarling and growling. Finally, he retreats, but not before grabbing a tube of Pringles from a basket atop the mini bar. This monkey knew exactly what he was doing. He's done this before. He snarls at me and runs off.

I lock the door behind him, breathe out a sigh of relief and hear the bathroom door unlock.

I turn around to see Margot holding her iPhone, filming me, a hand clasped over her mouth from laughing.

She opens the door and emerges. 'Sorry, but it was you or me.'

'Great, thanks a lot,' I mutter.

'I now have my viral video too. *Trust-fund baby fights monkey for Pringles*.'

I swipe out in an attempt to snatch her phone but she's faster and she wriggles out of my grasp, giggling.

'Delete it,' I growl. She waves the phone in front of me in a taunting fashion, then her eyes scan me and she looks away briskly. The giggling has stopped. She seems to have noticed I'm wearing nothing but a towel. Her cheeks are growing pink.

'I can't believe you made me go head-to-head with the monkey and then ditched me. If there's a jaguar at the safari today, I'll let him eat you,' I say. 'I'm quite a fast runner, and you're likely to be wearing bedazzled butterflies on your feet, so good luck with that.'

'Jaguars?' she says, her breathing growing a little quicker.

I'm not even sure there are jaguars here, but all the colour has drained from her face and I've only just noticed now that all she's wearing is a tiny nightgown. It's satin and hugs her curves tightly . . . a little too tightly. Averting my gaze, I reach for where I know the robes are in the hallway closet and hand her one and she mumbles a *thank you*.

'I signed up for a tour around the world. Not whatever *Crocodile Dundee* stuff this is,' she says grumpily, wrapping the robe tightly around herself. 'It's cute and all, but I've had enough wildlife to last me a lifetime.'

'I can go alone. I'll make an excuse for you. It's our last day, anyway – do something you like.'

'Really?'

'Yeah,' I reply. 'Like shopping.'

She shoves me playfully. My muscles tense at the contact and I straighten out and cough. 'Look, I need a little favour.'

She has the audacity to look suspicious, even though I rode in like a white knight and saved her just now.

'I was thinking maybe you could tone down the trial stories on your feed until we finish the Maison Partout stuff, just so they don't have a problem with it.'

I can't meet her eye as I say this because I'm a little embarrassed to be asking.

'I might be scared of monkeys and jaguars, Theo,' she replies. She stands on tiptoes until her face is close to mine. I'm hyper aware of her breathing, and that she smells of coconut shampoo. 'But I'm no coward.'

I look down at her, those insufferable green eyes staring back indignantly like I didn't just rescue her from a dangerous primate.

'Fine,' I say through clenched teeth. 'Then come face the jaguars.'

ASTROS, GREECE

The Thalassa Hotel by Maison Partout

welcomes you to the Peloponnese region.

During your time here, you will enjoy:

Visiting a monastery

Hiking up to the local castle ruins

Making your own olive oil

A day trip to Nafplio

Theme: Finding the beauty in simplicity.

CHAPTER 39

THEO

The town we are staying at in Greece is tiny. Like *only one main street* tiny. A quaint sandstone street with honey shops and fish tavernas, but so tiny that I just hope Yuri has the good sense to not be out in the open. Margot might suspect something if she sees the same man she saw in my room in Japan suddenly materialize in a town so small that everyone seems to know one another by name.

It was an extremely long leg of the journey and I'm tired as a result. Both from the flight and from waiting for Margot for three hours at the Athens airport as she threw fit after fit about them having lost her suitcase. They promised to deliver it in 'one to two days', but in the meantime I've had to lend her some clothes to sleep in because the shop in town was closed when we arrived late last night. On top of that, I seem to have injured my knee on a wobbly cobblestone outside the lobby. No amount of icing it last night has helped the pain.

The Maison Partout branch here is also the smallest one so far. An agricultural boutique hotel at the foot of a small mountain crowned with the ruins of an ancient fortress that looks like the dregs of a crumbling sandcastle. After the hustle and bustle of Hong Kong and Japan and the beautiful, immersive chaos of India, seeing empty streets and an empty blue sea feels like coming home somehow. Even though I've never lived by the sea, I always feel at home next to it – perhaps I feel at home in the peace. In the absence of chaos. Next to the sea I feel insignificant, anonymous, blissful. It reminds me the world is infinite, and we are blips. I wonder what Margot would think of this theory, and I receive my answer when I find her in a local beach club called Jupiter not long after breakfast.

Hair blowing in the wind, she looks a little like a Grecian goddess lying on a sun lounger in her bikini, which I recognise from the hotel's tiny gift shop, and my formal white button-down. I'm grateful she isn't looking my way and can't see me limp over. I stop a few feet shy of her sun bed.

I catch myself looking at her taut abdomen for a moment before realizing that she's violently chewing her nails and staring at her phone. So much for saying she wanted to switch off her news notifications. She doesn't look like she feels the least bit peaceful. Her finger flicks upwards methodically and I can tell she's following the timeline of yesterday's protests, following the new statements made in the trial. Ingesting all of it, like some hellish internet catnip. Yesterday, my father's counsel brutally cross-examined two of the victims. Discrediting them with cheap legal tricks in which they tried to paint them as unreliable narrators, questioning their life choices. I've seen this done before: if you make the jury doubt a witness in any way, even in a way unrelated to the trial, then they automatically doubt the story related to the trial as well

One of them, a farmer's daughter whose sister died from cancer likely caused by the water, broke down in tears on the stand. I only watched snippets, but what the lawyers did was vicious. I'm sure my father thinks they are worth every penny, though you couldn't tell a thing from his vacant expression.

I can't watch too much of the whole ordeal – it makes my stomach turn.

This morning, I tried reading the news at breakfast. I tried being responsible and aware, but each article I read left me with nothing but frustration and hate and nowhere to put it but to shove it deeper inwards.

I suddenly realize I'm being a massive creep standing a few feet away, so I move forward and sit down quietly on the lounge chair next to hers; it creaks in response. It's off-season here in the small town, and the beach club she chose is nearly empty. A waiter waves to me and I peek at Margot's foamy drink.

'What's good here?'

'I'm drinking a cappuccino *freddo*, as he called it,' she says, without looking up. 'Their take on a sweet, cold cappuccino.'

'Is it any good?'

'It's my second one,' she says by way of answering. 'But it's strong.'

I order the same and feel a little ridiculous drinking something that foamy and that sweet through a teeny tiny cocktail straw. I watch her continued frantic scrolling and feel a little bad for her. She reminds me of my mother, not living in the moment. Consumed. Or maybe I am the one who is too detached? Do I not care enough? I shake my head as if thoughts could be dislodged like coins from a piggy bank.

'In India, you said you wanted a break from scrolling,' I venture carefully.

She looks at me then, eyes reflecting the sea, and sighs.

'I know what I said. But it's hard.'

'Want to see the castle? Get our minds off it?' I cock my head in the direction of the mountain. 'It was on our Maison Partout itinerary as something they wanted us to add into the videos of the hotel.'

She taps her screen.

'You know in his latest examination he denied that they knew about the contamination up to a year earlier. Even though there were leaked emails that prove that he did know – he's just saying it's all fake.'

She looks at me expectantly.

'Margot.' I measure my words, not sure how I could explain years and years of context to her. 'He doesn't talk to me about this stuff. If you think that we sit at the dinner table and he tells me all his darkest trade secrets, you are mistaken.' I was lucky if my father attended one of my opulent birthday parties. The only work-related thing my father would be willing to discuss was when I would be coming to work at Eau Jeune, and I'd rather eat coals than that. On all matters, my father would expect blind loyalty and zero ethical questions.

'Can you . . . text him? Have you spoken to him about any of this? About the trial? I don't know. Isn't there, maybe, a settlement they can reach that he would be able to swallow?'

He won't care. I want so badly to tell her the truth but I doubt she'd understand. What would I text him anyway? *It's wrong to lie in a court of law, Papa! At least give these people some money.* Turn your back on billions and your boards of directors and shareholders and an entire empire you've built? To men like him these things sound like the altruistic musings of a child. Someone whose prefrontal cortex hasn't formed yet. And he'll tell me as much. Worse, he might cut off my mother entirely if pushed and I can't yet afford to maintain her on my own. Not in the apartment we live in. Not in the comfort she's used to. And if one more thing changes in her life, I'm afraid she might unravel completely.

Moreover, how do you ask someone to speak the truth when you know their victory relies on lies?

'No, I haven't talked to him.' I shrug my shoulders as she watches me.

'Will you?'

Her eyes are big and saucer-like, and for some odd reason I want to give her what she wants. So, I lie. A tiny white lie, a drop in the ocean of my father's lies.

'Yes, but I doubt it will change anything.'

'I'll hike up to the castle with you. But only because I was going to go right now anyway. And I need some help filming.' She gives me a smug look.

'God, you know how to make someone feel wanted.'

'I'm sure you have no problem with feeling wanted, Theodore Delacour,' she says with a pointed look in my direction, but it somehow doesn't sound like a compliment. Or is it?

'I need to get changed,' she says, tugging at my borrowed button-down, and I'm thrown by a sudden vision of her waking up next to me and putting one of my shirts on in the morning. I shake my head. It's a strange rabbit-hole image, one that couldn't be further from our reality in which she still hates me fifty per cent of the time. I try to erase it from my mind but it kind of sticks, as if pressed into the honeycomb of my brain.

'What are you going to change into? Your suitcase won't arrive until tonight,' I remind her.

'I have an idea,' she says. And it's the sparkle in her eyes as she says it that puts me on edge.

'Okay, but the thing is,' I say. 'I busted my knee a little on a loose cobble yesterday so I can't hike.'

'How did you expect to get up to the castle then?' She frowns.

I smile at her. 'You're not the only one with ideas, Margot.'

CHAPTER 40

MARGOT

We stop briefly to snack at a souvlaki place, where they stuff mixed chicken-and-pork gyros into fresh spice-dusted pita bread, then top it with red onions, tomatoes and French fries, before drizzling it with homemade tzatziki. It's divine.

After lunch, Theo leads me to an alleyway where he finds a derelict pink Vespa, rusty and sun-damaged. He mounts it and gestures for me to follow.

'You're joking. Where did you get that ancient thing?'

'It's not ancient, it's *tanned*,' he says. 'I asked the hotel manager for a means of transport to the castle on account of my knee and she let me have it for the day.'

I snicker as I take a seat on the rickety thing, wrapping my arms lightly around his middle to stabilize myself. It's an odd sensation, like I'm trying to hug him. I feel his muscles tighten under my grip – clearly, he didn't expect the familiarity either. I let go and steady myself on the back of the Vespa instead.

'Okay, Peloponnese Ken, full steam ahead.' I hear a low rumble of a laugh as he takes off in the direction of the castle.

We pass an ancient amphitheatre and two small cliffside churches, both blue, perched above the green cliffs as if keeping watch. We pass a lighthouse and then drive up an overgrown path flanked by wildflowers and dandelions. I think about how spoilt for history this area must be if the path to the castle isn't that well trodden. They must have their pick of ancient sights to visit, or maybe it's a little bit of a tourist thing to do and the locals don't come up much.

At some point we have to park, and I walk patiently next to him for the final bit, giving him and his knee time. I'm surprised I didn't notice his limp earlier. I'm holding a plastic bag and Theo's eyes dart to it with mistrust. But I have a vision. The same way he had a vision. As it is with many of my videos, I can see the content clearly in my head like a mini film. The ruins of the keep spread in front of us, and when we pass what used to be the door, I spot the cerulean sea flashing through the remnants of what were windows, and realize my vision was accurate.

I hear Theo exhale, taking in the beauty of the 360-degree view, visible to us through the cookie-coloured gaps in the ruins. I stretch out, letting the wind of the elevation wash over me – let it roll over my body like a wake-up call.

'This is perfect,' I say. 'I'm going to go change behind that tree.'

'It's carob,' says Theo, picking something that looks like a large dehydrated edamame bean off the floor and tasting it.

'Nerd.' I roll my eyes. 'Just no peeking.'

'You flatter yourself,' he says, irritation tinging his cheeks, and I smirk. Somehow, getting under his skin has become a hobby of mine.

I quickly change into the contents of my bag, a simple thin bedsheet, then clip everything into place and shove his shirt back into the bag.

When I emerge, he looks at me and scoffs.

'Seriously, a toga?'

'A sheet, secured with gold napkin rings from the hotel restaurant. Yes, it's ingenious. Thank you.'

'You look ridiculous.'

I push my phone into his hands, entirely disinterested in his opinion.

'It's my turn for a collaboration video. I want one camera set on you and one set on me. Okay?'

He nods and begins setting up as I lift the bottom of my homemade skirt and walk towards the castle's edge. I shed my sandals and gesture for him to start filming. With a rather grumpy expression, he begins, and I start to pose, walk around, turn and look at the camera in different combinations and successions that I know work best for me. To give him credit, he doesn't complain out loud once, just follows me with the phone, filming as I direct, but sometimes he improvises and I see him pan away. I don't mind; despite being the most irritating human on the planet, I know he is good at filmmaking.

'Now, start the camera facing you,' I direct him shamelessly. He obliges but has one eyebrow raised in speculation. He continues filming me, nonetheless. He would make a great Instagram boyfriend, though I feel bad for whatever poor girl has to contend with his massive ego. Theo only briefly stops filming when I climb onto a windowsill.

'What are you doing?'

'Just trust me.'

'It's dangerous, you're right on the cliff's edge.'

I stare down over the edge of my feet. 'And so I am.' I glance back at Theo, wink, and leap.

CHAPTER 41

THEO

'MARGOT!' Her name bellowing out of me like that sounds strange. I've only said her name a handful of times since we met, but never like this. Never with fear. I drop the phones as I sprint forward. A thundering pain echoes in my knee but I ignore it. It's a huge drop and even if it's straight into the ocean, with no obstructing rocks, the impact could break bones. I'm vaguely aware of calling out her name again as I skitter to a stop against the window and lean against the wall, only to be met by her jade eyes staring up at me from where she's hunched on a safe ledge. She grins up wickedly, dimpling her freckled cheeks.

'Got you.'

'You know that's not funny. In the least.' I pull a bundle of weeds from between two cobbles and chuck it at her along with the dirt, unable to use anything else to show my irritation. She just laughs in response. I reach out a hand and help her climb back up. Ignoring her dumb makeshift toga and the fact that she looks like a mischievous, albeit beautiful, nymph. Haunting the ruins. And ruining my life.

'Lighten up a little. It was nice that you were concerned for my welfare.'

‘I’m not like some cold-blooded gargoyle, Margot. I wouldn’t actually take pleasure in someone leaping to their death in front of me. Even someone as annoying as you.’

‘If not gargoyle, why gargoyle-shaped?’ she asks, and playfully pinches my cheek, making an exaggerated frowning face in some sad attempt to imitate my annoyance. What an absolutely infuriating girl. I look around for something else to throw at her and come up empty.

‘Is this why you had one camera on me?’ I ask. ‘To get my reaction?’

She smiles, helping herself to my phone and no doubt airdropping herself the footage. She laughs as she watches it.

‘Your face!’ She smiles. ‘Viral gold.’

‘I need to work now,’ I say grumpily, bending down and unpacking my drone. She hovers over me, arms crossed over her chest.

‘How come you’re so obsessed with that thing?’

‘I like a bird’s-eye view.’

‘Why?’

My head shoots up when I think she’s goading me but her brows are scrunched up; she looks sincere for once.

‘I like the freedom of flying, seeing everything on an equal plane.’

‘You are scared of flying,’ she says.

‘Pfft, no I’m not. I’ve flown hundreds of times.’ I bristle.

‘I watched you on the flights. Your hands tremble at take-off and you do this kind of weird meditative thing with your eyes closed, like you’re counting the seconds till the seatbelt sign is off.’

I had no idea she had been paying attention. That is literally what I do. Count time or listen to a song that lasts long enough till we are out of the most dangerous zone of flying, the first five minutes. A heat rises in my cheeks.

'After the first five minutes of take-off, the chances of being in an accident are drastically reduced. By eighty per cent,' I say. I've never admitted this to anyone. My habit of counting till I hear that seatbelt ding.

She brushes some errant dirt from her makeshift toga. 'Where did the fear come from?'

I shuffle uncomfortably. 'My dad's jet once had a rough landing when I was little.' I right away think she will mock me at the words *my dad's jet*. But she doesn't.

'My dad was so mad at me for screaming and crying.' I will myself to shut up but there's something about Margot which means I just keep offering up more damning information.

She searches my eyes. 'You know, I read that it's not always the trauma itself that traumatizes kids; sometimes it's the parents not comforting them afterwards. That lack of regulation causes the trauma, not the event.'

'That's interesting.'

She starts to make her way towards the exit of the fortress. 'Normally, I would think your fear of flying would severely impact this trip, but turns out my fear of monkeys came up even more. Who would have thought?'

'I didn't expect monkeys to be such a huge factor. Anyway, need to set up my drone now. To answer your previous question – I love seeing the world from this angle.'

'But you see the world from above on the plane too. Maybe you can learn to think of it that way.' She says this kindly, and I smile at her.

I don't know how to explain to her that on planes I'm still trapped. Still in a cage, just like at my father's house. And, in a way, at my mother's apartment too. I'm still caught in circumstances outside of my control in either scenario. With the drone, I'm in control. I'm free. Untethered. Or maybe I just like the way it looks on film.

I point at it as it rises into the sky. 'This was the first thing I bought with my own earnings.'

She seems to respect that.

'I bought a giant statue of Tinker Bell. But each to their own,' she says, wandering away from me and back to the cliff.

I launch the drone up, vaguely aware of her sitting down on the edge and staring out at the sea. I watch the footage on my control screen – the beautiful ocean, the castle, then I send the drone along the coast. But my eyes drift from the screen and back to her. She has one leg hanging off the stone wall, her toga billows out around her and she looks peaceful. Etched into the ancient scenery as if she belongs there. I watch her for a little while longer, as she watches the ocean, shading her eyes with her hand to get a better view.

Somehow, I've forgotten why I find her so annoying.

CHAPTER 42

MARGOT

The only thing my followers might hate on more than the Disneyland photos is the fact that the last TikTok I posted is entirely shot by Theo, and his priceless reaction when he thought I fell into the sea. But the numbers are intense and I've included footage of the hotel and even got Theo to share some drone footage with me. The video is already doing crazy numbers. I cross post it and put my phone away. I thought I would mind actively posting with the son of Pierre Delacour but Theo feels different to his dad. Saner and kinder and . . . *I don't know*, just different. Somehow, travelling across the world feels like we've left those identities at check-in. Like we can be anonymous, and I can forget for a moment that he's someone's son and just see a blue-eyed boy my age who's helping me film and generate content. Amazing content. Is that so wrong? I'm afraid to answer my own question.

I've agreed to have a shared dinner on the terrace with him in the Maison Partout brand restaurant. My suitcase still hasn't got here – so much for luxury travel! But I'm used to working with what I have. I'm wearing one of Theo's less offensive anime t-shirts and my embroidered Indian scarf wrapped around my waist as a skirt. The temperate climate makes fashion choices like that okay. I meet him at the hotel's fish taverna on a veranda overlooking the sea. The whole terrace is framed by lemon trees, thick and drooping with bursts of yellow. The waiter points out a passion fruit tree in the distance and tells us there used to be more but someone cut them down.

By the time we are seated, my mood is light.

'You're smiling,' he says.

'I do that sometimes.'

'Not really around me. Not unless there are deer around.'

'Some beasts bring it out more than others.'

Theo rolls his eyes and focuses on his menu. Maybe I've been a little unfair on him in all of this. I keep thinking about the ways he described his lonely childhood. The few things he has told me about his dad. Theo Delacour is … different from his father. And he said he would try to talk to him about the trial.

We are brought Greek salad, cooked beetroot, saganaki – a deep-fried cheese – feta wrapped in puff pastry and drizzled with sesame seeds and local honey, crunchy deep-fried sardines, pumpkin cheese balls and silvery sea bream each, covered entirely in lemons.

'Excuse me.' Theo calls the waiter over. 'Is there lemon on anything else?'

'He's allergic,' I say, trying to be helpful, and Theo nods gratefully.

The waiter looks carefully at everything and shakes his head.

'Do you want another fish?' I ask once he's left. 'Considering you can't even touch this one.'

'No, I love sardines anyway.' He pops one of the small deep-fried fish in his mouth and I can't tell if he's just trying not to be difficult.

I add olive oil to my fish and the salad and push the fried cheese in his direction so he can have the rest.

'All cheese should be fried,' I declare, biting into it.

Theo pops another sardine in his mouth. 'And all fish.'

After some chewing-filled silence, Theo speaks up

'So, what are your goals, after all the vlogging? Who do you want to be when you grow up?'

If you'd asked me when I first started doing this, I would say that it already feels grown up to be sitting on a veranda with a good-looking boy in another country.

I stare out at the horizon. Then back at him. He's wearing a crisp white button-down that is half open – he's more put together tonight than his usual anarchic style.

'I would sort of like to do *this*.' I wave my hand vaguely at the sea and the table. 'For ever.'

'Be an influencer for ever? Hmmm, *bold*.'

'You know.' I shrug. '*Get Ready with Me to Hit Up the Nursing Home*.'

'What's in my bag, end-of-life edition,' he jokes back. I grin at him.

'Come with me coffin shopping on the Upper East Side.'

Theo makes an odd sort of face and for a minute I think I've said something wrong. Maybe he buried someone on the Upper East Side? Confusion flits across his sharp features and he reaches for his tongue, touching his index finger to it. He clears his throat and pulls a little at his collar, even though it's unbuttoned.

'Theo?' I say his name but as he pulls on his collar again, I see the hives, splotchy and raised, spreading across his chest. I drop my fork. A panic is spreading in his eyes and his hands fly to his neck. He jerks to a standing position and gestures for something but I don't know what he means. He's growing redder and I shoot up from my chair, still uselessly clutching my napkin.

'Theo?' I say again, stupidly. My eyes search his, and my adrenaline surges.

‘Help!’ I say. ‘Help!’ This time I scream, my second attempt more desperate. The waiter rushes over.

‘Theo.’ I yank on his shirt but he collapses in my arms and I sink to the ground under his weight. His eyes are still open, lips swelling visibly. A fear seizes me, so deep it seems endless. Like a black cloud cascading through my body, filling every crevice with an acrid kind of smoke. A sense of doom.

A small crowd begins to gather around us, voices rise. *Ambulance! An ambulance! Asthenoforo!* I don’t know if they are saying it in Greek or English but suddenly, I’m screaming louder. And I can understand them, I can feel the urgency. Distantly I think about how when people are screaming and panicking you suddenly understand any language. Almost like deep searing panic needs no translation, it’s universal.

My voice is distant from my body. *Somebody help him! Please. He’s dying. Please.*

Theo’s eyes are searching mine in a blind panic. Then there’s a vacant look to them. *Please no. Please Theo no. No. No. No.*

A body pushes past the rest and a large man sinks to his knees before me, grabbing hold of Theo’s limp form. The man produces a syringe and sinks it into Theo’s chest. After a moment, Theo gasps and relief pours through me like ice – cold, sobering relief. Until the man’s eyes meet mine. The unmistakable blue eyes of the weird lawyer friend I met in Kyoto. He isn’t paying me much attention. He gingerly holds Theo up in his arms. Cooing, almost like a father would.

‘You’re okay, boss,’ he says, almost like he’s chanting. ‘You’re going to be okay.’

CHAPTER 43

MARGOT

We are going clubbing tonight, I text Dimitra who has agreed to drive a few hours down to meet me on my day trip in Nafplio. A small, historical town, thirty minutes away, that Maison Partout is chauffeuring us to as part of our itinerary.

I'm not sure there is clubbing in a town that small, she writes back.

Then we will go dancing!

I'm not sure they have that either (sweat emoji) it's very small!

Then you will hold my phone and play music and I will dance around you, for Christ's sake. I need to blow off some steam and move on from this whole Theo situation.

Say no more. Also, I'm bringing my cousin Kostas. He's fun.

I've told Dimitra everything that happened and she could barely believe it. The near-death experience, the bodyguard. She did ask if the bodyguard was hot 'like in the movies', but I ignored it – I'm not in a laughing mood. It was a traumatic experience and though I'm so happy Theo survived, I can't just get over this. So, I will dance like crazy and try to shake all of these cobwebs off from my overstimulated nervous system. The protests. The trial. The way

Theo looked when he was dying in my arms. Or when I thought he was dying. How scared I was that I would never see him again. How it made me feel. How I've allowed myself to care about someone I can't trust.

Now I wish I never had to see him again. I'm not about to forgive him for lying to me. That the man he had introduced as his father's lawyer turned out to be his bodyguard – who was following us the entire time. A freaking bodyguard! Another voice in my head says *thank god he was there and able to save Theo's life*. But the gratitude is short-lived. I feel stupid and lied to and naïve and like my privacy has been completely shot to hell, yet again. Like Theo thinks he can't trust me enough to tell me. We are not friends, we have nothing in common, and it's high time I stopped acting like it.

Enough of that! I'm in Greece and it's a cardinal sin to be depressed on the Greek coast. I taste like sea salt from my first dip earlier in the day, and so does the night air. I'm not speaking to Theo, so we did a silent tour of the beautiful local monastery in the mountains that morning, followed by some slow-living content I shot over the panoramic views. By the time we break for mid-day souvlaki, he's got the gist of our new arrangement. This is purely professional; I will travel with him and do my job. But any friendliness that had seeped in on our previous travel is gone. *GONE*. I don't want anything to do with a liar like that.

Sometimes, I spot glimpses of his bald bodyguard tailing us. He's given up on the pretence now, and the anger sets in all over again. But so does the pain of thinking Theo was near death. Though I don't let myself entertain that. It's been a roller coaster, and as I sit on another veranda having my cappuccino *freddo* in the sun, I decide that dancing is the only way to get over all of this.

I wordlessly take the shuttle to Nafplio with Theo, and, as soon as we are there, separate from him. I visit the wood shops, full of spoons and dishes carved from olive wood and at irresistible prices, fantasizing about the day we can renovate the inn a little, and how the olive serving dishes would look there. I visit a number of quaint jewellers whose shops are full of gold medallions and zodiac jewellery, and watch a cobbler work on creating Grecian leather sandals by hand. My suitcase has finally arrived and having access to everything I've bought during the trip inspired a new mantra, *Your bags are too full*, the entire way down the high street, and I only allow myself a pair of traditional wool house slippers with pom-poms on top.

I drift down the harbour, past the white superyachts that bob like glittering giant pearls in the black water. I don't know why I don't take myself out for solo dates more often; it's such a liberating experience to wander and eat alone, people watching.

More solo dates for me in the future.

I walk along the harbour and stop for some ice cream, opting for a flavour I've never tried called *kaimaki* – a white chewy sheep's-milk ice cream that feels stretchy and reminds me of the textures in Japan. I can't quite pinpoint the flavour but it sort of tastes like sweet aromatic herbs.

As the day turns to evening, I take photos of myself and my ice cream and my new fancy bag that is shaped like a seashell and cost more in the local artisanal boutique than I care to admit. I sent my mum photos from the shop and she encouraged me to treat myself.

It helped take the edge off my stress. The news today was mild: protests are slowly breaking out in different areas but not enough to amass, they still disperse quickly, and the trial still has no conclusion. I've messaged Alexandre and he said he's still struggling with exam week so my worries are lessened on that front too.

I text him again.

Eating an ice cream by a harbour in Greece. Even though I just had cheesecake.

Oh no, however will you cope? Next time take me with you!!! ;) I can't vlog but I have great hairy legs. I can model your brand deals.

I laugh, but it reminds me that I need to take photos of my dress and shoes – which were buried in the depths of my recovered suitcase – because they were gifted to me by an up-and-coming designer in France. I prop the camera up on a cobbled windowsill and set the timer. I don't worry about my phone here the way I would in a bustling city. Maybe people are right to live by the sea. It calms your whole body. I get a good few pictures of the dress, then my shoes, detailed sunset shots of my jewellery, and a few of my sparkly bag for good measure. Then I keep moving and do a little pan of the scenery.

Bustling restaurants, ice-cream parlours, children playing.

The harbour isn't huge and neither is the town, so it doesn't surprise me when my eyes meet his. We face each other, like a Wild West standoff, with ice creams melting quickly in our respective hands. His is pistachio; I can tell from the green-brown tint. Only snobs get pistachio.

His eyes bore into mine and I'm brought back to that moment when I thought he was dying. I flinch and take a step back.

'I'm trying to eat my ice cream in peace,' I say.

'And what am I doing? Eating it in violence?'

'Then have a nice evening.' I saunter elegantly past him, flicking my hair over my shoulder.

Suddenly, I feel a rush of wind and time seems to slow as my hand is yanked forward. At first, I think it's Theo yanking me back, but it's too rough and it hurts and I hear a commotion, the sound of an engine. Someone yells out. I trip forward, stumbling from the unknown impact and onto my knees. It takes a moment for me to come to my senses when I realize people around me are cursing in Greek as a young man on a moped speeds away from me, laughing, with my seashell purse in hand. I look at my empty palm. Then at my bloodied knee. Theo breaks into a run.

I watch his form shrink down the boardwalk. I must admit, he's pretty fast, but no man can outrun a moped and they quickly lose him and bank left.

After a few minutes, shoulders sagging, Theo makes his way back to me. His breathing is heavy, eyes full of searing rage.

'I'm sorry,' he says. I shrug my shoulders, unable to thank him for running because I feel like if I say something earnest, I'll break down.

'Can I . . .' He hesitates for a second, running a hand across his buzzcut. 'Maybe buy you a new bag?'

I wave my hand nonchalantly. 'Whatever, it's fine, it was cheap,' I lie through gritted teeth. 'My wallet and phone are in my pocket anyway, so no harm, just some make-up in there. I have to go, I'm meeting someone.'

I don't wait for him to stop me. The bag was near empty but it was so, *so* pretty and I don't want to admit to Theo that it was a big rare kind of *treat yourself* purchase for me. I also definitely don't want him to buy me a new one with his daddy's money. Or to feel like he can buy back my trust, or my forgiveness. Most of all, I don't want to cry in front of him, and tears are already threatening to stream down my face from the humiliation. I can feel the heat pooling in the corners of my eyes.

Screw the thieves. Screw the bag. Screw Theo. My phone vibrates in my pocket, undoubtedly signalling that Dimitra has arrived.

I need to dance all of these feelings away.

CHAPTER 44

THEO

I'm walking down an alleyway, feeling useless, when I run into him.

'Evening, boss.'

'I'm not your boss and you know it,' I say grumpily. Yuri falls into step next to me easily, ignoring my desire to change direction. The streets are narrow and there's just the two of us, and the distant jubilation and muted music of the harbour nightlife.

'Yeah, but you're the one I'm meant to protect.'

'I don't seem to need any extra muscle tonight.' I wave my hand in the direction of the quaint, deserted little street. This is our usual gist: I pretend I don't need him, when time and time again, I'm proven wrong. I can put up a front all I want but there were many times I was grateful to have Yuri's company. I'm just sad Margot had to see him. I doubt she's ever going to speak to me again.

'I'm meant to give you this,' says Yuri, handing me an envelope. Being my father's son, I'm used to having envelopes handed to me, but I never know if it's bank notes or a stern handwritten letter. This feels like something else. I peek in and it's an assortment of credit cards.

'Bank details and spending habits were revealed at the trial so your father wants you to switch away from French banking. These are some Swiss cards and Bank of Luxemburg, for emergencies.'

Instantly I think again of buying Margot a new ridiculous seashell bag when I remember how devastated she looked. But I've never wanted to be the guy who racks up Daddy's credit card bills for presents for girls. I learned early on with my first girlfriend, years ago, that kind of behaviour could be weaponized against me. Each item I've purchased thrown back in my face in reproach when my father wanted my behaviour corrected.

I push the envelope back to Yuri.

'I don't need it.'

He pockets it, knowing I'm serious. But I'm sure he'll try again later.

'You always have to make my job harder, kid.'

We turn into an alley and I come to a grinding halt. There's laughter at the other end of the street – a group of boys of a similar age to me, six of them in total. A few of them are half mounted on their mopeds; they are sharing a bottle of wine, Margot's bag slung haphazardly over the handles. They aren't even professionals, just random teenagers who decided to be assholes tonight – and Margot was on the receiving end of that.

'*Hmmmm*,' Yuri says in a long, mocking drawl. 'I saw the little redhead get robbed. Could have run for them. But you told me not to expose myself again.'

I stare down the alley, counting the guys again even though I know the number. My father loves judo, and so I took years of it. I have a red belt, but no belt in the world lets you take on six guys at a time. I'm not Jackie Chan. Oh well, screw it. I walk towards the group.

'Hey, asshole,' I call out and instantly swing. My fist connects and there's a commotion, but right when I reach for the bag I feel a gut punch knock the air out of me. Someone kicks me in the side. This isn't going well. Cursing rings out.

I feel another punch just as Yuri materializes in front of me. He makes quick work of incapacitating two of the boys, his military training on full show as both boys don't even understand what's happening to them when they suddenly find themselves on the ground. He hasn't injured them – he knows better than to hurt them – but he has scared them enough where both the guys he threw down and their wide-eyed friends all scatter into opposite directions. I snatch the bag from the ground.

'What was that about you not needing any of my muscle?' says Yuri, grinning.

CHAPTER 45

MARGOT

'You're a great dancer,' says the tall, handsome guy towering over me. I yell back a return compliment but the sound in the Friday-night bar gobbles it up. Dimitra's cousin Kostas has dark-brown flowy hair, impressive height and a tanned summer air to him that is easy and beautiful. Exactly what I need.

'Stop ogling my cousin,' Dimitra says into my ear before playfully shoving me. She's found someone to dance with too, and he's twirling her around.

'I thought you brought him to be ogled,' I say back.

'I brought him because my car is in the garage,' she says. Kostas is smiling unknowingly as he twirls me around again.

'I thought you kind of have a thing with Theo,' she says when she's back in earshot. I scoff and roll my eyes.

'When have I ever said that? That's ridiculous.'

'You two have chemistry!'

'Yeah, negative chemistry!'

'The distance between hate and love is small!'

'Not that small,' I yell over the music.

She shrugs. I've never said anything to give her this impression. Yes, I was scared when he nearly died but I would feel the same way about a dog. The last thing I want to think about on this dance floor is Theo.

And I'm going to prove it.

Winding my hands around his waist, I pull Kostas deeper onto the dance floor.

We dance for what feels like half an hour. He yells things out at me in broken English. He doesn't frown or smile when I tell him I'm from France, almost like where I'm from doesn't matter to him that much. All that matters is the music and the dancing.

He tells me his family owns a vineyard, and I joke that we have farmland too. Though I know this beautiful boy won't understand that farmland in my family is clucking chickens and endless mud with old bathtubs protruding from the frost, used for water gathering. It's not the twisting vines of Peloponnese rosé. Far from it.

'We make our wine in bathtubs in the summer!' I yell out, grinning.

The joke is lost on him and he twirls me wildly till I'm laughing and my vision blurs.

As an old Madonna song blares from the speakers, Kostas moves closer. He brushes a hair out of my face and behind my ear. I don't stop him when his pink lips close in on mine. The kiss is fruity and light and meaningless at the same time. But it's relaxing and it helps me forget. I kiss him back, hand tangling in his thick, wavy brown hair.

When we finally break for air, Dimitra is yelling my name and signalling at something. My eyes scan the bar and land on Theo. A current of shock slides through me as my eyes lock on his. I straighten up as I see he is holding my seashell purse with one hand. His left eye looks swollen and bruised, and his lip is busted. I seem unable to move towards him, like my feet are planted in the ground. I feel Kostas kiss my neck, before he starts dancing again, and I wish I could disappear as Theo watches us.

Theo puts my bag on a table, nods at me and leaves, something strange in his expression. How much did he see? I run to snatch the bag and then follow him out into the dark street, but by the time I get there, he's gone.

CHAPTER 46

THEO

People kiss people all the time. Why would I care? It's probably what half of Greece is doing on a balmy Friday night. But I can't shake the gross roiling sensation in my belly. Irritation? I was out getting her bag, fighting off a bunch of guys with Yuri, earning myself no less than three contact punches to the face. And she's there sucking on someone's face. It's just . . . it's inconsiderate is what it is. I kick at a rubbish bin near a closed ice-cream shop and it tumbles and spills a sea of half-eaten waffles and napkins into the street. I immediately pick it all up and put it back. I wander the streets a little aimlessly. I haven't eaten and my stomach is rumbling because all I've given my body in the last six hours is an ice cream and a brawl.

As I walk past a busy alleyway of restaurants someone calls my name.

'Theo!'

I spin and my eyes land on Ginevra Calinessa, daughter of an Italian tycoon, a young model and an acquaintance from my childhood. Our fathers were friends, if men that powerful can really conceive friendship beyond lining each other's pockets. They've had joint business deals, and with that come joint ski vacations in Maribel and joint family dinners in St Barts while our mothers would be shopping at Hermès.

'Gin,' I say, using her nickname. 'How the hell are you? What are you doing here?'

I fight the urge to sigh when she gestures to her and her friend's table and it becomes very clear they want me to join them. 'My father's yacht is anchored here for a few days,' she says, waving a hand at the shiny superyachts beyond the port. I follow her hand and spot her father's unmissable gaudy boat.

'Come join us,' she says.

I still have to get back to the hotel, and to do so I have to wait for the shared shuttle with Margot. But then an idea comes into my mind.

'Have you ordered already?' I ask, as Gin's friend watches me with a keen interest.

'Only drinks,' says Gin. I pull out my chair next to the two beautiful girls.

'That's great,' I say. 'Because I know just the place for dinner.'

'And that's when Dad fired the pool guy because he thought he had dyed the pool pink, but it was actually Theo and me,' says Ginevra to her friend, before breaking out into a fit of giggles. I laugh too, remembering what it was like to be fourteen and stupid enough to pour a bunch of dye into a pool in St Tropez as a prank. We've finished our slow-cooked lamb and moved on to dessert wine. It wasn't hard to convince the two girls to come back for dinner with me at the hotel that I described as *breathtaking*. Finding a taxi was easy enough too. I had zero desire to eat in that town, and leaving Margot behind to take the shuttle on her own was a bonus.

'No way!' says her lanky friend Francesca, whose ballerina frame and cheekbones declare her as a model too. 'That poor man,' she drawls, but her voice is devoid of sympathy.

I take another swig of delicious wine and flinch against the burn on my bruised lip. 'I remember that I had to convince my father to re-hire him.'

'Did it work?' says Francesca.

'You know I wouldn't be able to convince my father to drink water in a drought.'

I'm laughing when I spot Margot through the white curtains of the swooping entrance. She's looking for someone, and I know it's for me when her eyes lock on mine and she marches towards us like an army general. But by the time she reaches our table her resolve has flattened a little and she has taken note of my companions.

'Good evening,' she says wryly. She looks at me. 'I waited at the shuttle for you. For, like, thirty minutes.'

'I left early with my friends,' I say, gesturing. 'Gin and . . .' I hesitate for a second too long. '*Francesca.*'

'New friends, then,' says Margot through gritted teeth when I faltered on the girl's name. I gesture to the waiter for more wine.

'No, no. Gin and I go way, way back. And *this* is Margot,' I declare to Ginevra and Francesca. My voice slurs a little and Margot's green eyes narrow on me accusingly. What's she got to be grumpy about? I'm not out here kissing random Greek girls.

'She's my travel companion on our brand deal.'

'We know all about you,' says Ginevra. Despite being friendly there's something unkind in her tone. That superior type of invisible meanness rich girls dole out so easily when they think someone is lesser than them. 'From TikTok,' she clarifies. 'We heard Theo got *this*, saving your bag.' She runs a thumb gently over my cut lip which is a little too intimate for the circumstances, and she's never acted this way before.

'Yes, I've come to thank him actually.' Margot takes a seat. 'When did you and Theo meet?'

'Theo and I grew up together. Skiing in Courchevel in the winters,' says Ginevra.

'It's a place in France,' Francesca adds in Margot's direction. 'With the best skiing.'

'I know where Courchevel is,' says Margot dryly. 'I'm literally from France.'

'Of course,' says Ginevra. The two Italian girls share a meaningful look. 'Have you been?'

'Can't say that I have,' says Margot, pouring herself a liberal amount of wine. There's a nod of aggression to her movements. But a shyness, too – I know her well enough to recognize that. A shyness she is trying to conceal.

'Shame,' says Gin, in that saccharine way that is starting to grate on me. 'It's so close to Theo's house.'

Margot cocks a brow and refocuses on her wine. I'll admit, I wanted to punish Margot a little by leaving without the shuttle, causing her to worry, and, of course, I knew she'd likely see me with two beautiful Italian girls on the veranda. Which was a bonus. But I don't like them mocking her.

Gin yawns and puts her hand on my arm. 'Theo, darling, how big is your suite? Any room for Chezzy and me to crash out? The boat feels a little far.'

I clear my throat. I did not expect her to ask that. 'It's a small suite.'

'Even better,' says Gin with a wink.

What on earth is going on?

'What do your parents do, by the way?' Francesca asks Margot, just as her eyes narrow on Gin's hand still on mine. I feel like the temperature has shot up in the room.

'More wine, anyone?' I ask awkwardly, moving my hand to the wine bottle, trying to move the conversation along. Only rich people ask each other what their parents do.

'They are in agriculture,' says Margot, with a forced smile.

'Ooh, mine too,' says Francesca, excited. 'Fruit mostly, and some farmland. Yours?'

Margot downs the rest of her wine and puts the glass back on the table with perhaps a little less grace than she intended.

'Three goats, two pigs and four chickens. One sick cow.'

Margot stands up. 'I wish all three of you an amazing rest of your evening.' She throws one more pointed look at Gin's hand, which is now drawing lazy circles on my forearm, and walks away.

'Unpleasant girl,' Gin declares. 'You must hate travelling with her.' Francesca nods.

For the third time that night, I'm wondering what the hell just happened.

SEEFELD, TYROL, AUSTRIA

The family hotel Edelweiss by Maison Partout

welcomes you to Seefeld.

During your time here, you will enjoy:

Hot tub under the stars

Various hikes

Strudel tasting

A secret surprise

Theme: Love and laughter in the Alps.

CHAPTER 47

MARGOT

I watch the flickering screen as it announces yet another delay. There's a storm brewing and the hours trickle by slowly, like honey. Theo busies himself silently editing and I find myself drifting off in my uncomfortable seat by the airline gate. I think about how awkward our last days in Greece were, the pinnacle of which was an hour-long olive oil masterclass we spent in complete silence.

I close my eyes and will myself to nap.

Finally, hours and hours too late, a voice with a heavy accent announces that the storm has wound down and we can board our flight to Innsbruck.

It's nighttime by the time we reach our hotel in Tyrol with more than six hours' delay to our journey. The short cab ride from Innsbruck airport was spent entirely in taut silence. I hear Theo drift off into sleep on the backseat, his deep, rhythmic breathing making me sleepy. Maybe he's hungover from drinks with those unpleasant girls, maybe he invited them both to his room and is exhausted from *that*. Maybe he's just as exhausted as I am. Maybe he's a prick. I scoff, irritated. Either way, I make a mental note to tell him that he snores and it's annoying.

I check my connection in the car and hold my phone up, as if that might help. Nothing. Then I wait, eyes trained on the black landscape as if I could make something out in the forest other than the headlamps of the other cars. We drive through a quaint Tyrolean town with tiny shops, their windows displaying mountain products like hiking gear and colourful homemade soaps.

We pull up outside the hotel and I let the cab driver wake Theo as I stare up at a blanket of stars in the parking lot, breathing in the cool night air as Theo fetches our bags, still half asleep, and groggily heads for the reception. The air is as clear as water and I can smell the light hint of evergreen pines and cut grass. I bet the scenery is beautiful here in the winter. Part of me wishes it was snowing so we could enjoy the full alpine experience. I take a few final deep breaths of cold mountain air, steady myself, and follow him in, well aware the awkwardness from Greece hasn't subsided.

The hotel night manager takes pity on us because of the late hour, giving us the short version of the Maison Partout shebang before handing us our keys. He's a young night-shift guy and doesn't seem to know much anyway. He impatiently bids us goodnight and walks off, apparently unconcerned with our luggage and in a hurry to get somewhere. Maybe he's heading out for a smoke?

I follow Theo to the second floor, taking care to be quiet for the sake of the other sleeping guests. Everything around us is made of wood, and there's antique ski paraphernalia mounted on the walls and the odd deer head jutting out ominously. I'm sure this place is adorable during the day, but late at night I could do without dead animal heads at the end of every hallway.

Theo opens the door to his hotel room and I continue walking before checking the dangling piece of paper attached to my own key. I've gone too far and I backtrack, but then realize the number on my key is the same as the door he just opened with his key. Room 13. I check the piece of paper on his key: *13*.

'You have got to be kidding me,' I hiss. 'He gave us the same room.'

Theo sighs, looking utterly exhausted, and mumbles something about ineptitude under his breath. 'Okay, I'll go and find him. Stay here.'

I'm a little freaked out by the decor and dead silence so I stay glued to the spot, awaiting his return, equally spooked about entering the room in case there are more stuffed animal heads. Theo returns less than three minutes later, wide-eyed and with a sour expression on his face.

'He's left. There's no one there. The lights are off.'

'What the hell do you mean, there's no one there?'

'This . . . is just what happens in alpine hotels sometimes,' Theo says, pinching the bridge of his nose in exhaustion, or irritation.

'Well, go and find him,' I snap.

'No, you don't understand.' His tone is laced with frustration now. '*Gone*, as in he's left for the night. Driven away. His car isn't in the car park. In these chalets they check in the last guests at the end of the night and sometimes they leave until the morning. They don't just sit there in silence for hours. It happened to me when I was skiing once.'

'Oh god, no. Please. I'm way too exhausted for another Courchevel story,' I say bitterly.

'No need to be a brat.' His voice is ice cold, eyes flashing. I can tell he too is near breaking point. He opens the door wider for me. 'You take it. I'll sleep on one of the couches in the lobby till he returns.'

'Like hell you will,' I snap back. 'I'm not having you play the victim and villainize me in front of Maison Partout. And your giant bald bodyguard will come after me. You'll sleep in here.' I gesture to the room. 'I'm sure there's a couch.'

Too tired to argue, he nods and follows me in. To be honest, the lobby is far too cold for him to sleep in, though I do catch myself wondering where his burly bodyguard is staying and how these things work. Does he track his phone? How can he keep him safe from a distance? If I weren't there, would he just ride in Theo's car? And what is it Theo needs to be kept safe from? I'm sure I could ask him about the intricacies of having security, and how it works with being followed, but I wouldn't give him the satisfaction of knowing his odd life has piqued my interest. We haven't even talked about his near-death allergic reaction, about his bodyguard, or about my bag and how he got it back. The tension of things left unspoken hangs between us.

'Can you hurry up, please,' he snaps, holding open the door. I take one last look at the creepy hallway lined with heads and enter the room.

Wherever that large bald man is, he'll hopefully materialize out of nowhere to save us if this hotel turns out to be haunted.

CHAPTER 48

MARGOT

I cuddle up into my blanket. It's warm and thick and smells of lavender and cotton. Sleep starts to flicker at the edges of my vision, embalming and soft and so very welcome – like the cloud I'm sleeping on.

'This is the *only one bed* trope,' I say sleepily. The room is almost fully dark except for the dim light filtering through the curtains from a lamppost outside. I'm still incredibly annoyed with him, but my drowsiness and the comfortable bed have tapered some of the irritation.

I was wrong about there being a couch – there wasn't – but the bed turned out to be huge so we both took a side and we're now back-to-back and as far away from one another as we can humanly get. Theo's voice is muffled from the other side of the bed.

'The *only one* what?'

'In books and movies, when they get to an inn and the innkeeper is like, *"Oooh, sorry, but there's only one bed. Boohoo"*. You know, in fantasy fiction. Dragons—' my speech is fractured by fatigue.

'I don't read that type of fiction,' Theo interjects.

'Oh, sorry Mister I-have-to-carry-Jules-Verne-and-Sartrearound-in-my-back-pocket-so-everyone-can-see-how-cultured-I-am.'

'I read plenty of fantasy stuff, but there's never a one-bed issue. That's in romance.'

'Well, you're missing out.'

'All right. So why only one bed?'

I sigh into my pillow, exasperated by this boy and his stupid questions. I was just trying to make a harmless joke and distract myself from the animal heads above us.

'Because then they do *stuff*,' I say. 'And there's tension and barely touching hands. It's a plot device. Okay? They wake up with their bodies touching and it's hot.'

Why did I even say anything? He has no idea what I'm talking about and now I'm having to explain myself in the dark like an idiot. There's a long silence from his side of the bed.

'Are you worried I'm going to roll over three whole times and wake up pressed up against you? Because this bed is huge. You don't have to worry about that.'

He seems genuinely concerned but now that he's voiced it out loud, I'm imagining it. I'm imagining what it would be like to feel the bed dip as Theo edges nearer, to sense the warmth of his body close to mine, the sound of his gentle breathing. I imagine how it would feel to edge closer myself and rest my head against his chest, my head lolling up and down with each one of his breaths. *Gross!*

'Goodnight, Theo,' I say testily and hear a rumbling chuckle, but I'm too bone-tired to react.

When I wake up, Theo isn't pressed up against me. In fact, he isn't even in the bed at all. I check the time – 7 a.m. That's a new level of sociopath, even for him. Instinctively, I scroll through my feeds and soon see the reason why Theo isn't in bed. The French headline jumps out at me and turns my early-morning blood to ice.

Front page: *CEO of Eau Jeune attacked outside court.*

CHAPTER 49

THEO

I can't taste the pretzel the hotel staff brought me, nor the salty speck cut into thick chunks on my rustic-looking plate; all my senses have deadened as nausea roils in my gut. I pick up my phone, then set it down again. I've done that a million times already this morning. I've already had a text from my father's assistant, confirming he was not harmed. Slews of texts from my mother followed, each text growing more unhinged as they rained down like marbles, clattering against my brain.

Maybe we need to change your name?

Maybe don't come back.

What if you delete your social media accounts?

It doesn't matter what I do. I can change my name but I can't change where I come from. I can't change my skin. The sensation flooding my body at the moment is otherworldly, like I've climbed out of myself and I'm standing far away watching it all unfold. Yet at the same time, I feel possessed: something creeping behind my teeth and in my brain like an infestation of sorts. It's one thing to hate on my father for the man that he is, but it's another to imagine him dead or injured. To imagine going through the rest of my life without him. To imagine that he would just cease to exist. I push away my coffee and notice my hand is shaking.

A manager materializes with an apology about the room mix-up and another apology about the fact that they seem to have rented out the only other available room. He tells me he will speak to Maison Partout corporate and see what they can do. Although, short of throwing someone out onto the street, what *can* they do? It's not long before another fruit basket materializes. This time accompanied by a complimentary tray of various strudel – berry, cheese, apple.

'Please give us a minute,' I hear Margot say as she pulls up a chair beside me. She's wearing what looks like a pink hiking outfit. I'm forever mesmerized by her ability to produce themed outfits at every destination, even though Maison Partout didn't give us the full itinerary of places we were visiting. We only find out the night before we head out. Whether by marketing design or logistics, I don't know, but our followers enjoy being surprised alongside us.

'Don't worry, we'll share the one room. It's just a few days. It's fine,' she says to the manager. He looks relieved and slinks off before she changes her mind. I go to say something but she's already turned her attention to me.

'We're going on a hike,' she says, pulling my phone out of my grasp. I let her.

'No reception. No noise. No news. Just us.'

Right. So, she already knows about my father and that's why she's being so kind. I nod, because the lump forming in my throat makes it too hard to speak. I don't think I could even put my gratitude into words – I'm too scared of what would come out if I tried. Maybe I'm in shock, but the swirl of emotions in my gut is indescribable, like a bird's-eye view of the inside of a blender, a million thoughts and feelings merging together in a sinkhole until I can't tell if I'm relieved or afraid or just nauseous. But I do know that if I speak, I'll throw up.

Margot gestures gently for me to come with her and I gratefully follow her out the door and into the crisp, clean alpine air.

CHAPTER 50

MARGOT

My chest expanded like a balloon when I saw him at breakfast, sitting alone and staring into space with his phone grasped in his hand so tightly his knuckles were growing whiter than his face. I don't know what to say to Theo; it's not like people try to attack other people's fathers every day, so I say nothing at all. Actions speak louder than words, and all that. I didn't plan to force him on a hike with me, but I'm glad I did because now that we're outside I can see the colour has returned to his face and he looks nearly human again.

It's a long and gorgeous hike up to the top of the mountain that the manager recommended to us. He told us that after about an hour's hike we would reach a famous restaurant at the summit, and I can't wait because I've had nothing to eat but a dry, errant pretzel I grabbed off Theo's plate as we headed out.

I keep stealing glances at Theo, wondering what he's thinking right now, if he's even able to put a coherent thought together. What he's going through brings back faint memories of my father's incarceration. I flinch as I remember the way that phone call made me feel, the way I stepped outside of my own body and watched my family break apart right in front of my eyes when my father was arrested for a second time. It's not the same though, and whatever Theo feels is probably worse, because no one ever attacked my father outside a courthouse in broad daylight. Whatever comeuppance I believe Theo's father deserves, I don't want it served like this. Never like this.

The sky is an impossible blue, dotted with cartoon clouds, the grass so green it looks like it's been coloured in by a child and their crayon set. We walk past jagged rock, slick with water and moss. Tiny waterfalls trickle down on both sides, creating an ethereal soundtrack. We hike past yellow meadows full of edelweiss and alpine rose, and then back into the dense woods of pine, spruce and fir. The air smells heavenly, like flowers and the spice of tree bark, and for a minute it's easy to forget why we are here and what we have left behind. In the midst of nature, I'm more than an influencer, more than the daughter of a broken family; I'm part of the world and everything feels like it's going to be okay. Like this is why we are here: to just be. I wonder if Theo is experiencing the same sensations. I hope so, because he needs the respite . . . even if just for a moment or two.

We finally reach the top, where an alpine hut rests in the middle of a clearing. Cows are grazing nearby and a horse-drawn carriage that seems oddly out of place trundles past. It's like we've been placed in the middle of a painting from a chocolate box. There's an empty table outside the hut and we take it, both of us breathing out in relief at the rest.

'So, did the hike make you feel any better?' I ask.

Theo shrugs his shoulders squarely.

'I'm sure he's safe. They will tighten his security.' I have no love lost for his awful father but neither do I want someone to go through that kind of loss. Theo is kind, and sensitive, and many other things his father is not.

'When your dad is that important . . .' Theo starts cautiously, 'you think more of the implications of the loss and not the loss itself.'

I'm not sure what that means. Is he trying to say he wouldn't mourn his father so much as he would be afraid of the consequences of the loss? I need a drink and crane my head for a server.

'Isn't that kind of cold? Don't you . . .' I want to say *don't you love him?* But I don't because maybe that's too intimate a question. 'Wouldn't you be sad if he was gone?'

He thinks about it, turmoil passing across his dark blue eyes. His hand runs across his buzzcut, which, over the course of our travels, barely qualifies as a buzzcut any more, having grown thicker and unruly. I can tell he's nervous and thinking. His eyes finally lock on mine.

'I would be sad. Of course, I would. I love him. Or, at least, some parts of me love some parts of him. Some parts of our history. But he's a very complicated man.'

His voice drifts away as he continues to stare off into the distance.

'I know what you mean,' I say by way of encouragement. I loved the parts of my dad that were strong and courageous. I didn't love the part that came home drunk after he was released from prison, rambling on and smashing plates left and right, scaring us all because he couldn't face the demons inside of himself.

'What would be the implications of him being gone?' I ask.

'The lives of his new family. My mother. What happens to the empire. And my identity, I guess. Who am I without him.'

His question is rhetorical; I don't think he's expecting an answer. He looks sheepish, like he regrets saying anything at all.

Before I know what I'm doing, my hand shoots out and cups his.

'You are so much more than just his son, Theo.'

He blinks twice, looking at our fingers intertwined, and I let go immediately. I didn't expect to say that either. Mercifully, the innkeeper interrupts us.

'What can I get you?' she asks.

I clear my throat and point at something on the menu called *Kaiserschmarrn* because I heard a couple next to us order it and it smells heavenly. Theo orders the liver meatballs and convinces me to try one too – even though the words liver and balls shouldn't go together in my opinion. Not this early in the day.

'Two of each,' he tells her finally. The innkeeper scurries off and that's when I notice there aren't any lights on in the lodge, my eyes following the trail of smoke rising above the stone building.

'You know, I don't think they have electricity here,' I say. Theo follows my gaze and leans backwards so he can peek into the dark building.

'Shall we go and see?' he says with a mischievous grin.

We wander around the dark house and see that it's an old family home which, in fact, doesn't have electricity – probably more to maintain their cutesy tourist image rather than because they can't get any. But what do I know? It's incredibly atmospheric and I feel like I've stepped back in time to a simpler era, without phones and Wi-Fi and endless news cycles. Maybe this is what Theo and I need for a change – a chance to think for ourselves. I watch him read the plaques beneath the black-and-white family portraits nestled between vintage sleds and jagged wooden shelves filled with copper tankards and copper pots. There are sheepskins slung on wooden dining booths and many wooden cuckoo clocks in various shapes and sizes hanging on the walls.

Something flutters by my feet and I jump back, surprised to see a chicken stride into the house. I'd rather that than a monkey!

We walk beneath the awning to the back of the house where we discover hay bales and a woman in an apron cooking soup in a large cauldron over the fire. I smile at her but she ignores us, undoubtedly used to wide-eyed tourists taking in their lifestyle and home, mouths ajar.

This slow and simple existence doesn't feel real to me – it's one of the most atmospheric things I've ever experienced. Instinctively, I reach for my phone as another chicken crosses the stone threshold and jumps out into the misty road, then I stop myself. Theo's words from the Kyoto Kobe restaurant drift to the forefront of my mind like paper floating on water.

Some things are just for us.

The idea of this remote cottage being full of tourists because I made it go viral horrifies me. I want it to stay this way for ever, a moment in time that only Theo and I get to experience, together, preserved as if fossilized in amber.

'You want to take a video?' he asks.

'No, not now.'

He gives me a look like he knows exactly what I'm feeling, making something warm pool in the pit of my stomach. I look away from him, scared that he'll see the colour rising in my cheeks.

'It's so peaceful here,' I say.

He nods, both of us aware that I'm saying much more than that.

That I finally agree with him on something. That this moment is more precious than the likes it may generate.

We head back to our table and arrive just as our food is brought to us. I carve the liver meatball with my spoon, eyeing the grey hunk sceptically, but when I finally taste it, I'm surprised by how delicious it is. It has the metal echo of liver yet it's salty too, and the broth is hearty and warm.

The temperature has dropped and wordlessly the innkeeper brings us woollen blankets as slowly the mist begins to spread over the horizon in front of our table, obscuring the nearby white carriage horse who doesn't seem to mind the drizzle.

We sit in silence as we eat, the two of us cocooned beneath one giant blanket, the heat of the meatballs warming my stomach as the cold mountain air pinches my cheeks. Even if I wanted to, I couldn't capture this feeling in a TikTok.

When we are done with our liver balls, the innkeeper sets up a fire in the outdoor hearth near us and brings out a massive age-worn cast-iron pan. When it's heated to her satisfaction, she pours a mixture in and begins tossing it around in the pan, letting it solidify and separating it until it looks like small lumps of dough.

'Is that the *Kaiserschmarrn*?' I ask, staring at the lumps cluelessly. It smells like a bakery that has just taken pies out of the oven.

'Yes, it's tossed pancakes,' she explains. 'And it's called *Kaiserschmarrn* because the emperor, the Kaiser, referred to it as the "chef's mess".'

She serves us two hefty portions and a dollop of plum compote to accompany it.

'This is heavenly,' says Theo, digging into his shredded pancakes.

I'm always pleasantly surprised when he's impressed by anything because I assume he's seen it all, eaten it all, had all the *Kaisershmarrn* in the world. But when I bite into my dessert, I know he's right. The slightly sour compote on the butchered pancakes is divine and, paired with the cold outdoors and the burn of the hike, it's pure sugar-dusted heaven. My hands itch for my camera again but I resist, trying to bring myself back to the moment.

We sit for a while longer, watching the fire burn out, until the bad weather threatens to overtake the valley and we agree that we don't want to hike down in a storm. I watch the horse shake off the dew of raindrops, again and again, then I look at Theo. He appears calmer now, more relaxed, like the hike and the food has made him let go of the weight he was carrying. When he catches me watching him, he smiles and pulls his hoodie up, blue eyes gleaming.

CHAPTER 51

THEO

The next few days at the Maison Partout Edelweiss hotel follow a simple rhythm. We hike and we eat – enjoying alpine cheese boards, speck selections and goulash soups.

The room mix-up has ceased to be irritating and we've grown used to each other's presence, except perhaps the number of clothes Margot has. I have literally no idea how she's able to carry all of this around with her. And even though the hotel is apparently fully booked, we haven't seen a soul the entire time we have been here – except for the staff, who have not stopped apologizing for the room mistake. Under Margot's watchful eye, they've brought us more fruit baskets, without citrus fruit, as well as alpine cheeses, local chocolate truffles and snacks, until our room resembles a pantry.

'I'm really enjoying this Maison Partout guilt train,' Margot says as she pops a Maison Partout-branded chocolate macaron into her mouth. 'How much longer do you think they'll keep this up?'

'Not long enough,' I say, side-eyeing her piles of clothes. She gives me a lewd gesture. The truth is, I'm happy to be in a room with her. It makes me feel less alone, and less scared. Every night since the news about my father broke, I've been having nightmares about my parents. In the nightmares about Mum, I see her overrun by demons, engulfed in darkness. In the nightmares about my father, I see him engulfed by flames. My nightmares never wake Margot though; instead I just sit there in the dark listening to her breathing and it lulls me back to sleep. In my half-asleep state, I wonder if it's natural for kids to be consumed with thoughts of something bad happening to their parents.

The Alps and the progression of the trial have made me especially reflective. I keep thinking about the province I'm from and the people that made me – almost like I'm trying to decipher what I am made of too.

Margot clears her throat as she finishes tying the laces on her hiking boots. How she managed to pack those, along with everything else she's been hauling around, is beyond me. All I'm wearing on my feet is white trainers which look like they've seen better days – Rishikesh and Greece having coated them in a layer of well-earned dust and grime.

'What's on the agenda for today?' she asks.

I glance at a note Maison Partout sent us.

'More hiking, and then we're supposed to film nighttime footage of their spa.'

I'm a week late posting on YouTube, which means the Greek content still isn't up, and now my memory cards are bursting with the epic scenery of Austria. I tell myself that I haven't quite got the editing right, but the truth is that I haven't posted because I know there will be a barrage of abuse. As the trial and protests continue, so does people's disdain towards me, and towards my beautiful lifestyle content in fun new places. On an article about the attack on my father, someone commented *Well done. Shame you missed. #wedeservecleanwater.*

Margot got a small taste of what the abuse was like after Disneyland, but the comments on my social media posts have been way worse than that. I'm being sent links to videos of people sick in hospital, and loads of comments telling me the world is better off without me. I half expected it. *Nepo baby touring the world while his billionaire father is on trial for concealing a water contamination . . .* Doesn't really have a great ring to it.

When we return to the hotel hours later, my legs are burning and I'm looking forward to the spa for once. I know how much Margot loves her petals-in-water content and I normally avoid the whirlpools and saunas, but this time I can't wait to unwind.

The manager leads us down to the humble underground facilities that are less luxurious than their Japanese and Balinese counterparts, but quaint nonetheless. I start to unpack my filming gear, wondering if Margot would be willing to appear in any shots because empty spa footage is a little boring. But judging by the stern look in her eyes, I decide to not press the issue and carry on filming angles and close-ups, like the condensation on the cucumber water, and the crushed lavender ice. It will all look good paired with music anyway.

The manager explains some of the history and features of the hotel, giving us a mini presentation on the essential oils they hand-make in-house. This is where Margot excels, craning her neck and moving this way and that, taking her time capturing the right angles of the essential oils. When she disappears for a little while, I have a sneaky suspicion she's gone to do some on-camera stuff about the oils and spa but without the added pressure of me watching her film.

In the past, I never would have consumed her content, but lately I've been watching some of it, taking in some of her stories from my anonymous burner account. I have my reasons. One, because it's interesting to see the trip I'm on through someone else's eyes. And two, because I'm beginning to grow accustomed to her content and find it relaxing. The tap of her long nails, the way she eats, it's all oddly comforting. I can see why she's sky-rocketed to such popularity.

Not that I'd ever admit that to her . . . or anyone else.

'If you're done with the interior, we have a little surprise for you both outside,' says the manager as soon as Margot returns.

We pack up and dutifully follow her to a large green space overlooking a lush valley framed by mountains. There's a hot tub in the centre, which I previously clocked from one of the upper decks of our hotel. They've filled the entire wood-lined hot tub with flowers.

I don't know whether to laugh or groan at their lack of originality. This is Bali all over again.

The sun is setting, pink over the closest peak, giving us the perfect shot for our videos. Wordlessly we start to unpack our equipment again and begin filming, exhausting every possible angle until we realize the manager has left us for 'another surprise she needs to get'.

'Now what?' I say, staring at the petals bleeding colour into the swirling water.

'Now we get in.'

Excuse me?

I don't have time to reply before Margot is stripping off her dress, revealing a blue crochet bikini beneath that she must have picked for her Instagram essential oils shots.

She hands me her phone.

'Can you film me getting in, centred of course, and then pan out so you get the view of the sun setting behind the mountains behind me.'

I nod awkwardly and take her phone. I aim it, making sure my hands are as stable as possible. Margot wanders into shot in her bikini, expertly looking around as if she's not being filmed. Then she gracefully walks over to the hot tub and climbs in, using the railing. She settles in and tips her head back aesthetically, her long red hair fanning out into the flower-strewn water. I swallow, then with a jolt remember I'm supposed to *pan* and not just linger on her. Quickly, I pan out to the sun setting over the mountains then switch the camera off.

'Done,' I say, depositing the phone on the edge of the hot tub. My voice sounds strange, thick and gruff. I clear my throat and put my hands in my pockets, watching the flowers drifting on the water's surface in answer to her languid movement.

'They did this in Bali too. Waste of flowers,' I mutter.

Margot still has her head tipped back, her delicate face pointing up to the darkening sky, her eyes closed. 'Hmmm,' she says, completely unconcerned.

'The flowers just mush up and then don't drain properly. It creates a lot of mess and it stains your clothes, you know.'

'It's not a waste if you enjoy it,' she says, opening her eyes.

My gaze snaps onto hers and I can see flashes of the sunset reflected in her irises. Half her body is submerged in the water, and half out of the water, like a mermaid. I look away, as if I've just witnessed something I shouldn't have, when I feel water on my shirt. She just splashed me.

'Stop acting like a grumpy old man in a supermarket line on a hot day and GET IN,' she shouts. 'Or it's your beloved drone that's getting into the water next.'

She splashes me again and I do my best to keep my face serious.

With a sigh and a roll of my eyes, I strip down to my trunks and weave my way through the colourful flowery mush.

I settle on the opposite side of the whirlpool to her, with my back to the sunset. The water is warm and my initial irritation fades instantly as my shoulders drop back against the border of the tub. Margot's profile is illuminated against the fleeting light, her delicate nose and rosebud lips outlined like a Victorian silhouette portrait. The flower dregs stick to my torso but I no longer care.

'*The moment is all we have*,' she repeats what I've said to her in the past, without looking at me, wafting her fingers through the flowers. 'I wish I could learn how to live that way. I still struggle so much with living in the moment.'

'Don't worry, I don't really practise what I preach,' I tell her. 'My head is elsewhere half the time too.' Even here, in the bubbling water beneath the alpine peaks, our brains are wandering to other problems. To the trial. The internet. Our families. To everywhere but here. It's just how we're wired these days.

'I'm going to learn though,' she promises. 'Despite all odds.'

'Well, when you learn how, will you teach me?' I ask.

She nods in acknowledgement. I look up at the stars that are starting to appear and will my brain to calcify this moment. To seal it in the amber chambers of my brain so I can revisit it later. It's almost an active exercise to still my brain and bring it back to this moment, and I'm surprised how challenging it is to be present. But at some point, my brain stops travelling and settles, *here.* In the moment. Where there's a beautiful girl. A hot tub. And a blanket of stars.

CHAPTER 52

MARGOT

I'm watching Theo sit there with his eyes closed. Submerged in thought or in the blissful absence of thought, I'm not quite sure, when I see the manager materialize behind him with a few unexpected guests. I don't say anything and bite down on my cheek to stop myself from grinning.

With a start, Theo seems to feel something wet and cold on his shoulder and he yelps out. He looks at me first, then twists his head and comes face to face with a large furry body and giant eyes.

'What the . . . !'

He scuttles towards me like he's trying to get away from an anaconda in the water, and I can't help myself any more and break out into a hysterical, high-pitched laugh. The manager points proudly at the two long-necked beasts beside her.

'Alpacas!' she announces, as if we don't both have eyeballs. 'That's my other big surprise!'

It takes me a few minutes to get over Theo's reaction. Him scuttling back from an alpaca is going to be cemented in the comedy archive of my brain for all eternity. Which was a welcome relief from my other reaction to how Theo looks in just his trunks. The dip of his v-line that seems to be even sharper than it was before.

I had seen him with no top on before in India, but that was at night, not as the sky filled with pink and purple and the golden light of the sunset settled on his taut abs and cut torso.

He looks the complete opposite to what I imagined a pale manga-loving trust-fund baby would be. Not overtly muscular but enough definition where his body rippled and flexed as he got in the water, and it took all my willpower to keep my eyes trained on anything but him. All of which makes it even more hilarious that this ripped Adonis got so startled by a cute, fluffy alpaca.

'It's been, like, ten minutes already,' he says, stroking the head of the alpaca whose name we've been told is Benji. 'Are you done laughing?'

'Never. It was like you were in a horror film – *Attack of the Alpaca 3*,' I giggle as I pet the back of the white alpaca's head. This one is called Christoff.

We've also been given cute little buckets full of food to feed the animals with. The manager explained that they've been running this alpaca gimmick for two months now, but they think if filmed properly it could go viral. I have to admit, it's hilarious and one of the cutest surprises I've ever had. We've given up on filming specific shots, but I've popped my camera on a tripod to get the full video of the experience later. Enjoy now, edit later. That's my new motto.

'It's going to rain soon,' warns the manager as she comes to collect the alpacas. She lets us say our goodbyes and we hurry to get our clothes on before the storm sets in. But it doesn't take long for the light drizzle to turn into heavy rain, which apparently is very common in the mountains.

Even though I'm already wet from the tub, I still shriek when the rain starts to lash at us, because, unlike the floral hot-tub water, this is ice cold and stings as it pelts down on my forehead. We scramble to collect our film equipment, the rain falling heavier. We assess the distance between the safety of the spa and the hotel. Theo looks at me. 'Shall we run for it?' And so we burst into a run all the way to the hotel, Theo on my tail. Just as I reach the door of the hotel, my foot suddenly hits something and pain rings through my leg. I'm stuck. I've stepped onto a loose cobble and wedged my sandal in between two stones.

'Theo!' I call out, panicked, as he runs past me. I try to pull but it won't yield, my ankle bursting with searing pain. Soaking wet, Theo turns around and runs back to see what the problem is.

'I'm stuck. Help me!' I cry out.

He looks at me, raindrops dripping off his long, dark lashes. The downpour is streaming down his face, rivulets collecting along his collarbone and down his chest.

'Help me . . . *please*,' he says slowly.

'This is not the time. Just pull my leg out, you idiot.'

'Pull, *please*,' he corrects again with an added smirk.

'Pull, please, you idiot,' I screech. Theo turns to walk away.

'Fine. Please, please help me. It hurts.'

As soon as I say I'm in pain, he moves quickly and shifts the cobble easily. I yank my foot out, hobbling from the throbbing in my toes. He drops to his knees in a puddle, his hands warm and gentle on my ankle, turning it slowly side to side to see if it's broken. It's not, I don't think it's even sprained, but I still can't put pressure on it. Theo puts his arm around my waist and helps me limp back towards the hotel. I pause as we reach the covered shelter outside the lobby, rain drumming down behind me, camera equipment on the floor.

'This is your fault,' I say, leaning against the doorframe, soaking wet, turning my ankle from side to side and checking it's not swelling up. I grimace against the pain, but I know from previous experience it will be fine by tomorrow. Theo is looking at me, his t-shirt soaked and sticking to his skin. He's out of breath from half-carrying me, his chest rising and falling, drops of water running from his wet hair down his pecs to his flat abdomen. I try not to stare.

'How is this my fault?'

'You're the one who said that we should run!'

'And you're the one who decided to wear *sandals* on a mountain,' he retorts. 'I don't know why I keep helping you every time you get yourself in trouble. First with your bag in Greece, now this.'

'I didn't ask for you to go and get my bag,' I say. 'In fact, I didn't want you to.'

'No, because you were too busy ignoring me, because I had an allergic reaction.'

'No.' I grit my teeth, furious now as to where this conversation is going. 'I didn't speak to you because you *lied* and told me your bodyguard was a lawyer.'

'So what, Margot?' he thunders. 'I hid Yuri's existence because I didn't feel the need to give you even more reason to mock and humiliate me.'

'I wouldn't have mocked you.'

'You mock me for everything. Blame me for everything. You think I'm some spoilt rich kid, but I'm not.'

'Aren't you, Theo? Hunting with Daddy? Skiing in Courchevel?'

'Is this about my father or is this about Gin? Because you didn't speak to me for two days when I ran into an old friend.'

'Oh, she was *really* friendly.'

'You sound jealous.'

'Jealous?' I scoff. 'As if!'

'See? You can't even admit it. You can't even imagine that you would feel anything but disdain for me.'

'You didn't need to bring them back to the hotel, did you? Didn't need to take them to your room.'

His eyes widen slightly. 'Just admit it.'

'Fine. I *was* jealous,' I say, my heart pounding. 'At least I can admit it. At least I'm not a coward. You can't even admit you hated seeing that guy kiss me! At least I didn't take him home.'

'I was out getting your bag back for you while you're just sucking on some guy's face.'

'His name is Kostas. He's Dimitra's cousin.'

His eyes flash darkly. 'I don't care what his name is, Margot. And I didn't invite Gin or Francesca to my room. I sent them home in a taxi.'

'I've admitted I was jealous.' My breathing comes fast, anger rising in me. 'And you can't even admit it back. Coward.'

He whirls on me, closing the space between us, water dripping from his hair onto my lips. 'If you call me a coward one more time, Margot, then . . .'

'Then what?' I step closer still, until his heaving chest is nearly flush against mine. 'Hmm? You're all threat, no follow-through. That's why you didn't take Gin to your room.'

Theo is towering over me, his breaths so heavy they're hot against my cheek. Rage is emanating off him like static, his whole body tense, his jaw twitching like he's holding back everything he's been wanting to say since we started this crazy adventure together.

'I didn't take Gin to my room,' he says slowly, 'because I was thinking about *you.*'

His eyes are locked on mine, his pupils growing so dark it's like the light has left the room. I can feel my own breaths growing heavier, my chin tilting up to meet him, his fingertips just inches from mine.

'Are you going to kiss me, Theo? Or are you going to stay a coward for ever?'

His eyes don't leave mine as he cocks his head in the direction of the rain.

'You want me to kiss you in the rain, like we are some cliché?'

'Just because everyone likes something, doesn't make it bad, Theo,' I whisper, my mouth nearing his. 'Pretty yoghurt bowls, selfies, flowers in a bath . . .'

I don't get to finish my list as his lips gently brush against mine. He kisses me slowly at first, hesitantly, and I kiss him back. But only for a few seconds before I push him away again.

'No. You're right, that was cliché,' I say, stepping back and flipping my hair as I go to walk away. I take my first step and attempt to steady my heart, which is thundering out of my chest, but I don't make it to the second step before he's grabbing my hand and spinning me round to face him. This time he pushes me up against the door and kisses me like he's been wanting to kiss me since the day he first saw me.

CHAPTER 53

THEO

Margot is in my arms, my fingers running through her silken hair, her beautiful lips pressed against mine. I'm here. Right here. For the first time in my life, I'm fully present, enveloped, my mind and my body and everything that I am is here, with her, and it's all-consuming. I cup the back of her head, bring her even closer to me, causing her to release a light moan. And I'm undone.

Her hands roam over my damp back, clawing at my neck. I close my eyes, breathing in the mango scent of her shampoo and taste of her wet skin. I don't know how we managed to make it back up to our hotel room, but I don't care. Rain batters at the window beside us but I can barely hear it any more. All that exists is her and me, and the small spaces between us that we're closing with every second that passes.

Finally, she lets go and I step back, her leaning breathlessly against the door, and me struck dumb. She looks up at me with her large round eyes, so vibrantly green and beautiful that I want to dive into them and drown myself.

'What now?' she says quietly.

But she's saying a lot more than that. It's more than a simple *what now?* She's asking *Are we no longer enemies? Do we like one another? Who are we now?*

With my index finger, I tilt her chin up and lean closer, grazing my lips against hers. I dig deep for the hatred or caution that was there before, searching her eyes for repulsion or hesitation, but all of that has gone, replaced by want and a breathless need. I kiss her, and this time the kiss tells her everything I've been wanting to say for such a long time. And I know she feels it too.

'I want this, but it's a bad idea,' she says, burying her face into the crook of my neck.

She's right. We come from different worlds – nothing good will ever come of this. Yet I don't want it to end before it's properly begun.

'How about this,' I say, our foreheads touching, my mouth inches from hers. 'For the next few hours, it's just *you and me*, and we keep the rest of the world out there.' I cock my head to the sheet of water at the window. 'All the reasons we should say no, all the issues this might bring . . . none of that exists while we are in here together. The world out there isn't burning. Time isn't moving forward. There's nothing else. For the next couple of hours, nothing else exists but you and me. Okay?'

I sound like a madman bargaining with his gods. There's no way to stall time or block out the one million reasons we shouldn't be doing this, but when she reaches up on her tiptoes and kisses the side of my mouth, her face still wet from the rain and her fingers tracing the curve of my neck, I forsake every one of those one million reasons. Let the world burn.

CHAPTER 54

MARGOT

I giggle into his shoulder. There are no hours any more, days no longer exist. Sitting with Theo beside the fireplace, eating cheese and watching stars appear from the balcony, this is all there is in life for now. I could spend eternity in this moment. Maybe this boy *can* stop time. Or maybe it's just me who loses all concept of before or after when I'm in his arms.

I lean into him and his lips close on mine for the hundredth time. All we have is the now. We aren't infinite, we are made of moments, and just for one night I'll allow myself to bask in it.

'Fine,' I whisper against the freckles on his chest that appeared in the Peloponnese. 'I guess you can stop time for a while.'

'You're the only one that makes me want to stop time.'

'Cheesy,' I whisper, holding up a piece of brie.

But I don't mean it. My heart is breaking and seaming itself up at the same time, tightening stitch by stitch, held together by this beautiful boy and the delicious absence of time. I reach up and kiss his chin, and neck, hearing him groan in response.

'By the way, how *did* you get my bag back?'

He chuckles, pulls up my chin and kisses me. 'Fought a few guys over it.'

My eyes widen. Outside, the rain batters our wooden balcony.

'Well, Yuri fought a few guys. I gave emotional support and got hit in the face.'

I know he's being facetious. Something tells me Theo can hold his own in a fight.

'Yuri is the name of your bodyguard?'

He nods, looks sheepish.

I kiss his neck again, unable to resist the temptation of being so close to him. 'Hmm.' He groans again. 'Stop that,' he says in a voice that suggests that's the very last thing he wants me to do. I continue my trajectory upwards till I meet his mouth again. Theo kisses me wildly against the cushions in the wooden breakfast nook. Hands on my hips, then on my waist, then cupping my face. I can't stop. I don't think I'll ever be able to stop. He lifts me up with ease and carries me to the bed.

The rain stops at some point, but neither of us cares because time has stopped. All we can do is kiss and kiss until the sun rises and our lips ache.

LAS VEGAS, NEVADA

The Vegas Maison Partout Hotel

welcomes you to the neon capital of the world!

During your time here, you will enjoy:

Tickets to Cirque de Soleil

Dinner by the Eiffel Tower

A visit to our casino

A celebration check-awarding ceremony

Theme: Wild nights in the city of lights.

CHAPTER 55

MARGOT

I run my thumb across his palm and he laces his fingers through mine. The sky outside is a stunning blue at ten thousand feet elevation. It feels weird to think we've been on planes before together. But not quite like *this*. Not holding hands and looking at each other. This particular plane structure allows for you to sit at the opposite end across your flight partner for a meal by spinning the seat inwards. And that's exactly what we are doing. Theo did wait for me to gleefully film the set-up.

'Are you feeling better now?' I ask, continuing to stroke his hand. I held his hand through all of take-off, telling him it would be okay. I do feel like it helped a little.

'Best take-off I've had in a while.' He smiles and it really brings out the blue in his eyes. Blue-grey with little yellow flecks in them. I'm studying them now, in the light of the cabin.

'Scallops with a pumpkin purée,' says the flight attendant as she puts the plate in front of me. I let go of Theo's hand a little too quickly. I'm still not used to other people seeing this. To other people sharing *this*. Theo notices.

'Relax, we are not as famous as you think we are.'

I smile at him and dig in. It's not that I'm embarrassed of him, but this just happened and I'm not sure I'm ready for my followers to know that I have a romantic thing with *the* Theodore Delacour, even if they already assume as much from our collaboration videos.

Hottest couple ever alert.

I'm so sat for this.

Hmmm, guess a hot guy makes you forget your morals. #keepourwaterclean

That morning's comments were plentiful and varied. But we don't discuss them. These are just the comments from people *assuming* we are together. If we hard launch, I'm sure the comments would quadruple. Even though some would undoubtedly be obsessed with the concept of two popular influencers dating, there would be a lot of unhappy people in the comments too. And they don't know that Theo is so much different than the internet says he is, the way I have discovered during this trip. Besides, this is new, I want to savour it. I want to keep it just for myself.

'I feel like we've wasted a lot of time fighting,' I say.

'True, we could have been doing much more interesting things.' He winks at me, and I blush, tossing my napkin at him. This light-hearted cheeky side is new to me, and I can't say I object.

'Speaking of fighting, I don't want to fight any more. But I have something I need to tell you,' he says. His expression grows more serious, nearly frowning.

'Go on.' My chewing has slowed. He looks uncomfortable.

'When I asked you to stop posting trial stuff, that was because Yuri had told me my father asked for that. Or that I'd have to go home. And, to be honest, I thought it would be safer for you. But I'm sorry I asked.'

I take a moment to think about this. It doesn't feel great to know that Theo was doing his father's bidding and trying to influence me. It feels even more odd that billionaire Pierre Delacour knows who I am.

'Well, why are you telling me this now? And I didn't stop posting, so why weren't you sent home?'

'With what happened over the last few days, I wanted to start clean. No more lies. I also think he changed his mind about sending me home after the attack. Maybe he thinks it's best that I stay. What do I know? It's not like I speak to him directly.'

The flight attendant refills our drinks, clears our mains away and takes our dessert order. I opt for the chocolate lava cake.

I look at him, eyes locking in. There's a little bit of indignancy and rage there, in the pit of my stomach, but that last phrase, *it's not like I speak to him directly*, is heartbreaking. And beyond the lies about Yuri and about his father, I just see a boy that's been left to his own devices. To figure out things entirely on his own, kind of like me. And it shouldn't be that way. And in that moment, I too want to start fresh more than anything.

'No more lies,' I agree. And clink my orange juice with his.

We spend the rest of the flight buddy-watching films. *Mamma Mia* – my choice, and *Paddington 2* – his choice. Then whatever time is left beyond that, kissing inconspicuously, or what we think is inconspicuously, in his seat. I try to not blush too hard when the flight attendant clears her throat for the second time and reminds me to go back to my seat for landing.

Theo scrolls through his phone as we pass security. His brow furrows and, for a second, I tense. What if he just found out something terrible about home? The internet on my phone isn't working.

'Is everything okay?' I ask, but my stomach is already tightening.

'Yeah, everything is great,' he says and I exhale in relief. 'My friend Jodi, from the Bali competition, is in Vegas too.'

CHAPTER 56

MARGOT

Our hotel in Vegas is as I expected, large and opulent, and though it's laced with gold and marble and Vegas kitsch, it pales in comparison to the rest of the hotels on the strip. I've bought myself a tiny notebook, the size of my palm, in the gift shop and have taken the liberty of writing my own itinerary outside of the Maison Partout one. Jodi is meeting us for dinner and then we are having a night out on the town before our award ceremony tomorrow where we will be given our grand Maison Partout cheque. Then we can go home.

As I scribble some notes in the lobby, I find myself thinking what my and Theo's life might look like back home. Will I have to sneak into the château? Will we get found out eventually? What will his dad think of me? What will my parents think of him? And what about his mother – he's told me so little about her beyond her sickness. I make a mental note to ask more about his family and what might be waiting on the other side of the Atlantic. Maybe I'm getting ahead of myself, I think, as we head out to explore the strip. Jet-lagged but otherwise giddy.

'What are you thinking about?' he asks, wrapping his hands around my waist.

'Just . . .' I hesitate briefly. 'What it's going to be like back home.'

'In regard to what?' He looks nervous.

'What?' I put a hand on my hip. 'Are we going to not talk any more back home?'

'Huh?' he says, affronted. 'Oh, you mean *us* back home?' He smiles lightly. 'Of course not. You're going to have a hard time getting rid of me now.' He nuzzles into my neck and my stomach fills with butterflies, tapping their wings against my rib cage.

'But if I want to see you, how will I come to your house if your dad hates me.' *And I hate him.* I don't say the latter part.

He looks surprised. 'I don't live at the château.'

'What? Where do you live?'

He looks hesitant. 'You know how my dad is with that actress?'

'Yeah, the lame soap opera one with the yellow hair.'

Theo looks grateful that I'm downplaying her fame. 'Well, when my father and her got together, my mother had to move out of the château.'

'She had to move out of her own home with her child because the lover moved in?' I'm shocked. This titbit never made it into the press and it's even more awful than what I do know about his dad's relationship.

'I was allowed to choose.'

'And you chose your mum,' I say. 'Where did you move to?'

He puts his hands in his pockets, clearly not enjoying this part of the conversation.

'We moved into one of his smaller flats in the city. The one he used with his *lover.* God, I hate that word.'

Oh. 'I'm sorry, I didn't know that.' I take his hand. There's not much I can say in this moment so voice the only thing that comes to mind. 'I dislike your dad even more now.'

'That's why I need the money,' he says, shrugging. 'My mum isn't doing that well after the divorce and I need to get her a new place at the level she is accustomed to, and to get her away from all of this. Anyway . . .' Theo glances mournfully at the wide, open doors. 'Can we change the subject now? I'm bumming myself out.'

'Okay, well, housing aside, people will recognize us. And what if the trial doesn't go well . . .' My voice trails off because he kisses me.

'We will figure this out, Margot,' he promises as we merge into the heat of the strip.

'How many more fountains do I have to film you next to?' Theo makes a mock scowl as I force him through yet another fountain-side photoshoot.

I smile and pose. 'As many as it takes.' When we are done, I take the camera and flip it and take a selfie, my head posed on his shoulder.

'You know that's our first photo together,' he says.

I shrug my shoulders, but I do know. Weeks and weeks of travel together and this is the first snap of us. I doubt I'll share it anywhere but it feels like a gem, tucked away on my phone. I like having it there; I like that it exists. A record of our perfect time here. Even if it's fleeting. I hesitate but then send it to my mum, with a cryptic note saying that we are getting along now. *He seems lovely, beautiful eyes*, she writes back. And my body relaxes further. I'm so grateful she's the kind of person who can see past the hate. I'll think about my father's reaction to me dating Theo Delacour someday in the very distant future, but definitely not tonight.

We've given up the pretence that we might be recognized and Theo kisses me often and everywhere. We take pictures by the iconic

Vegas sign, and we have brunch at Sadelle's Bellagio. As the sun sets, he twirls me around in the glow of the Paris Las Vegas hotel.

Everything is hot and so kitschy, streets teeming with tourists clutching palm tree plastic cups full of daiquiri. I'm sweaty beneath my white dress but I don't care. I'm wallowing in this moment. In his company.

'Let's go to Paris one day, you and me,' he whispers into my ear when we are standing outside Vegas's Eiffel Tower. I close my eyes and let him twirl me once more.

Jodi meets us at dinner in a posh restaurant of his choosing, that has *influencer* written all over it. There are mirrors everywhere and the tables are nestled on tiered platforms as if they were a beehive. Jodi is sitting opposite us, watching Theo feed me a bit of his carbonara that he wanted me to try. I didn't get to know Jodi at the Bali place but now that I am, I can see why Theo likes him.

'Never have I been more of a third wheel,' he declares, two courses in. Theo has been paying him attention, and I've listened heartily to his stories of doing a brand deal in Capri and being the face of Magnum ice cream at a film festival. But in between I've been stroking Theo's hand across the table, gazing into his eyes. And we may have shared a quick kiss or two.

'You know I called *this*,' says Jodi, pointing his fork at us.

'How come?' I say, trying to pace myself with my raspberry New York cheesecake to not look too greedy, because it's freaking delicious.

'Sometimes people hate each other so much it's basically just love in an ugly coat. *Chemistry.* That energy needs somewhere to go.'

'Well, for a while I thought all that energy would go into homicide,' says Theo.

'Really? You wanted to kill me?' I arch a brow.

'No.' Theo laughs that low rumble of a laugh I've come to adore. 'But I was pretty sure you might kill me.'

Jodi buys us a round of shots and we set off into our last night.

We dance across the Venice canals and take photos by the Sphinx and the pyramid. We take hundreds of silly photos and videos, likes ones of Jodi and Theo doing the Egyptian dance in front of the pyramid. We kiss by the slots and after a while a kind of melancholia seeps into my bones.

'What's wrong?' says Theo, noticing. He tucks an errant strand of hair behind my ear.

'I can't shake the feeling that this is all a dream – fragile, and breakable somehow.' I look out at the slots spinning wildly. Everything feels so surreal, and I'm hyper aware of this being our last stop.

'Life is only beautiful because it's fragile.' He kisses the back of my neck.

'I know, I know. I just don't want it to end.'

'It doesn't have to end if we don't let it,' he says against the skin of my cheek, noses nearly touching.

I kiss him wildly against the rising sun, by the Bellagio fountains – like we are in a two-person remake of *Ocean's Eleven*. We aren't the only couple there with the same idea, and no one pays us any mind. Jodi has long since abandoned us. By the time we tumble into our California king bed at the Maison Partout hotel I feel like I could sleep for a hundred years and it wouldn't be enough.

CHAPTER 57

THEO

The trite ceremony draws on and on as we look out at the room full of strangers. Mostly staff paid to be there, some journalists, a few people from Maison Partout corporate who were introduced to us in a slew of shaking hands. Corporate events where I look out at a room of people I don't know are not new to me. There is often a new building opening that I must attend with my father, or worse, a charity function where I am sent in his stead. But I do catch myself wondering what the point of these ceremonies is. The money will exchange hands either way, charity or not; what does the pageantry bring? And what is the point for the attendees? Are people gathered here today just for the buffet? Or were they expressly told they had to come and watch some random influencers get handed a hefty amount of money? I'm cynical this morning, like there's something in the air. Or maybe I'm just scared my trip with the beautiful girl next to me is coming to an end. I'm scared whether or not she will still see me in the same light at home.

The manager says a whole lot of floral nothing about the history of Maison Partout and then reads off some stats from our brand deal with a tricked-out presentation on the wall, graphs and all. I'm actually impressed when I hear what a global impact we have made for the Maison Partout brand. Their bookings are up. Their viewership has skyrocketed, and Margot and I are responsible for at least six viral videos, including her clever *How to Live Your Life Like a Grecian Goddess* and my aerial videos of the Alps. The alpaca stories have also made a big splash. Staff members clap politely. A sea of pantsuits and clipboards and name tags stare back at us. I'm grateful the buffet they might have come for is actually very generous, as I eye a tower of shrimp and cold cuts, and a rotisserie chicken station in the back, and even a soft-serve machine has been rolled out for the occasion. I am learning that everything is bigger and more intense in Vegas. We are underground, in what seems to be an events hall – one of those naked spaces customized with ribbon-backed chairs for anything from weddings to plumber conventions.

'And without further ado,' announces the main manager dramatically, carving me out of my stupor. 'Please bring out the one-hundred-thousand-dollar cheques!' A couple of members of staff carry out two of those comically large white cardboard cheques and everyone cheers. Margot is too excited to share my sardonic look, and flashes me a giant smile. I return it, even as I awkwardly clutch the side of the cheque for photographs. The flash blinds me. I wonder what my father would think of me now, accepting a comical cheque like this, pennies to him. He would think I look stupid. But this isn't about him. I can finally help my mother. And that's something to celebrate.

We snack on the buffet like crazy. Even though it's not the best buffet in the world, my hunger seems unstoppable. There are fish cakes, and tiny turkey wraps, and shrimp cocktail. Margot eats as if possessed too, almost like being this happy has made us both ravenous. We are in the adjacent room to the ceremony, as we wait for them to cut the opulent five-tier cake with the words *Maison Partout Cares* iced on top, the new slogan they launched yesterday.

A manager takes some time to walk us through the T&Cs of the competition and what's expected of us in the next few months. There are a few televisions on in the back, next to a resting section by the soft serve. The televisions are on for no particular reason, as I've noticed is common in America – TVs in lobbies, in waiting rooms, at the airport – like it's a lifestyle to stay vaguely aware of what's on the television at all times. We are standing next to three of them, showing BBC, CNN and EuroNews, listening to the manager conclude his explanation, when Margot sees something and moves away from us. A minute ago, they were all showing different uninteresting things, but now something familiar flickers on the left television. Images of home. Images of *our* home. There's a block of fat red where the headline drifts across in white – and when I read it, my stomach plummets.

I watch Margot drift to the televisions like a moth to a flame.

CHAPTER 58

MARGOT

I'm watching the EuroNews screen but I feel like I'm not seeing anything. Or maybe my vision is going blurry. I walk up too close for comfort and look up at the moving picture, as if staring at a riddle. *Protests.* Many of them clashing with one another, a sea of people ploughing into rows of uniforms outside a courthouse, and I can't make sense of anything except the ice pouring through my veins like anti-freeze.

The headline reads *Violent protests erupt in France as water billionaire acquitted of all charges in trial.* Acquitted of all charges. *I'm going to be sick.* I'm distantly aware of someone talking to me but I can't hear anything except a high-pitched ringing sound. I need my phone and a toilet. My phone. My phone. My phone. And a toilet.

I locate my phone in my bottomless purse and shuffle to the toilet. Even though I hear Theo say my name, I'm gone. Moving forward as if summoned. I feel woozy, and when I'm finally alone in the stall, the vomit comes quickly, once, then twice. My body contorts and contracts and I feel like I'm being turned inside out. Then relief washes over me as all the cocktail shrimp is gone. I wipe my brow; it's slick with sweat. I hear someone bang on the door.

I yank down my finger on my phone to refresh my messages and a few come in on WhatsApp. One from my mother. I blink, and a single tear jets down the right side of my face. I'm staring at myself in the bathroom mirror. Theo materializes before me and reaches for me, but I push him away. He shouldn't be in here. He shouldn't be in the women's toilets.

I don't want to be touched – not by him, not by anyone. I can't breathe. There's not enough air in this basement. Not enough air in this tight gold dress I've chosen to wear.

I run up the stairs and into the lobby. I hear Theo following me as I nearly collide with his bodyguard, Yuri. There's no air. I jolt forward into the elevator but turn to find Theo and Yuri entering after me.

'I saw you running, I got concerned,' says the bodyguard. I feel like laughing but my hand shakes as I press our floor.

'Leave us alone,' Theo snaps at his guard, who seems alarmed.

I keep pressing the button hysterically until finally it kicks in. Other people filter into the lift. My breathing grows hitched. People talk and their voices melt together.

'Are you okay?' says Theo. 'Margot, look at me.' But I think he knows the answer. I sink to my knees in the elevator.

My mum's voice pounding in my head like a growing headache as the WhatsApp voice note plays.

Alexandre has been arrested. Come home.

CHAPTER 59

THEO

She's crying on the edge of the bed. I reach for her but she pulls away, and I feel like she's melting through my hands. Sand slipping through my fingers, swept away by the sea.

'Don't touch me,' she says.

'Margot.' My voice is gentle. 'This isn't my fault.'

'Nothing is ever your fault, people like you, like your father, *that man*,' she spits viciously. 'You're all blameless, just existing.'

'That isn't fair and you know it.'

'Did you even speak to him?' she says, her voice rising angrily, and my guilty silence results in a gut-wrenching sob. 'Acquitted of all charges? Seriously? Every last one. Like he never even did anything. Like he never ruined all of those lives?'

I reach for her and for a second time, she pulls away. I flinch. Something sharp twists in my belly.

'I hate you,' she hiccups, expression turning dark. The words sting and I blink against them, trying in vain to still my heart.

'So, you hate me just because of where I come from? Just because of who my father is?'

I'm hyper aware of her whole body shaking and I don't know what to do. She rises and starts throwing things in her luggage indiscriminately. I watch her for a few moments, a pain spreading through me like ink blotches in water. I watch her pack against the backdrop of the symbolic and enormous cheque that was brought up after we left it, noting the awful irony. Knots are twisting in my abdomen, tightening themselves around the unspoken rot there.

'I'm going to go home; my cousin was arrested in the protests,' she says.

I shake my head. 'I'll help. I'll find you a lawyer. Please don't leave.' She ignores me. I rise to my feet. 'I won't let you.' I reach for her arm and she shrugs it off.

'I'm really sorry about your cousin, but you can't just . . .' I don't know what I want to say. Can't just leave me? Us? The brand deal?

'I can do whatever I want. Men like you think you own people. You know what? They only wanted you because of your dad. Head Partout management ... Because they want investment in the failing Maison Partout chain, and an oligarch, one of your dad's friends, is the one bidding. I overheard Georgina saying that before they chose Vincent. You were a pawn.'

I try to conceal the pain from the blow she just dealt. But I believe her.

'We are all pawns,' I say sadly, 'but don't be a stupid pawn that just leaves everything behind.'

She becomes incredibly still. 'I told you if you ever called me stupid, we'd never speak again,' she says simply, and I can tell her mind is made up. There's an incredibly tight silence but when she speaks, her tone is resolute. 'I will always hate you, with every fibre of my being,' she says into the silence of the room. 'I hate what you represent.'

'Great,' I growl back. 'Sins of the father and all that? What a fucking cliché.'

She turns and I reach for her. '*He's* the monster,' I say. When she seals her suitcase and looks back up at me, her eyes are full of tears.

'And you're just as bad – you know exactly what he's like and you let him do it. You could have spoken up, done *something.* So yes, that makes you a monster as well.' I get close to her, hovering over her the way I have a number of times before.

'So the boy you've been kissing across continents is a monster then?'

She averts her gaze and I can feel her chest contract. For a moment I think she might fall into my arms, change her mind, realize she's wrong. But her eyes flick up and meet mine. Cold. Set.

'If the profile fits.'

Then she walks out the door. I'm still standing by the bed.

I don't chase her. And maybe I *am* a cliché because I just watch her go, words building and dissolving on my tongue like tablets. Until there is no one left to hear them.

PUYFLEUR, FRANCE
CHÂTEAU DELACOUR

CHAPTER 60

THEO

I wake up in the château and can almost imagine I'm a child again. It's funny how something can look the same, and smell the same, and sound the same – but you are no longer the same and therefore none of it is, it's all different now. Different and wrong. The absurdly high thread count of the Egyptian cotton feels wrong on my skin. Like an unearned luxury amidst the chaos of what's happened. The protests are still raging, and when I arrived at the airport, the tinted vehicle sent to get me drove straight to my father's house instead of my own. I wasn't even asked.

My mother was already here waiting for me. Father made the decision that neither of us could stay in our apartment because it's a security risk in the wake of the trial verdict. My mother hasn't been back since the divorce and I cringe to think what this will do to her fragile mental health. I cringe to think how they got her here.

I get dressed and eat the breakfast which is delivered to me. Eggs Benedict, served on fancy crockery. Which feels even more absurd but I'm too hungry to prove a point. I wander the gilded halls, full of oil paintings and *trophées de chasse*, stag and hog heads poking out from the walls reminding me of the Alps and causing a dull longing ache in my stomach.

I walk towards my mother's old bedroom. I know there are two panic rooms in the château; I used them both when I was little – a few times to play in and only once when the masked vandals came in the middle of the night. They say *absolute power corrupts absolutely*, or at least I learned that quote in school, but I've also learned firsthand that absolute power renders someone absolutely paranoid. Sometimes with good reason.

The château is beautiful, I have to admit, even after visiting the iconic locations we have in the past weeks: the Venetian plaster, the exotic displayed gifts from abroad – Chinese hand-carved room dividers, marble busts, endless gold-rimmed china cabinets that require round-the-clock dusting, and hallways full of Persian rugs. They have a visceral effect on me. Both beautiful and haunting. Both familiar and completely foreign to me at the same time. It's been a while since I've been back, but it's always been like living in a museum, and about as lonely as living in one too.

I find my mother sitting by a television and I kiss the top of her head. She's watching the news and doing sudoku. She told me once the sense of the numbers calms her down when she's nervous.

'Hi, *Maman*.'

'*Bonjour, mon lapin*,' – *hello, my rabbit*. I smile at my childhood nickname.

She pats my hand distractedly. It feels like she's happy to see me but not really aware of the time that has passed since I've been away for the brand deal.

'*Ça va, Maman?*'

'I don't like being back here,' she tells me when I ask her how she's doing. And I know no one asked her if she wanted to come – undoubtedly Yuri was sent to collect her and pack her bags. She's always trusted him. Though I guess I should consider myself lucky my father bothered to send for her at all. It's not like they are on good terms.

Yuri left Vegas before me. Summoned by my father no doubt in wake of all this craziness. I scan my mother's face.

'Did you eat?'

'I don't want to eat any of the food here. But Yuri brought some of my food from home.'

I thank the stars for my bodyguard. She would undoubtedly have refused most of the château's cooking and just starved herself.

It's impossible to tell whether my mother's escalating anxiety, her marriage falling apart or the water contamination happened first. Impossible to know which domino fell and caused all the others to fall in its wake. All I know is she found out about his affair and about the water making people sick relatively close to each other; then she quickly found out she was hated by most of the region. People would say things to her in the street. It wasn't long after she found herself served with divorce papers, moving with her tween son to the fancy inner-city apartment where her husband had his affairs. Because that's where she was relegated to.

I feel for her. It's hard to lose everything and not lose yourself in the crossfire.

I kiss her again on the head as if she might disappear. I look upwards and I'm face to face with an enormous crystal chandelier, sparkling like one of those Swarovski statues in airports. Why does everything need to be so opulent here? I hear Margot's voice almost instinctively. I feel like she would say something along the lines of *people who hoard wealth like to display it*. Or *collectors like to show off their collections.* Then she would give me that look, like she's seeing right through me.

I've seen my mother twice since I arrived, once the night I landed from Las Vegas and once for breakfast. I've not been summoned yet to see my father. The protests have grown overnight and he's meant to be holding a press conference tomorrow, no doubt gloating in his innocence. It's no wonder I haven't seen a glimpse of him yet . . . he's probably planning the whole thing with his team of publicists now.

The rise in protests is his personal PR nightmare but I know what he would say – *control the narrative, you control everything.* If only I too could shift the narrative, I would. I think of what Margot said. *You could have spoken up, done something. So yes, that makes you a monster as well.*

'Did you sleep okay?' my mother asks. She is a waifish woman with blonde hair and a tiredness that set in soon after the divorce and never leaves her, even when she's resting.

'Slept fine.' I cock my head in the direction of the screen. 'I feel like they are lying about the numbers of Yellow Vests in the centre.'

She turns to me, blue eyes searching mine. I haven't told her yet but I have already contacted a clinic in Paris. Already sent them all of her information after Margot flew back home. And I've paid the deposit for her evaluation with the leading therapist. Now all I need to do is convince the woman that is scared to go outside that we need to go and live in the capital for a while.

'Your father lies about everything,' she says, startling me. She sighs at the screen where his face is currently appearing as they replay him addressing the press, post court victory.

'He's always lied about everything,' she continues. 'Since you were little. He knew the water was poisoned long before they made any announcement. Told me not to drink it. I did anyway.' This is news to me; I've never heard her talk about the contamination. Before Margot, before the trial, it was an untouchable topic in our house. Even when we moved away from the château.

'So that's it then, there's no winning in this,' I say, almost to myself.

She fills in another number on the sudoku grid. 'The only thing a liar fears is the truth,' she says simply. She's always been this riddle of a woman, doling out wisdom that seems both brilliant and confusing. *The only thing a liar fears is the truth.* So, exposing his lies would be the solution but how could I ever achieve that? And what would be the consequences?

Coward. Margot's voice is crystal clear in my head. I know she's brave. The few glimpses I caught of her socials since landing show her in the main square, in a face covering and a yellow vest, fighting smoke and tears. Chanting with the hundreds around her.

'*Maman*, am I a coward?' I lean close to her, inhaling her scent and letting my head rest on hers. Letting her be my safe space.

'No, *mon amour*, Theo.' She strokes my hands on her shoulders. 'I've never been brave. Never gone places on my own. But *you* have. I'm so proud of you. You show people bits of the world; you show people places they don't get to see.' I hug her tighter and she sighs, letting tiredness overtake her.

'I need to lie down,' she says and I nod, helping her to the bed.

My brain is racing. *The only thing liars fear is the truth.* I've made a living of showing people things. Of showing people places. And I could show them the truth too . . . The thought is half-formed at first, like many of my content ideas, but it quickly starts to crystallize.

'*Maman*,' I say. 'Do you remember when I got caught clubbing when I was fourteen? And the paparazzi took those photos of me?'

She nods. And the plan crystallizes in my head. It might be the worst idea I've ever had. But it might just be an idea that could work.

'I'm here to fetch you, little boss,' says Yuri, towering in the doorway of my room. I make sure not to react on impulse and close my laptop abruptly. Yuri can't see what I'm doing from where he's standing and I don't need to give him reason to be suspicious. I trust him, but I'm not sure I trust him enough to choose me over my father. And that truth hurts the tiniest bit.

'Fetch me for what?'

'Big boss wants to have a word.'

I sigh, rolling my eyes, giving Yuri the exact response he would expect. Then I slowly close my laptop and follow him out, never betraying that this is exactly what I was hoping for.

My father sits at the head of a long mahogany table, going through paperwork. He's an older, understated man, with most of his hair intact and an appearance that wouldn't make it easy to spot him in a crowd.

He's not someone who screams billionaire, unless you know to look for the signs. The understated vintage Patek Philippe watch that sold at a Christie's auction. The minimalist Loro Piana vest that might, to the undiscerning eye, look like Uniqlo but actually cost seventeen hundred euros – and the man has ten of them on rotation so he doesn't have to think about what to wear day in, day out. The disappointed scowl. The new wife whose surgeries are so well done you would have to see a 'before' to know there was an 'after'. The whole package screams wealth, but only when you know what real wealth looks like.

'Good morning, Father.'

'*Salut*, Theo,' he says in a more jovial tone than I expected from a man acquitted of murder. He smiles at me with his perfect teeth and for a moment I'm back to being eight years old, craving his approval more than any Lego set in the world.

'Are you done with your little trip round the world then?'

'Yes, one and a half months was enough.'

'A hundred thousand prize money . . .' He lets out a whistle but doesn't stop looking at his paperwork. 'Not bad. Though you could have access to a lot more in the family business. But hey, you know all that already.'

'That's what I've been meaning to talk to you about. I think I'm done vlogging for now and would like to take you up on that position you offered me in the past.'

He eyes me speculatively. 'Why now?'

'I'm not enjoying the hate online and I will need more money for Mum if she ends up needing treatment.'

He sighs, and for the first time puts down his paperwork entirely. 'Theo, I can pay for your mother's treatment now. I couldn't before. She probably has a neurological disorder from exposure to the contamination. But I couldn't deal with it before, you understand? Now that the trial is concluded, I'm happy to help. Has to stay discreet, of course. But the money isn't a problem.'

I couldn't deal with it before. A hatred brews inside of me so strong I think I might vomit. Not only does he admit not wanting to help entirely, but he's also admitting the water might be connected to her disorder.

'Did you know then, when Mum started to not feel well, that the water was contaminated?' I ask, mapping out the timeline.

'I'm not sure which came first.' He waves his hand as if it's inconsequential.

'She started having symptoms that spring,' I remind him – the season etched into my brain as if branded there.

He has the audacity to shrug. 'We developed a new filtration method that was more efficient, a cleansing agent. We had no idea that microplastics were entering the water at that rate because of the product. It was as much a surprise to me as it was to the public. You can't control these things, Theo. One whiff of it and the Eau Jeune stock would have plummeted.'

'So you knew, and you didn't warn the public, that's what you're saying.'

His eyes snap to me with irritation. 'Grow up, Theo. Of course I knew. What was I supposed to do, let the entire business collapse? How would that benefit you, or your mother or Josephine?'

'You want me to care about the welfare of your new wife?'

'Theodore, we have been married for years. She's hardly my new wife.'

I try to leash my deep anger, bubbling in my belly like water boiling in a kettle. I need him on my side. I need him to believe me.

'Okay, I apologize,' I say. 'It's all said and done. But I'm serious about that position. Maybe I could work at the northern plant – it's closer to the apartment.'

'That one isn't operational,' he says. 'I want you at head office.' He seems pleased, satiated. 'You're going to love it.'

I school my features into an artificial hesitancy. 'How do you know?'

'I know you, Theo. I know you better than anyone,' he says.

I smile at him and nod. As I'm dismissed and I leave the room, the smile doesn't leave my face.

Because if that man truly knew me, he would have known that I recorded every single word he said.

When I was a teenager, I used to sneak out across the grounds and throw my SIM cards away by the edge of the forest. Then I would locate a weak point in the fence, deeper in the forest, and hit the nightclubs incognito. That's why Yuri calls me *Theo the escape artist* – he has a history of fetching me from nights out because my clubbing would be bad for my father's image. And that's why, when I was caught by the paparazzi at age fourteen, drinking, my mother had a hacker remove all footage from the internet. Including from news sites. It didn't really stop me from sneaking out.

Even though this was years ago, the familiar night crawl is so nostalgic that I can feel muscle memory kick in. I bend under the windowsill of the games room, use the shadows of the staff quarters to my advantage, and head towards the forest via the path of trees. There were a number of holes in the fence that could still be there – if not, I have wire cutters on me. Yuri always caught me but never sealed the holes and always covered for me, back then anyway.

Once I've cleared the small lake and am approaching the stables, I breathe out in relief. That is until a familiar shadow moves by the hay bales and Yuri emerges, a smirk on his face.

'Up to your old tricks, eh?'

'God,' I say nonchalantly. 'You've upped your game. You usually only catch up with me by the hunting lodges.'

'You know I was always aware of you sneaking out and chose when to intercept you.'

I lean against the stable wall, aware that the only difference this time is that I'm carrying a conspicuously large bag which Yuri knows contains my drone, and in the other hand I have another large bag which he will know is unmistakably a Starlink. Yuri's eyes scan my bags.

'Is this wise, boss?'

'I'm not your boss.'

'I know, and you know that means I have to stop you. Or I'm the one that gets fired.'

There's a long silence, and though I tell myself maybe I could outrun Yuri, or maybe I could fight him, I know that's a big fat lie.

'So, what now?'

'I thought this might happen,' says Yuri. He pulls something gun-shaped from his bag and I balk, taking a step back and feeling the wall behind me. Surely, he wouldn't shoot me over this? What if my father found out I recorded him and has given orders to just get rid of me? My breathing hitches, but instead Yuri hands the item over to me.

'Here,' he says as he passes me a tranquilizer gun.

'What the hell, Yuri?'

'It has to look like I put up a fight, so I'll say you stole a tranquilizer from the hunting lodge when they find me. Shoot me right here.' He taps his shoulder. 'You still remember how from when I taught you?'

I stare at the item in my hands, dumbfounded.

'Why are you doing this?'

'I stood up for something in the army once. Stood up for the little guy. And it cost me my position, before your father hired me, but I never regretted it. You know? I think every man has a right to stand up for something they believe in. I knew that girl would change you, but didn't know how much.'

My arm goes slack as I stare at him.

'Come on, kiddo,' he says with a sparkle in his eye. 'Don't be a coward.'

I take a deep breath in and shoot one of my favourite people.

It's another hour till I reach the water plant. I make the taxi drop me off a good walk away, and I pay cash. Then, using the cover of shadows, I get to the tree-lined edge and up to the security entrance. I run my card in the slot that lets me into the larger car park. Once inside, I go a little further and hide behind one of the parked cars. I say a prayer. Then I bend my knee and I send my drone soaring up into the night sky.

I'm in the thick of the barricades. No one notices me in my black baseball cap. The police aren't out in full force yet. The smoke is thick. The protest is growing by the minute – it's a Friday night and it's almost like the crowd outside of city hall, where the verdict was reached, is a living, breathing thing. Pulsating outwards, rolling in waves. The barricades are mostly built of walls of tyres. Some of them have been set on fire; the smell of burning rubber is acrid and makes my nostrils flare. I join in the chants for clean water and bide my time, waiting for the crowd to build to its crescendo. I send a text to the hacker. What I've asked him to do is going to cost me over half my Maison Partout money, but it's okay. I have a few more months to make that money back, and I will. Of that, I am sure. It's only half an hour till my father's press conference on the local news.

This . . . this is going to be good.

CHAPTER 61

MARGOT

I'm getting dressed to collect my cousin from jail in a similar way as I would for an outing around the countryside, mostly because I know I'm going to the protest right after. Before that, I have clear instructions to drop Alexandre off at home. I'm wearing a canvas jacket to ward off rain, trainers to be fast on my feet, pepper spray in my pocket just in case.

Mum stands in the doorway, an apron around her as usual. I sniff at the air and smile. She smiles back but it's a heavy smile, a burdened one. Too much has happened.

'There's a brioche in the kitchen,' she says. She's tired and heartbroken from the results of the trial.

'Chocolate?'

'Of course, we aren't savages.' She flips her red braid over her shoulder. A lighter red than mine.

'*Merci, Maman.*'

She stretches a little in the doorway to my room. 'I'm really sore from all the farm work.'

'I'll help now that I'm back. And we can afford some external help too. You can relax.'

She smiles before walking back to the kitchen, and I make myself a silent vow to email all the all-inclusive resorts in the

Mediterranean and convince them to give my mum and me a free holiday. She needs it. And I have the Maison Partout brand deal as my new calling card. I don't think anyone is going to turn me down now. Not to mention, I have a fat Partout discount as well. Maybe we need something even more epic than the Mediterranean after everything we've been through.

'*Maman*, how do you feel about going to Mauritius with me?'

'Hmmm, I mean, there's a lot of work around here but I might be persuaded to take a break for the white sandy beaches.'

'That's the spirit. You know I spoke to Maison Partout about our inn,' I say, following her into our large country kitchen. I tear off a piece of warm brioche and pop it into my mouth.

She laughs. 'It's nearly twelve, *mon amour*, go get Alexandre.'

'Fine, but listen to me. I did speak to them and they said they would take a meeting with me. I could put a business proposal together for La Voile Rouge to become a Maison Partout boutique hotel in the region. That would come with some financing.'

'You remind me of your father,' she says, and I'm still for a moment. How can someone try to be so different to their parent and yet still be compared to them? My body stiffens and she runs her thumb across my cheek. My shoulders sag. She pulls me in, and it feels good to be back in her arms

'His obsessiveness was his downfall, but it was also his superpower,' she says. 'It's a good plan but you just got back. Have a breather. Anyway, I have cows to milk. You pick Alex up and take him straight home. And come straight home yourself,' she says, brows furrowed.

'Straight home,' I echo. But we both know it's a lie.

*

Half an hour later, Alexandre slips into my tiny French car. A hand-me-down from my father. His wheat hair is tousled, and his round cheeks are pink. His green eyes sparkle as he takes me in. He looks surprisingly chipper.

'How angry is your mum? And how angry are you?' he says, looking well rested for someone who was placed under arrest. Though there's a big blue bruise under his left eye, one that reminds me of Theo's back in Greece. 'We are working on a one to ten scale,' he adds, helping himself to a roll of Petit Prince cookies I put in the side of his door for him.

'Mum's a seven, I'm a five.'

'Well, that's not too bad.'

'Yeah, the words *murder* and *dismember* both came up.'

He sighs, looking less amused.

'If you were a cat this would mean you officially ran out of lives.'

'I know.' He nods, resigned. 'I just needed to get it out of my system.' I nod in return. I understand exactly how he feels, and I'm planning on getting it all out of my system today. But he doesn't need to know that. I pull out of the car park.

'Movie night this weekend?' he asks.

'Absolutely, if either of our mums hasn't killed you. I'll bring the snacks.'

'Your trip looked pretty awesome. Shame you had to share it with that tool.'

'It is a shame.'

I let anger roar through me like a melody, and it feels so much sweeter than sadness or missing someone. Someone you shouldn't miss at all. Someone you should have never stopped hating. Even when your heart told you to.

*

Bodies smash against me. The echo of chants. The slice of speeches. But mostly I hear feet hitting the ground.

We will not be silenced. Our voices will be heard. I chant, thinking just as I say it that it's not catchy enough. I hear the sound of rising drums.

The more days I spend going to these, the more resolute I become. Theo told me not to be a pawn, but I don't feel like a pawn. I feel like someone who has refused to play the game altogether. Who stepped out and did *something* even when I knew it wasn't going to be enough. My heart hurts a little when I think of him. Someone next to me is watching their phone instead of paying attention. When I look over at the screen I skid to a stop. He's watching Theo's account.

Frantically, I pull out my own phone and tap on Theo's profile. I've unfollowed him but of course I find him easily. He's posted a new video and the views are rising like wildfire. More and more people around me are going on their phones to watch. I try and refocus; the video is of drone footage above the water plant, showing that part of the plant is still closed. Showing a person walking in a hazmat suit. Footage that exposes the water plant as still being contaminated.

Rumours spread through the protests like rattling rocks.

It's his son who posted it.

Theo, yeah, that one. His own blood.

What a legend!

At the end of the video, there is audio footage of Theo's father, paired with imagery of the water plant and images of victims. Suddenly, Theo's father's voice is broadcast across the speakers of city hall.

Grow up, Theo. Of course I knew. What was I supposed to do, let the entire business collapse?

There is more audio of Theo talking to his father. Of his father admitting everything. And it's broadcast over the city's loudspeakers. Loud enough for everyone to hear. Suddenly I see that Theo has gone live and I click on the circle with his face. It's footage of the protest. He's here.

I break into a run.

CHAPTER 62

THEO

She materializes like a dream. Through the smoke, like a vision, an angel. Looking for me. The gas is burning my eyes but I see her instantly. She runs and I break out in a run too. We push past people, being swallowed up into the crowd, but I keep my eyes on her. She's all I can see. Until we are only a few feet away from each other and we stop. She flings herself into my arms and I squeeze. Holding her tightly to my chest like I've never held anything, or anyone, before.

'I couldn't just let you hate me,' I say into her ear, brushing her hair aside. She kisses me feverishly. Another water cannon goes off somewhere.

'What about this.' She points at the speakers, on which I've made sure the hacker loops the audio recording of my father. Long enough that everyone gets the point and that the news cycles pick it up.

'There's going to be a price to pay,' she says.

'I'll pay it,' I say, nuzzling against her neck. We are shoved from side to side as the protest rages on. She looks wide-eyed and scared for me.

'I could never hate you, never. Ever. I'm so sorry,' she sobs.

'Hey, hey.' I wrap my hands around her, shielding her from more movement in the engulfing crowd. 'Look at me.'

Tears cloud her beautiful eyes.

'I don't care about what was, or will be,' I tell her. 'I only care about the right now. This moment. You and me.'

'The moment is all we have.' She repeats the words I spoke in Japan back to me.

Then she tucks something into my hand, and I look at it. It's the tiny gachapon toy of a hippo from Kyoto.

'I kept it for you,' she says. I kiss her again, and again, like she's the only person in the world, and not like we are standing in a swaying crowd of protesters. My Instagram video will play over my father's press appearance, on loop. The hacker made sure to buy me at least ten minutes of national footage as he hacked into the mainframe of the TV channel. Now everyone in the country will see the truth. What he's done. There will be a price to pay, but as I hold Margot I realize I will gladly pay it. A hundred times over.

You're brave, Theo. Mum's voice rings in my ear. I just hope that *she* doesn't have to pay any price in my stead. A siren rings out somewhere. And then a chant grows and builds from a distance. We join in, hand in hand. Raising our fists into the air. Part of the wave of people. There will be a price to pay. But not now. Not yet. For now, we are infinite. We are just a moment in time.

EPILOGUE

PARIS, FRANCE
ONE YEAR LATER

THEO

I'm quiet as I hear Margot recording a yoga session in the other room. The Parisian apartment has tall ceilings and large rooms but there's an acoustic echo. I know she's been looking forward to this session so I tiptoe to my desk. I check my watch – I'd warned her that we only have an hour before we meet my mother for lunch. She emerges, sweaty and regal.

'How did it go?'

'Good.'

I've learned to see something deeper in her eyes. Something darker dwelling there.

'Just good?'

'A couple of mean comments, but only one death threat!' She's aiming for light-hearted sarcasm but she bites her nails and it's a dead giveaway. I pull them out of her mouth and kiss her fingertips.

She smiles up at me as I wrap my arms around her, breathing in her scent.

'If you want, I'll have Yuri hunt every last one of the commenters for sport.'

She giggles into my chest. We both know Yuri doesn't work for me any more, but he has secretly come over for dinner. And it's fun to joke about it.

'That's a little bit of an overblown reaction to a comment,' she says.

'Fine, but I will be sending them all *angry* GIFs.' But also, death threats and influencing go hand in hand, unfortunately. Because people take the internet too seriously. I've had my fair share of them since I whistle-blowed my dad. But I brush them off. People who threaten others behind the safety of a screen have bigger things to worry about.

I kiss her again, taking my time now. It's been a year and I still can't get enough of her touch, of her fingers interlaced with mine. It's almost like I feel that it can easily be taken away so I hold on tighter. I have homework for university, a six-page paper on Nordic noir. Not to mention the extra work I have to do for my internship at a local film studio that's doing a documentary on the Bois de Boulogne.

'Stop thinking so hard,' says Margot. 'You'll never get out alive.'

I wink at her. Marvelling that at least we are here together. Homework is a small burden to carry.

'What time are we meeting your mum?'

'At four. She'll need something sweet after her blood draw.'

She gets on her tiptoes and kisses me. 'Good thing I know the best patisserie.'

She goes to get dressed and I scroll mindlessly, even though I've deleted most of my socials. Margot has decided to continue influencing and I respect that. But I'm done.

After the protests and the drone footage went viral, my father was removed from his position by his own board. Another younger guy, a protegé, has been put in his place. A man made of apologies and condemnations and promises the past wouldn't be repeated. But there are reparations to be paid and they've already begun. Victim pay-outs, major clean-up operations, new legislation and a new board. My father will be fine as a silent shareholder; men like him always land on their feet. I'd say that to him, but he no longer speaks to me after what I did – whether that's through an aide or not. I don't know if he ever will. In a way, I miss him. In another way, I don't miss him at all. Our relationship continues in this complicated vein.

We made our voices heard and that's what matters, and now we can move on. My punishment was light, all things considered. No more trust fund. And no more apartment for my mother. So, Margot and I cashed our prizes in and moved to Paris for my mother's treatment, after we got Margot's farm and inn back up and running. I always thought her cousin would hate me when he met me, but turns out we have a lot more in common than I thought.

Paris is great for Margot's influencing. She continues to rise and her Parisian agency is working hard on growing her platform. I support her, as long as she doesn't force me to go to any brand deal events. My mother and Margot get along very well – a little too well sometimes. It took a while to convince my mother to leave her apartment and move to Paris with us. We rented her a small apartment across the hall; that way she's still with us but everyone has their privacy. A privacy Margot and I have been enjoying a little too much.

My mother had treatment for agoraphobia, and a lot of exposure therapy, and though the apartment is humble and not what she's used to, somehow putting physical distance between us and the problem has healed us all. Also, she loves Paris, just like Margot, and they both love shopping, which is a whole other problem. There are still dark days when she doesn't want to leave the house, but then there are light days, much lighter than anything we've had in years.

'Six more nasty comments,' says Margot, emerging from the bathroom with her towel on.

'What do I always say?' I grab her into a bear hug till her breath is hot on my neck. And it feels like home, though home is something distant I can't access any more. Now home is in my mother's eyes. Eyes that are improving every day. And home is in Margot's arms.

'Don't let it ruin the moment.'

'It's all that we have,' I echo back. And though it's half a lie, beyond the internet there is the reality. But in that moment, I choose where we are. *Here.* I choose her arms and my mother's eyes and to be there, present, against all odds. To stop scrolling once in a while and be in my skin, looking out at the things I can touch, smell and feel. The things I can change in that moment.

Because the moment is all we have.

ABOUT THE AUTHOR

Jacqueline Silvester has lived all over the world including Sweden, France, Germany, LA, London and New York. As a result, she speaks four languages. She studied at the University of Massachusetts and Royal Holloway, London. After graduating she wrote her first novel and began writing cartoon screenplays. She is the author of self-published Wunderkids trilogy and the co-author of The Blood Web Chronicles under the pen name Caedis Knight. She splits her time between London, rural Greece and Vienna with her husband, her excessive vintage clothes collection and a husky named Laika.

ACKNOWLEDGEMENTS

A book takes a village, and so I would like to thank mine. Thank you to my fabulous agent Clare Wallace at Darley Anderson for signing me and believing in my caffeine-fuelled pitching and for "standing on business," as Justin Bieber would say. Thank you to my former agent (now friend) Kesia Lupo for getting my foot in the tightly locked trad door. A huge thank you to my editor Arub Ahmed for her attentiveness and helping me shape this love story. I think we've succeeded in creating something wholesome and yet nuanced together, a love story that feels like a plane ticket (I hope!). Forever grateful for your encouraging margin notes. Thank you to Lucy Pearse, my former editor, for commissioning my love stories. Growing up nomadic, I spent a lot of time in airports so to have seen my own book in airports was amazing, thank you. Thank you to the whole editorial team and eagle-eyed Lauren and Petra. Thank you to the S&S Rights and Sales teams for your support and Miya and Ellie for the M&P magic. Thank you to the design team for the whimsical cover and adding in the cherry blossoms and my favourite country in the world.

To my mother, thank you for making travel a non-negotiable part of my character and life. And for teaching me the flexibility it takes to be nomadic. To my brothers Misha and Nicky, the best plane ticket in the world is the one that leads me to you. To my departed dad and grandparents, you inspire me endlessly. To my living grandparents who plaster their walls with my milestones and always cheer me on, the cheers keep me going. To author Natali Simmonds, for all the free therapy and for basically being there every step of the way. To the besties around the world keeping me sane, love you Nat (again for emphasis), Emily, Yulchik, Bry and Stace. To wonderful authors Marve, L.J, and Sophie Jo for the support. To Rachel, Kirsty, Demet and Elizabeth for being so supportive for so long. To giants Jennifer Niven and Lynn Painter for the kind blurbs that led to amazing things.

To Trisha Silvester, who passed away three days before I sat down to write these acknowledgements, I just want to say thank you for being you. For chatting to me about books and reading my work and for sipping drinks with me poolside in Mexico. I'm really lucky to have known you and been in your family.

To my love David, the window to my aisle, traveling with you is the best part of my life. When we were teens you wrote in my birthday card that you wanted to show me the world and you kept that promise. To Ezzy, our day cycling through the deer parks of Nara has made it into this book, so have our midnight Hong Kong dim sum, and I just want you to know that every 'best day ever' in my life includes you. To Laika, I know no other doggy that would put up with this many a mile, from the alpine peaks to the Peloponnese beaches, you've never once complained. And to you dear reader, thanks for reading to the end.